AF375012

OTHER TITLES BY SUSAN MERSON

FICTION
Dreaming in Daylight
Oh Good Now This

NONFICTION
When They Go and You Do Not
Your Name Here: An Actor and Writer's Guide to Solo Performance

HOW WE SAW THE MOON

Susan Merson

[blocpress]

How We Saw the Moon is a work of fiction. Some incidents, dialogue, and characters are products of the author's imagination and are not to be construed as real. Where real-life historical figures appear, the situations, incidents, and dialogue concerning those persons are based on or inspired by actual events. In all other respects, any resemblance to actual persons, living or dead, events, or locales is entirely coincidental.

Copyright © 2022 Susan Merson

Cover design by Lilliana Winkworth

ISBN: 979-8-218-11825-9

LCCN: 2023901934

All rights reserved, which includes the right to reproduce this book or portions thereof in any form whatsoever except as provided by the U.S. Copyright Law.

Names: Merson, Susan, author.
Title: How we saw the moon / Susan Merson.
Description: [New York, New York] : [Blockpress], [2023]
Identifiers: ISBN: 9798218118259 (paperback) | 9798215961230 (ebook) | LCCN: 2023901934
Subjects: LCSH: Estranged families--Fiction. | Mothers and sons--Fiction. | Older women--Fiction. | Writers' workshops--Fiction. | Interpersonal relations--Fiction. | Mentoring--Fiction. | Loss (Psychology)--Fiction. | LCGFT: Domestic fiction. | Romance fiction.
Classification: LCC: PS3613.E7774 H68 2023 | DDC: 813/.6--dc23

"How have you managed to live so long and remain so pure?"

Prologue

Signs of the Apocalypse

This all happened before the plague and after and looking back at it now—it's like the dream about teeth falling out of your mouth. No amount of sinew or tether would keep them stuck.

We all watched Trump bully his way into the channels that had long been stopped up. He opened the floodgates but then, the flood was always there. We all came unglued, in every part of our lives, trying to keep everything from banging against the tilting cabin walls. It was like a dinosaur encased in blacktop, as it rumbled into life, it sent everything and everyone around it spinning. Some went screaming into racist tropes, some gave up and pretended the Messiah had arrived. And others marched and marched and stood their ground, balancing the roiling ground beneath them.

And then it stopped. Everything stopped.

And all the debris that was whirling stopped, too, and landed in a pile at our feet.

We sheltered in place. We quieted and hid. Masked ourselves to others and revealed ourselves to who we were in the quiet days behind closed doors and in front of Zoom screens.

And slowly spring came again, and flowers dared to poke their heads into the contagion free air, and we dared to sniff them, mask free. Almost.

But the Trump election started the ball rolling, cracking and thrashing, revealing things best kept inside Pandora's box.

It was the beginning full of cues. But roadmaps, not so much.

Let me start with that.

Chapter 1

August 2016: The Descent

My son, Jordan, had been gone a year that month. August 2016. He took the money his dad left him and said, "I'm going as far away as I can."

He said this with fierceness, like a warrior expecting a volley of fiery torches. I wasn't surprised. I was hurt. I wanted to run away as well.

I replay the story of his departure too often but I can't get it right. I think this is what happened on the day he told me he was going.

We went out to the Botanical Gardens. It was April and a month before Jordan's graduation from high school. Ty, his dad, my husband, was gone two years already.

It had been rocky since Ty passed. But, of course, it would be. There were the usual things. Ty was the good cop and I was the bad cop. Ty was the one who had patience for Jordan's silence, his recalcitrance. It was me who wondered if my son was on the spectrum, who sent him to learning specialists, made him go to after school homework practice. I was the enforcer. It was my job, I thought. And my boy, my Jordan, was a "special learner." He scribbled between the lines in his second grade workbook and I freaked out, meeting with the teacher, the principal. Insisting on special help, tutors and the rest. It helped. I mean, it really did.

We put him into a wonderful school for "learning differences" and he thrived. He got on the robotics team and made the most amazing structures. I was so proud of him. But then, his dad was not there and Jordan wouldn't give me the satisfaction of watching his success.

I had made him feel odd and other. I think he said that to me. In between, when he was coming and going from school, and I was doing the same thing, trying to earn a living as a teacher, putting aside my own writing for practical reasons and forgetting I had a "problem son" and a dead husband. The times we would pass in the kitchen and speak volumes without opening our mouths.

I loved the jaguar connection of his bones as he grew tall and taller, leaving trees behind, and often folding those long legs beneath him to sit on his Zazen pillow. Like a secret forest, he had made his bedroom pristine, sealed in immaculate light. His temple. He did not wear robes to math class, but he might just as well.

I would stare at him sometimes when he slept. Like most mothers do at some time in their lives. I wondered at the way a night of boozy sex, years before, had coalesced into this living breathing animal. Certainly, Ty and I had left off that kind of behavior by the time Jordan was conscious.

Jordan had been a product of our abandon and our caution. He had sensed the perimeters of safety and the faux boundaries agreed upon to survive together. He flaunted them. As children do. Knowing we had dulled the world to make it livable.

I would think of those things as I watched him breathe, even when he was a sweaty teen, looking like he did years before. He had no lines on his face in sleep. No contortions. I noticed how much closer his eyebrows were to his large eyes when he slept. They were not lifted in alarm. A boy resting. An imprint for me.

I marveled at the way I understood him. How he missed the ease of his dad. How my electric scrutiny shocked and jigged him. I understood why he needed to get away. And I let him stumble upright to standing. I was willing to do that. I was sorry. I was sad I had nothing with which to hold him. Maybe I envied him.

Jordan and I kept our rituals. Going to the Garden was one of them. We often went to the Japanese teahouse. When Jordan was little, Ty loved to hoist him on his shoulders. His legs barely hooked under his dad's arms, then. Jor refused to come down when I insisted. I saw how Ty would gasp for breath.

So, this April, just before his graduation, my son said to me, "I am not going to college. I am going to Japan. Dad left me my college money. I'm going to go away. For a long time."

I remember the words. "We don't fit."

And then, "You always wanted me to be somebody else."

Then, I think he said something like, "Dad is dead." I must have blinked at that one. It hardly covered the moment we were sharing.

Maybe he said, "You are, too." That would be the flaming arrow meant to burn our connection. I still stood there and he said, "I fucking hate this. I fucking hate you!"

It doesn't matter. He left, angry, sad, desperate.

The memory was on a nonstop tape loop. And it was August again. A year since he took off. And since I had come to Boston to take a new job. The date was on my internal alarm calendar. The day Ty passed. The day Jordan left. The day I knew I had to keep moving to stay ahead of my feelings.

I woke to the news of Trump gaining in the polls. Michigan was shaping up to be a battle ground state in the election. I had been born there, raised when it was the car capital of the world, before the rage and rape of the car industry took all the good people and made them nutty. I had been there when everything worked, people fit, most lives mattered—in one community or the other.

The country had been riveted by Trump and his Melania. Venal, they floated from the heavens with their brittle message of faux beauty and dripping racism.

My classes had ended for the summer. The season of Jordan gone. The country fascinated with its demise. No one remembering the rise of the Nazis. I wondered if they'd take me, the Democrats. Let me help, feel connected.

"Glad to have you on the team," the young Latinx voice said to me on the phone. "We'll need your life experience!"

"I'll be there," I said.

And I got on a plane to Michigan to organize for Hillary. God help me.

Chapter 2

September 2016: Orientation

Around the table in the Union Hall on Warren Avenue in Dearborn were twenty young people. I was there, too. I came ready to work where I had grown up, but I was assigned across the state. Family and friends disappeared when I tried to volunteer them.

The city and state I remembered was lost in the mess of the scandals of Kwame Kilpatrick, the eager, greedy crook who led Detroit through its demise, and the swift departure of union jobs to offshore locations. The state had not recovered. The union hall had the taste of rusted metal. My eyes glazed over as eager millennials explained the myriad number of computer programs we would need to master to register voters, report responses, run surveys and input data.

I shook my head at my own foolishness. I had the romantic notion that working on a campaign meant shaking hands and talking to neighbors. The last night of training I was on the phone with my landlord and friend, Hattie, back in Boston.

"I can't do it. They want me to master all sorts of programs and figure out how to plug numbers. I shouldn't be here."

I heard her deep laugh. "Ms. Smith goes to Washington, 'cept

Washington is a rotting union town where they're not so impressed with your storytelling abilities, eh?"

"Am I that ridiculous?"

"Close, I bet." Why did Hattie always remind me of that old movie star, Marjorie Maine? Did anyone even know who Marjorie Maine was? I heard Hattie rip a pop-top, pour a drink.

"You drinking a beer? I thought you were laying off that comfort?"

"That was when you were here in town to keep me on the straight and narrow. I miss you, Annie. If you wanna come back, I can kick out your subletter. I have plenty of phone bank work you can do right here."

I looked at the quilted bed spread under my legs and noted all the places where the threads had been torn.

"I guess I want to revisit the scene of the crime," I said, pulling a long white string from the surround of a machine-quilted fleur-de-lis. "This Econo Inn has seen better days."

"Haven't we all?" And Hattie hung up.

The pharmacy was still on the corner, and it was a block and six houses down. I pulled the car over to the curb but didn't recognize the light that flooded the street. That's when I realized that all the old growth elms, that had shaded our front yards when we were growing up, were gone. Now, many years later, the street was bald and the sound of crunchy piles of autumn that had burned at curbside was a thing of the past.

When I was a kid, the city sent a truck with a guy on a loudspeaker. Through the static, he told us to stay in the house. "Do not come out for twenty minutes. Keep pets inside. The treatment remains in the air for twenty minutes. It can irritate human lungs." And then, that truck would rumble past and make its announcement at the other end of the block. "Do not come out for twenty minutes . . ."

Then, the spray truck would follow, like the elephants after the clown car, and lift its trunk, letting its brown spittle spurt across the trees, tobacco juice heading to the spittoon.

"Stay away from the window, Annie," my brother, Charlie, said to me. "This can't be good for anybody." But, he was just my big brother, and I thought it was magical seeing the brown mist shoot across the springtime sky. Surely the liquid would save us all, a little inconvenience to save the trees. It was my first lesson in seeing poison spread for the good of the people.

The trees were gone now. The house still had all its numbers and panes of glass but someone had taken off the shutters. Another little girl stared down at my car from the upper window. She was Black and looked at me with curiosity. I saw her turn and bolt, yelling out to someone as I stared up at the window, waiting for my brother to appear, or maybe even my own image.

The front door opened. I could hear the clunk of the storm door as it framed a curious woman, looking critically my way. It was not my mother, or anyone I recognized. Of course, it wasn't. The Dutch elm trees were gone, the chalk dolls I had scratched into the cement walk were gone, the evergreen trees long ago replaced.

I pulled away and continued down the street. Past the place where Johnny Beckman told me he had eaten my pet rabbit and it had given him super powers. A cruel story for a little girl.

I could make it to Kalamazoo and my assignment by five if I kept driving.

Chapter 3

October 2016: Swastika

There was a black swastika spray painted against the Hillary sign. It was on the right side of the road, next to the Fairgrounds Entrance. I saw it on the way to the Fair View Nursing Home. Life went on around it. Folks pretended not to notice.

I had to go to the Home, first stop of the day, to make sure the residents were registered to vote. The theory was that if they were registered and actually voted then we would be fine. In the election. Everyone knew it was just a matter of getting out the vote.

I came through the front door of the Home leaving the fresh air behind me. In the central gathering room were three women in sour bathrobes, their chairs pulled up to a card table, the smell of urine and yesterday's wash cloths surrounded them. They looked up, suspiciously. One of the women started cawing.

"*Caw, caw,* get me outta here! Get me outta here!"

Francis, the social worker, came into the room.

"Beatrice. It's okay. This woman just wants to make sure you can register to vote."

"*Caw! Caw!*" Beatrice was having none of it. And for emphasis, her body shrugged to the side and her colostomy bag filled with a brown foamy liquid.

"Maybe now is not the time," Francis said to me apologetically. "Just give me the forms and I'll get them to their loved ones. We'll handle it that way."

Though I wanted to be bold and neutral, I was relieved to hand the paperwork over to the social worker and get back out to the autumn freshness.

I drove the Mitsubishi across the street to check on the registration stand at the fairgrounds. It seemed strange to be driving a Japanese car in the former land of GM and Ford but American cars had vanished. I ignored the swastika that lurked like a rabid clown as I looked for a parking spot.

Walking past displays for combines and shredders, I glanced into the hall that held the pies and handcrafts. Three badly pieced Mickey Mouse quilts and a black velvet painting of the American flag hung above a folding table. No blue ribbons to be found. No one had time for crafting. They had to get in extra hours at the Walmart or the dollar store to get the mortgage paid. And the frozen apple pie was usually on sale.

Bobbie Carroll and Jean Williams were at the registration booth. They smiled cheerily when I came in. Jean's sister, Jenny, was working at the phone bank at the Church of the Nazarene this afternoon.

"We're here, fearless leader!" Bobbie smiled.

"Got everything you need?" I said.

"Oh yes!" Bobbie smiled.

"Except a machete," Jean added dolefully. "The other guys, the one supporting the other guy, they been sniffing around. I swear to God I want to chop off their goddamn . . ."

"Forget it!" smiled Bobbie. "When they go low, we go high!"

Waving away my doubts, I replenished their supply of Hillary yard signs and headed back to the car. The swastika was still there. Now it was screaming at me, boldfaced, fondling its cock.

A dusty red pickup honked at me, then pulled around me in the exit lane. I could see the woman in the driver's seat stick her middle finger in front of her rear view mirror. "Fucking Jew," her lips formed the words.

I am a Jew, of course. Were all the organizers for Hillary automatically part of my tribe?

I drove to the nearby town for some food. At the diner, there was a large table of farmers, rugged, tired, beat up. They had the hard bead of turkey vultures, looking for prey. The woman with the itchy middle finger clattered my BLT onto the red Formica table, bread and butter pickles bouncing into the napkin holder. Better to eat it on the way to the Church of the Nazarene. At least there I would be a welcome sight.

Jean's sister Jenny was there with two friends, brave women who made calls for Hillary while their husbands did not know. I pumped them up with smiles, thanks, and M&Ms and headed to my next stop in nearby Sturgis.

Sylvia Gonzalez Moustafa was in charge there. She was working as my second in command, a local, street wise and savvy. From a Texas border town, she met and married her Muslim husband while they were both getting their small business MBAs. She fell for him, and his already flourishing network of family owned businesses, converted to Islam and wore her hijab proudly. Fareed brought her to Michigan where his network of 7-Eleven franchises flourished across the state. She looked every bully who came near straight in the eye and that's where I found her when I pulled up in front of Lowry's Bookstore.

A stocky blond kid was hovering over the table where she sat, trying to bounce her eighteenth-month-old into an afternoon lap nap.

"I'm trying to get my kid to sleep," Sylvia said to him. "Could you back off, please?"

"Hey, you registered to vote?" I stepped in and between them.

"Naw. Not yet." He turned his attention to me reluctantly. He reminded me of my son, Jordan, with the wall behind his eyes that hid a mystery no one who loved him would find out.

"But I'm not gonna let anyone take away my guns!" he said.

"I'm not sure anyone's fixing to," I said, handing him a form to fill out. He leaned down to scribble his name and address. "Great! Your rights are represented!"

He spit at the curb, his bile even too noxious for him to hold. He hiked his pants and headed off. "We're watching, bitch," he threw over his shoulder as he walked away.

"Shithead, tough guy," Sylvia said, kissing the head of her now sleeping baby.

"Yeah," I agreed. "Asshole." Dismissing the whole encounter.

Who was I kidding? The gangbanger rattled me.

Chapter 4

October 2016: The Basement

I confess to being careful to watch my rear view mirror when I drove back from Sturgis, just in case that kid made good on his surveillance threat. Exhausting, navigating all the fury. Everyday walking through downpours of glass shards. It was more than I had bargained for. There was little time for reflection. I went from task to task too worn at the end of the day to digest affronts, remember I wrote stories in my real life, and taught others how to do the same.

The basement at the Church of the Nazarene was deserted when I got back around seven. My volunteers had disappeared, long gone, to make dinner for their families. I saw a note to check the fridge and found a plate of American cheese sandwiches that were left from the community senior feed that happened every Thursday just before the phone bank. My volunteers made sandwiches, put out chips and juice, made their phone calls in Jesus's name, Amen, and headed home to their gun toting husbands, who were all just doing the best they could.

I buried my feelings in the 150 calls I made that evening, the required amount to stay on the campaign. The demands were linear and rigid. Numbers counted. People not so much. I ticked off the hang ups, the "fuck you, bitch—don't call again" responses and confess to crossing off a few extra names that had cycled back to my call list from the day before.

I hadn't eaten, my head was pulsing from the challenging day. I hadn't checked my email yet for group meetings but I lingered in the linoleum basement of the church. I could hear the clanging of the gates as the maintenance crew emptied the dumpster outside. There was an old piano in one corner, a bulletin board with messages about Sunday School and fellowship trips, missions to Africa. There was an American flag on a raised platform and a rocky lectern where I imagined Scout leaders stood, hands on heart, "I pledge allegiance to the flag." It was a great scenario. The setting for the ice cream social, Sunday school white elephant swap, that I fantasized about. I shook my head at what was embraced as ideal when I was growing up. Funny, I never noticed that Jews were rarely included in those scenes, let alone BIPOC or LGBQT folk. But the dream dies hard. It felt safe here in the quiet with only the dusty past. I felt like a fly caught in Midwestern aspic. But the aspic was melting.

Time to make my way back to my room in the basement of Barb and Jeff's house a few towns over. They had put a dehumidifier in the small room and my things were not smelling of mildew as much as they had in my first weeks here. Before I turned off the church lights, I stocked up on cheese and mustard sandwiches and lunch sized bags of chips. They would come in handy during these last hectic days of getting out the vote.

Chapter 5

October 2016: Scarecrow Gun Shop

I must have taken the wrong turn at the Scarecrow Gun Shop. The GPS failed around Berryville. The gas gauge slid over to empty. No cell reception. And there was something under my left rear tire. The car had been limping since the last turn a few miles back in the black night. I was too tired to pay attention and I was now somewhere in a matrix of little gravel roads that spilled through the farm fields.

During the day the farms were bucolic. Vistas of ripened corn and loaded apple trees sang "Howdy Neighbor" as loudly as the gunning pickups playing heavy metal. The trucks followed a little too closely on the country roads, I noticed, with their Dixie flags flapping in the wind, motors revving when they saw I was on Hillary's team. Now, those pickups were parked somewhere nearby in the darkness, hiding in sheds and barns, panting from their days labor but always eager for a little bat bashing fun. My car slowed and I let it roll to the side of the road to get my bearings.

The swastika, the gun-toting kid in Sturgis, the phone bank women scurrying home to their unsuspecting husbands, the colostomy bags, the stale cheese sandwiches, the threatening MAGA campaigners, the seventy-five hang ups on my nightly calls all lay at the feet of a growling Cerberus, guardian of the Gates of Hell. He was sniffing the offerings mightily. I was lost and didn't know what to wish for.

I tried to start the car again. It strained to find the last gas fume at the bottom of the tank and groaned at me. I could not see much over the dashboard but what I could see were rows and rows of dried cornstalks teased by wind and moon glow, ghouls rising, ghosts skateboarding on barn board memories. Ghosts out of joint.

Not sure what to do, it made no sense to find a farmhouse and knock at its closed doors. That smacked of *The Rocky Horror Picture Show* and bad movies. I locked the doors. The sandwiches were filling the car with fumes so I grabbed one and started eating. Two bags of chips later, I found myself defeated with sticky fingers. The only thing my eyes would do is close.

I imagined what Jordan would say to me, of being a do-gooder, caught in my own 'compassion'. I had sent him an email telling him I was going to the campaign, but no response. He was fully immersed in his Zen studies, learning Japanese? Yes, his last email said so. Several months now. I made a note to check with my nephew Eddie to see if he had heard from Jordan. He connects with Eddie more often than I do.

I pulled my jacket up around me. I double-checked the car doors. A pickup passed after the moon was gone. I slid down in my seat as it slowed a bit, but then sped off. There was nothing to stare at that didn't stare back at me.

I woke to the sound of a tractor on the road in the grey dawn. I turned the key one more time and the car started out of pity. While the farmer watched, I pulled out and was able to coast down the hill to the highway and a local gas station. It looked deserted but a woman sat behind glass, gazing out at the pumps. She noted my arrival and pushed some buttons, letting the gas flow. She was unwrapping a candy bar while the smoke from her cigarette surrounded her face.

She wrote something down. Made a note. Pushed a button, the gas stopped. I waved a thanks through the glass. She nodded, chewed her bar, took a drag on her smoke.

It was cold. Steam from my mouth, smoke from hers obscured our goodbye.

Chapter 6

November 2016: Election Selection

On Election Day, I drove out to the headquarters where I had an all-day team of local women coming in to make the final phone calls. I had the church brigade ready to provide rides for voters stranded at home, Sylvia had M&Ms at the ready for the children of the phone bankers, and balloons and coloring books with crayons. Anything we could do to encourage the calls to go out, for the voters to be moved. Some women came at 7:00 a.m. and stayed all day. The only African American town councilperson was there with her grandchild until five in the afternoon, and a representative from the local tribal council came as well.

I closed the office at eight when the polls closed. Sylvia had already left to go make dinner for her family. I made my way back to Kalamazoo and the Headquarters. I went into the ballroom at the Marriott and watched as the algorithms paraded across the screen. Florida fell, as state after state, one after the other tallied cockeyed totals.

I couldn't stand to be there. People were leaning, casual, against tall cocktail tables and pretending that this was normal. No one panicked or screamed. Instead there was a slow caul that fell over the room, over the workers, over the monitors that gave us the news. Everything went to slow motion and half sound.

We were being branded by that cocky swastika, the angry hurl of the gun-toting boy, the dead looks of the women making coffee behind deli counters, noting license plates. No one said anything. Disbelief, I guess, kept exhausted workers from acknowledging what the screens above them were running over and over. I looked around and could find no eyes to meet. Just gin in tall glasses being poured and emptied, poured and drunk.

An hour later in my hotel room, I got a message from my boss that I was to join a busload of other workers to head to Detroit where voting machines had failed and something was wrong. I fielded desperate phone calls from friends from both coasts, screaming at me as if it was my fault that the election went haywire. "Breathe," I wrote across my Facebook page and turned off my cell.

I sat up 'til four in the morning in my darkened hotel room, slid low under cover, like that night in the cornfield, not sure where to find the light to the road home. Then, it started to rain. A note was slid under the door. "Go home for now. They'll do a recount in a few weeks. It's over for now. Thank you for your service."

And that was it.

In the morning, I went to the headquarters and cleaned out the paper cups and sandwich wrappers that littered my desk. I shredded my voter call lists. I said goodbye to my boss and called Sylvia.

"I'm heading out, friend. Take care of yourself and your family."

"How are you, Mami?" she said, using my pet name. I wasn't good. And neither was she. "My husband wouldn't let me come back for the party."

"Right. Not really a party. Not really a wake. Like everyone had been hit by an asteroid but was pretending they had another planet to inhabit."

"A real zombie dance, yes?"

"Yeah. I'll go with that. Love you, hija."

"Support your local 7-Eleven and think of me." She clattered the phone down unceremoniously. And that was over.

I got in the Mitsubishi and started the drive back East. By midafternoon, I made it to Pennsylvania. My eyes were closing. I pulled over with a few truckers at a rainy truck stop and covered myself with my quilt. I slept 'til it was dark again. Drove home. Burned my campaign book. And slept for four more days.

First, there was Anne Frank sitting on my bed, shaking me, telling me to get up, the Nazis were coming. But when I managed to turn over, Anne was gone and there was her grandmother or one from a Steven Spielberg movie.

"Shh," whispered the old woman. "Don't move! Don't let them see you. Just hide here. There are candlesticks under the floorboards!"

No GPS. Stuck in the cornfield, waiting for dawn.

Chapter 7

Women's March

My bag jumped and growled with each new message. The vibrate function told the story. Everyone was buzzy and scared. I was dreaming and waking, never sure which state I was in. I chose limbo.

My Facebook page was deluged with rants from the disappointed. The gist? *Who were we, if we were wrong?* I wasn't sure. I buried my bag, I needed time out of time.

On the fifth day, the phone rang and rang. I dragged myself from bed. The phone was not going to shut up. I followed the cord to behind the coffee maker in my Pullman kitchen.

"Annie?" It was my nephew Eddie. "Been thinking about you. When did you get back?"

I shook my head and tried to form sentences.

"I think a couple of days ago. I've been . . . in retreat."

"Hattie, your neighbor called me. She's been knocking on your door. No answer."

"I'm cocooning." That was who had been knock knock knocking at my chamber door. Hattie. My landlord and friend, too, I guess. Maybe it was time to make some coffee. I padded over to the front windows and split the curtains. There was a day outside.

"Hattie is worried and so am I so, are you okay?"

"Oh, Hattie wants the rent. I didn't send a check."

"Maybe, but are you okay?"

"Oh yes, of course. Indulgent liberal syndrome. I'm getting up now. Thanks for calling."

"Right. There's a big march planned in DC for the week of the inauguration. Hattie's going. Call her."

I had marched in the Boston Common during the Vietnam era. I had planned to go to DC for the big November march in 1969, but my father chose that weekend to die. So, I was pulled back from school in Boston to the bleak landscape of first grief.

I dressed slowly and then realized, it was time for a bath instead. Somehow, relaxing into freshness felt an odd betrayal. I peeled off the yoga pants I had been wearing for almost a week, and my black T-shirt and went into my small bathroom. There was the full-length mirror behind the bathroom door. It startled me when it reflected back a woman of a certain age, with some shape left but grey-skinned and hollow-eyed. My hair was snarled and lopsided. I didn't hazard a smile. I turned and brushed my teeth, the cold water signaling the first new feeling I had had since my return. Okay, I could avoid that woman in the mirror and sink into a tub.

There were still bath salts. There was hot water. There was lavender shampoo. There were no spiders in the tub and the water ran hot after a few minutes.

I lay long in the claw-foot tub, remembering it was one of the better things about this apartment not far from Central Square. The water ran through my head, through the strands of my hair, around my toes and over my stomach. A hot washcloth over my face, across my chest.

I heard knocking at the door. As the water drained, I grabbed my large, soft towel and Ty's old robe from the hook, avoiding the cool draft from the bathroom window.

"Coming! Hattie? Is that you?"

"Answer the door. Where the hell have you been? Answer the goddamn door." The voice always felt like it ran through a grater.

I pulled the door open, fresh-faced and with a fake smile, and there was my landlord. She was in her mid eighties and tough as nails. I didn't know her politics, but she had years of dealing with tenants and she did not mince words.

"Where's the rent?"

"Hattie. I just got back. I'm sorry. Come in and I'll write you a check."

She harrumphed inside and took note of my bags and the fact that my table was smooth and unused and the counter was cleaner than it had ever been when I was in residence.

"I thought you died in here and I am not interested in getting the 9-1-1s to haul you out."

"I just got back. My apologies. It was a rough . . ."

"My mortgage payment is due on the fifth. It's now the ninth and I'm late. Do not pay me late. I am old and cranky and I'll evict your ass, no matter how long you been here."

"Yes, Hattie. Okay. It won't happen again."

"While you been lolling around licking your wounds we have been organizing. There's a march in DC day after Inauguration Day. I left you the sign-up."

Hattie turned in her sweatshirt and sneakers. "Don't be so indulgent, Annie. Get to work." And she turned around and headed toward the door, but stopped. She had a brown bag with her. "Here. Coffee and a bagel. Get some nutrition in you. You look like hell."

We were a predictable crew of older women who had remained fierce in our youthful convictions. We had lived through the sixties but did not own up to our years or admit to the wear and tear of our lives thus far. We left at dawn, arrived by ten and joined the many who clogged the streets, flaunting homemade signs.

Descending from the bus, I got only a block before I was stopped by the crush of women ahead of me. It was a crisp day. The sea of pink hats buoyed us all but any forward movement was halted. I ducked into a small coffee spot where I spied a corner table, the only seat left for miles in DC.

"You're a lucky one," I heard a groggy voice beside me. "You got the last hard stool in the city." A large paw of a hand, connected to a very tall, very red-faced woman dressed in flannel, reached out to me. "Nice to meet you. Marg Willis. Chicago. We drove all night."

"Annie. Boston. Only a few hours."

"You want some coffee? My friend ordered it for me and took off. I only drink matcha."

"Thanks," I said. "I'll take it." I grabbed the cup and brought it to my lips. It was cold.

"Oh. It's cold, by the way," said Marge. "But it's wet."

"Thanks." I set it down and was happy for that when I saw the ring of sloppy lip-gloss on one side of the cup. "I'm okay."

"Glad you are. Because the rest of us are fucked."

I winced. I wasn't sure I could stand another diatribe, wedged into this crowded coffee stand with this now hostile stranger.

"Look," I said, launching into my standard speech. "He didn't win. Just remember that! She got three million more votes. And I was there, I worked the election. It's so fishy."

"Fishy?" Marge held her nose with two big fingers and grinned. Her big teeth glared at me.

"Fish business, as my grandfather used to say. He had a partner who had a fish store and who screwed him out of money and he never trusted a fishmonger again!"

"A fishmonger?" Marge leaned back into her corner, giggly, rocking the small table between us. Her eyes were beginning to close. I was losing Marge. It did not distress me, I was talking at her more than to her, anyway. Still, I could not stop.

"Someone was fucking around. The algorithms were set on a standard response. They shut down the recount. We'll make this right." I murmured my mantra.

"Yeah. Right." Marge didn't argue with me but she wasn't convinced. "I was a Bernie person anyway. I hated that cunt." I looked at her in amazement. "I wasn't going to support her. No way."

I didn't say anything, remembering Thumper's mother and her admonition about keeping yourself from snide remarks.

"Well, I'm here aren't I?" Marge moaned at my wide eyes. "God, I'm exhausted."

It was all I could do to keep myself from repeating the trope my writing teachers always threw at me when I protested after the thirteenth rewrite. "It's not enough," they would say.

"It's just not enough."

"Look I'm gonna close my eyes for a few. Move yourself around in front of me and maybe they'll let me sit here. Besides we couldn't get out of here if we wanted to. The streets are jammed."

I was happy to oblige. I turned my back on large Marge and felt her settle into the corner. Soon there was a light rhythmic snore behind me like a clogged respirator, grabbing for air.

I tried to get up and move out past the crowd. It was true that there was nowhere to go.

"What's happening?" I shouted out to anyone who would answer. A statement I would repeat for the next four years. A voice came back from the street.

"They have the end of the street blocked. We can't go anywhere. Just sit tight."

And I made my way back to the corner where my chair was still empty. I sat there for an hour or two, just watching the false cheer, the self-assured catcalls that thought the old tricks would kill the new rat.

Finally, I made it out the door and into the women, standing, signs waving above them, stamping their feet now and then but clogged in this side street.

"What's going on? Why can't we move?"

A voice from Brooklyn, loud and strong, "Da cops closed da street! There are so many people here they can't handle them all."

"They won't let us onto the mall, y'all." *This one had to be from Georgia*, I thought. Soft as a peach and hard as the pit inside. "They closed access to the front of the White House, my oh my!"

And a young man now, too. "My girlfriend called me to say kids are cascading down the hills around the Washington Monument."

I stood stuck in one place, silo-ed by signs, in the middle of a symphony of faceless voices shoving at the bottleneck, more bemused than beleaguered. I was still so tired, wrung out from the election and its aftermath, it was hard to stand. I don't know what I expected, but maybe more inspiration, more solidarity, more sense that we had this as a country but instead I couldn't breathe.

The crowd was dense and slotted. Cattle directed into pens. My legs ached, my neck couldn't swivel, my back refused to support me. And then it got harder to breathe and my limbic brain kicked in. It connected directly to my strongest subway voice, one I had cultivated during a summer course at NYU. "Out please. I need to get out please. Out please!" and with this rhythmic rat-a-tat I was able to finally find a way through the maze of dazed troopers and come out to a clear space above a major city street. There was a line of people moving forward in that stream. I climbed up the side stairs and finally found a perch on the overpass. I closed my eyes and started to breathe deeply again as I saw the forward movement.

Below me passed the Bread and Puppet Theatre walking on stilts as Uncle Sam and Lady Liberty. The young women there looked at the puppets with wry amusement. They didn't see what I saw, what my generation saw.

The Puppets had made many a statement in the seventies. It was their magic that raged against the machine, against the war. They stirred the marchers, larger than life and bold in image. But today, in this crowd, they were a circus act.

"What a day!" I heard the murmurs of the women as we reconvened on the bus at 5:00 p.m. "Did you see that sign that said . . . ? Did you believe how many people were there? They can't ignore this! There were more people for the march than there were at the inauguration." The self-congratulatory messages cascaded off the carpeted walls of the Greyhound.

I managed to snag my favorite seat, the first row with no one ahead of me. An easy distance from the bus driver. The tall Black man climbed aboard and placed his coffee thermos and sweater in place. He smiled over at me.

"Have a good time?"

A good time? "Well, I tried. I mean we tried. Hopefully, it will make a difference. Put them on notice!"

He smiled quietly. "That so? Well, maybe all you angry white ladies will affect the Man. I hope so. But I'm used to a different result, you know what I mean?"

"Yeah," I smiled up at him. "We're an idealistic bunch, us privileged white women! I hope we can make a dent."

"Good luck, young lady. Good luck, then," and he turned, settled in his seat and set the engine to rumble.

I heard the scuffle of Nikes behind me and the crush of a North Country parka.

"I'm Margaret. Okay if I plop down here? I get seasick in the back."

She was grey-haired with a little band that kept her thinning hair out of her eyes. Her black eyeglasses were skinny and I could see that she moved like she was used to being agile.

"Think we did any good today?" she said to me, looking wistfully out the big bus window.

"Well, we did what we knew how to do. Right? I mean we marched, right?"

"Right," she said. "I'm just not sure the 'fight the pigs' attitude of our youth is going to cut it. People are too tired. Too blasé. And we're all too old." Margaret sighed. "Maybe the kids will create their own underground resistance. Wear berets and sneak around the countryside hiding secret filled baguettes on the backs of bicycles."

"That's a nice idea."

"Yeah. I'm a writer."

"Me, too."

"It's not enough," she said. "It's not going to be enough." She closed her eyes.

Chapter 8

Rachel Maddow

I watched the news. God bless that Rachel Maddow. She was as stunned as the rest of us. I didn't miss any of her broadcasts. With everyone stuttering under PTSD she managed to explain what was happening and at the same time, feel it with us, for us. Thank God for her. I don't think we could have managed a way to hold on to the facts, let alone figure out our feelings without her as a mirror.

Tonight she played a news clip of Trump. "The president implemented a Muslim ban today," she said. The clip played and he stood at his lectern, blue suit, red tie and an almost Betty Boop expression on his face, wide-eyed. He shook his head and in a singsong said he will keep the ban in place until "we can figure out what the hell is going on." The clip ended and there were shots of groups of people gathering at airports. Grandmas caught in the airport in Pakistan. Children asleep on benches in Dubai, their journeys to America interrupted.

I grabbed my phone to call Sylvia.

"Sylvia! I just saw the news. Is your family okay? Your husband's family? Is anyone affected?"

"Hi, Annie." Sylvia's tone was even.

"Rachel Maddow says that lawyers are already volunteering to help out stranded travelers."

"Thanks for calling."

"Well, yes. Of course." I could feel her distance, but maybe that was just steadying herself around the facts. "How is your husband? Are you concerned about the business?"

I was sorry to feel that everything I was saying felt a little off. Intrusive even.

"We will be fine. Fareed is pretty philosophical. He already got a call from the Anti Defamation League in Kalamazoo offering him legal help if the fallout gets bad."

"Well, that's good, right?' I said, eagerly.

I could feel her smile. "Well, sure, but Fareed immediately told me how the Jew lawyers were already lining up customers."

I wasn't sure if she was shoving at me or just reporting in. "Should I not have called? Will he think I am lining up customers?" Sylvia heard my silence.

"Oh, Annie! It's just . . . it made him laugh, is all. Jews are always there, first in line! Fighting the good fight! I mean you told me yourself the reason you wanted to volunteer for Hillary was because of that Jewish thing . . . what is it called?

"*Tikkun olam.* Charged with being mindful of helping to repair the world."

"Right! That's what I love about you. You walk the talk."

"I can live with that," I said and quickly added, "the main thing is that you are safe, yes?" I stepped back a bit. Returning to a more neutral stance.

"Yes. We are safe. Fareed has a TV set up behind the gun-proof plexiglass at our White Lake location. And he told me to get used to the gun in the cash drawer. He's prepared."

"And you?"

"I'm looking for work," she said, nonplussed.

"Please be careful, my friend." I said. "Please tell Fareed I am thinking of you all. Just because I care about you. Right?"

"Right. Talk soon." She said, realizing that she may have insulted me. "Thanks for calling, Annie. We'll be fine."

I hung up and went back to the news. I remembered how Sylvia juggled her duties as a Muslim wife with her real street smarts as a Latinx kid from Texas. She joined the campaign to find a way to be in the world in a way that would respect all her realities. She had lots of tools, certainly more than me.

A few days later we heard that two Muslim girls were attacked on a train and defended by a vet who ended up dead. I didn't call again. Everyone was getting used to the new normal.

I realized I was made of American dreams and "howdy neighbor" commitments. I think that's why I went to the campaign in the first place. These skills needed to be sharpened.

Chapter 9

Finding Balance Again: Kauai

The stripping of my nerves, that started on the night of the election, had only continued and would no doubt get worse through the term of Trump. I could feel the needles in my spine, prodding me, not allowing me to stay in one place. Nothing felt right. I struggled to describe the feeling. Princess and the pea with the pea a pile of delirious fleas let loose?

This had already been true with Jordan's departure, but now, with the news piling brazen realities on us daily, finding a place to hold my itchy body and soul seemed to be paramount. I needed to work. I needed to earn some money and get back to teaching. Not sure how to find normal, I thought maybe nature was a good place to start.

I remembered I actually had a friend, who had an avocado and papaya farm on Kauai. That was part of my former life. Knowing people with avocado and papaya farms on Kauai. It was odd to think of such luxury while living in my sweet one bedroom in Cambridge. No matter, life was all about blending the old with the new, the possible with the impossible and I knew that Tora's place would be a great spot for people to refresh and come together. And the touchstone of beautiful places has always been how I managed to grow from one place to the other. Kauai would be a good first stop. And there were memories. Not all bad.

"Perfect. We're heading back to Milan April fifteenth. Come for May. Cesar will be here handling the trees and taking care of the grounds. Danny will be around but then, I think he has always had a crush on you, anyway." Tora was married to an Italian and spent only winter on the island. Happy to have a project, I wrote back an enthusiastic "yes."

The prospect of walking the groves with Danny, their old golden retriever, was an added perk. The last trip was tough, but the place was beautiful. It had a way of taking tough truths and making them palatable. At least that's what I remember. It had been ten years since I had been to Kauai with Ty and Jordan as a pretty little family. But, wait, Jordan was thirteen. I take it back, not so pretty.

I crossed my fingers, put an ad in *Poets and Writers* and hoped I could get a group together for a writing retreat. I made sure to write some nice copy about the beauty of Hawaii and the chance to ruminate on the beach facing Bali Hai. I figured everyone needed a break after the election.

David was the first person to connect with me.

Dear Annie,

*I read your advertisement in Writers and Poets and I am very inter-
ested in joining your writers workshop. I love old movies. Bali Hai is
a place I have always wanted to see. As you will see from my resume,
I am not an artist or even a writer. I write computer code but I have
something to say, in words, and am looking for a way to say it.*

I am retiring this year. I have no family and no hobbies, but rather some keen interests.

I have a friend who has encouraged me to take the workshop. She is not a writer but would like to come with me to experience the challenge. Would that meet with your approval?

Please tell me the next steps in registration.

Sincerely,
David Diamond

Slowly the confirmations came in. A doctor from Spain who had a friend in Hawaii. A woman writing children's books who needed some inspiration. A mysterious young woman from New Jersey, Amanda, who said she had a story to tell and hoped that Hawaii would be a good place to begin. Jerry and Anita, an older couple, who had a house on Maui, who finally wanted to write the story of their love affair. And Cesar's wife, Kelley, a school teacher on Kauai, wanted to attend the week to freshen her 'perspectives.' My nephew, Eddie, recently graduated from the Iowa Writers Program, was happy for the few hundred dollars and an airline ticket to Kauai. He would organize and teach a few sessions. I was set.

The island was more beautiful than I remembered it. It was the ink dark skies that startled me. I had forgotten how vast the expanse. The first night I could not sleep. The full moon kept poking at me asking me what was next, and it was all I could do to stand up, ignore the question and walk toward the sound of the ocean at the end of the road. Danny, the dog, never left my side.

We walked to the large rock that marked the entrance to the farm. I leaned against it, the rough edges poking at my legs, solid and strong, and at my back and buttocks through the slim nightgown. Was it here that I scraped the fender of the rental car and Ty was so furious at me? Or maybe this is where Jordan would perch when I turned off the television on him in the main house. The memories came like the shooting stars rocketing through the expanse above. Whoosh and then gone. And they did end up shoving the more recent drama of the election and its resulting upheaval to the side. Maybe I could set aside some of that turtle shell that I could feel growing to encase and protect me.

I looked down to the main house as I returned. There was a light on in the kitchen and I could see a figure of a man at the sink, drinking a glass of water. He sent his glance all the way through the fruit trees 'til it landed close. Near me. I could feel his glance all over my body. It was unnerving, like a heat seeking missile sniffing at my jeans. I kept the glance from returning to its sender and took it in instead. It was a shimmer of imbalance that tossed me somewhere else beside despair and memory.

Tora had an outdoor bathtub that sat sheltered in a nest of bougainvillea. I undressed slowly, shivering just the slightest bit in the night air. Dropping my robe, my gown, and slipping into the warmth of the water, bumping into the reflected star shine. I shook my head from side to side and water ran from my eyes. Morsels of mess and disarray that I had sported since Ty's death, since Jordan's departure, since Trump's election fell into the warm liquid. The electric glance from the window had sparked me. Foolish, but true. I wept with relief, at being able to feel something else. I felt my body again for good.

Everyone arrived safely. Kelley made our meals and got free tuition in exchange. The couples were embarrassed in class together. Writing for themselves in front of partners was intimate and strange. Jerry and Anita decided the best remedy was wine before every session so one or the other of them ended up with their eyes closed as the others attempted to free write an impression, a sound, a memory or an object to the gentle rhythm of a discreet snore. The doctor never showed up. Barb did not attend after the first session with her friend, David.

"I'd rather not, Annie. I hope you understand. I think it's good for David to have an outlet but honestly I feel so foolish." She squinted a little behind her glasses, rubbing her very white arms against the strong sunlight. I confess to wondering what it must be like to be her and to snuggle in with a big man by her side. Why did I constantly think about that polyester housecoat that Hattie always sported when she pulled out the trash bins?

"How long have you two been together?"

Barb blanched and smoothed one errant curl at the back of her neck. "Well, we are friends but I wouldn't say we're together. David can be a difficult fellow to please." She laughed weakly. "He offers his opinions," she said to me, as if it was a code between gals. Like, I guess I should know what it is to be scrutinized by a computer programmer for correct choices.

"Opinions?" I said. Barb sniffed and turned to her straw bag where she had some very important Kleenex.

"David and I are friends, period. That is his opinion, his firmly held truth. Anything more is foolish to contemplate, so it is my own doing." She smiled bravely at me. "I'm going off to see the orchid farm down the road. And then I'll catch the van to the airport. Can the van take me to the airport?"

"I am sure Cesar could arrange it. But it's quite a ride."

"It's most important. I'd like to make it a priority. I will pay him."

"Of course. It's really up to him."

"Well, I won't be stranded here. That's for sure. I can call a taxi!"

Barb was getting more insistent. Almost challenging, like I was trying to keep her here against her will. "I'll do my best to persuade him. Really," I said.

She softened but she was definitely in bristle mode. "Yes. Yes, of course, you will."

And she turned abruptly on her heel and was off, elsewhere. Anywhere, far from me was the goal.

The transaction between us did not work. She scurried away like a small rodent and I was surprised that I wasn't more sympathetic to her plight.

"She's not very realistic," David said to me at lunch, a little frustrated, when I asked after his companion. "And she's not interested in any input." He said that with a straight face and I did not react.

"Really?" I said, instead. "Is she entitled to your opinion?"

He looked at me for a minute before he smiled, understanding the tease.

"I am set in my ways, one could say."

I received this statement with equanimity. Then, he looked up at me. "I often say the wrong thing. I mean it's not wrong, it's just too blunt. It gets me in trouble." He wasn't glib, just honest, and he blinked his eyes as he reheard what he had just said. "That's a good reason to come to a writing seminar. To learn how to say what I am thinking. No. What I mean. Yes?" He struggled to fully describe what he was feeling and then gave it up. "She is someone I've known for a long time. We both would like it to be easier but it is not. How's that?" And he smiled, simply and openly. Like all the workings he had gathered to try to explain himself flummoxed him and he lifted his hands and grinned instead. "I'm so sorry, really. I'll try not to be the focus of any problems. And I will keep my opinions to myself. How's that?"

He looked at me so genuinely. He had been here before, I could see. But he was willing to own up to it and go along to get along. He seemed to know where he faltered and had some ways of dealing with it.

I had noticed him jogging after our first session. It was twilight before dinner, others had retired. Next day, he wrote about it in class. Something about the rhythm of the road against his feet and legs connecting him to new possibility. If he kept moving, feeling himself against the earth, there was a chance of redemption. That's what he wrote. I believed him and more than that, I agreed.

And he knew I had been watching him. He put that in the piece. How eyes followed him, curious, surprised that his muscle and bone still propelled him along black top. A bit vain, but then, he was a handsome man and was probably used to being a fascinator. He was alive and reckless and clearly had nothing to lose.

He was right. I did watch him. I envied his movement, the muscularity that he displayed. I wondered if I could match him. He watched me thinking all those things.

As he watched me I could feel that electricity sparking again. My spine tingling and the itch of this new post campaign state. I needed to get my arms around myself. Nobody had been interested enough in my reaction to them in some time. Older women assume the invisibility cloak, but he wasn't allowing that. Whatever gated community I thought I could live in dissolved when David looked at me so clearly. The doors flung wide open. I resented his easy shift of attention to me from the woman with whom he had arrived. I was glad to have the resentment to lean into, but all bets were off as to my staying power. This, too, was new.

I felt him assess all my baggage, the transparency of the contents of my strewn suitcase made me want to scamper away and pick up my underwear from where it had landed on the surrounding bougainvillea. And he could see all that and it made him smile, almost wickedly.

David could see he had struck a chord in me and he liked it. He was curious, intrigued. And I think I might have blushed.

"I'm learning a lot here, Annie. It's great to be able to download some of my images onto paper, you know?"

"I'm glad it's working for you," I said, wondering what images he was downloading and what he already had in his archive.

"Yep," he said. "Now, I'll try to be a nicer guy."

I found myself counting the potato chips on my plate. Wondering what they would sound like if I crunched them with my mouth closed. Sometimes I did that so I wouldn't say the wrong thing in a conversation. Like when I tried to talk with Jordan and there was nothing I could say that would land within a circle of warmth and acceptance. But I wanted to meet David on equal footing.

"Sometimes that can be refreshing," I said. "Being able to just speak your piece. Especially these days." I said.

He looked at me, assessing.

"These days different from others?" he asked.

David wore a white dress shirt, like he was going to corporate head-quarters. His nails were clean and I noticed, as he put down his coffee spoon, how carefully he had folded up his shirt cuffs, revealing thick wrists and watch with a metal, stretch band. He had the soft scent of lavender soap that swallowed up the fresh breeze from the ocean. I found myself wondering if he ever took that watch off his wrist, and what he would look like with a stripe of white highlighting his hands.

"I'm recovering. Finding my balance. I worked the election in Michigan and have been reeling ever since."

"Why'd you go?" It felt like he might really want to know.

"Do my bit for democracy."

He laughed. "You're kidding, of course?"

"No, actually. I'm not. I thought I could make a difference."

He laughed again. "Really? That's charming." His look was steady.

"Charming?" I said. "That's a little patronizing if you ask me."

"Oh, no! See, there I go, offending again." I said nothing and thought it better to sip my tea and get ready for the afternoon session. "I bet you wore one of those pink hats and went to Washington as well, yes?" He was grinning now.

"Yes, actually. I am rather proud of that."

"Pussy hats, they were called, right?" He looked right at me. I wasn't sure why the word felt intimate and embarrassing in his mouth. "I did my share of David and Goliath marching back in the day," he said.

I couldn't let it sit. "Well, what are we to do? Sit back and say nothing?"

"Tut, tut," he said, lifting his finger.

"I beg your pardon?"

"Tut, tut." And he looked at me, lifting his chin, a sparkle in his eye. "It's actually a literary expression I really enjoy! Stops an argument before it happens."

David could see I was a bit confused. And I was. I started counting the slats in the picnic table to focus myself again. He continued, "It's just that I have lived long enough to move aside when a crushing wheel is heading toward me. After eight years of Obama you gotta know the white folk were going to raise their own Jesus."

"What are you saying?"

"Oh, surely you will not tell me that we are a country post racial and ready to accept all. Tell that to my step son who lives in Georgia and is a favorite punching bag for the Valdosta police patrol."

"I didn't know you had a son." Since Jordan was part of the reason I did everything these days, I said. "I have one, too."

"Stepson," he said, ignoring my confession. "Hoping for work with the post office, like his mother. A good job. But that does not stop the police." He shifted back to his point. "In my experience, when the lower classes gain equity with the upper classes, the upper classes are not about to let that stand."

He was right. I knew he was but I couldn't let it stand, "I still believe that people are really good at heart. Anne Frank said that."

"I believe Anne Frank was murdered," he retorted. And then that grin, again.

Cesar and Kelley came out from the kitchen to the picnic tables where we all sat finishing lunch, cracking the last potato chip, washing it down with frozen papaya drink.

"Cesar will take folks over to Bali Hai this afternoon. We'll be there for a couple of hours. Everyone can write their assignment, or sketch or swim. Right, Annie? I mean we are in Kauai." Kelley spoke with an over-broad grin, reminiscent of a girl game show model of the 1980s.

I watched as the group assembled. Anita and Jerry, the couple from Maui, were ready for the beach, of course. Their faces covered in sunglasses, zinc oxide and floppy hats, and somewhere in all that muumuu fabric their arms and legs emerged like stalks of birds of paradise. They were first in the van. David had no hat and he wore wing tips, but he had found a folding chair in the garage for himself. He glanced over toward me, but I turned and headed into the grove of trees. Edith, the plucky blond woman who wrote children's stories, sat in front with Cesar, dressed in khaki shorts and a pith helmet, ready to charge ahead on the adventure. Eddie climbed in, skinny and dear, and they were off.

I walked slowly back to the bungalow, looking up at those electric papayas, wondering if they would ripen differently with the change all around us. They were still green and impenetrable, the avocados, alligator ugly. The fruit strained to grow, resolute that it had nothing to give until it was ripe.

I saw Amanda on the stairs of the yoga temple, sitting carefully in the sun, her hands on either side of her gripping the step, her face turned up to the sky. "No beach for you?"

Startled. "Oh! No," she said. "Is that okay?"

"Of course. Sorry to disturb your sunbathing!"

"Oh! No," she said apologizing for her presence.

Tightly wound, Amanda had been tentative most of the week, but then only Eddie was near her age in this group. And he had been strangely distant and moony-eyed all week.

"You're from New Jersey?" I offered.

"Yes," she said. "Yes, I'm a librarian. A recent librarian. Just coming back into the work force, you could say."

"Congratulations."

Amanda laughed a little. "I love books. I mean, books saved my life."

I smiled, "Yes, I feel that way sometimes, too." Amanda shifted and relaxed a little. "Who's your favorite?" I asked, looking to smooth her path a little.

"Writer?"

"Sure." A gear shifted and her neck softened.

"I read a lot of Willa Cather, last year. I know you said you liked her in our class. Read everything. I loved *Song of the Lark* the best, the part where she camps in the Grand Canyon all alone and safe and protected by those red rocks and the night sky." That was the longest sentence I had heard her utter since she had arrived. It fell out of her like it had been precarious on a shelf, pressured by others close by.

"I was never much of a camper but I always thought those red rocks had something to say," I offered.

"Yes. Right!" She grabbed hold of her tightly rolled up newspaper and tapped a few times on the steps.

"Anything interesting in the news?" I felt like I was talking to someone practicing English and I wanted to give her another opportunity to speak.

Amanda furrowed her brow. "Our new president wants to expand the prison at Guantanamo. Makes you wonder who he's planning to put in it." Her eyes shifted

"Well, we're nice and safe here." I was trying to be comforting but I heard my own tone grow ironic.

"You spent time here before?"

"Just once," I said carefully. "I have to admit it wasn't the best of times. But times change," I said. "And here I am again."

Amanda looked at me with her lovely green eyes, and then smiled. Right into them.

"Yes, things change," she said. A mantra.

"I need a nap," I said. "See you later."

"Yes." She blinked and I heard her release her breath when I stepped away.

As I closed the door of my bungalow, I watched as Amanda rocked back and forth in the sun, making sure that the sun she might snatch would cover all parts of her wary body.

I woke, chilled. I had thrown the pillows and bedclothes onto the floor, the pile wild and unceremonious. A mote of swirling dust hung in the air like a pointillist painting. The afternoon breeze came through the skylight, bringing layers of light to the stillness and gently shoving the dust into new doorways.

The van pulled up in front of the main house and I got up to peek through the window. Quiet, bedraggled, they were eager to get away from each other, quickly scattering to their rooms before dinner. I saw Barb come out of the house with her bag. She'd been waiting. Cesar stood to the side while she cornered David. David didn't look directly at her. He rubbed the top of the garden chair he was holding, clearly agitated. There was one sentence he did say, though I could not hear it, and then he turned abruptly and went into the house.

Cesar discreetly picked up Barb's bag and set it in the van leaving the door open. He closed the door. The sound stood by itself, a question, but David did not come back out. The van crunched the driveway stones and Barb looked out through the window. A prisoner leaving detention.

When the air was still again, David came out of the front door. He had a soft garment with him, maybe a woman's nightgown. He strode to the mulch pile in the middle of the grove and tossed it in. Slung some other branches over it. Wiped his hands on his pants and then stopped. Like at an altar. He stood quietly, shook his head. His strong frame wilted. Then, upright again he organized his bones to walk back to the house where he disappeared.

Danny nudged at the door and came to sit next to the rattan lounge chair that faced the small bungalow garden. He sat neatly, his head up, his paws crossed waiting for me to come and pet him.

"This place, so full of endings and beginnings." I said, putting my hand on his body. He put his head on his paws and waited patiently.

Chapter 10

Ten Years Earlier in Kauai

Danny had been a constant presence when Ty and Jordan and I had come to the farm to rest and play, ten years earlier. Fool that I was, I had thought my thirteen-year-old son would love to spend the days on the beach while I devoured my pile of bedside table books under my umbrella and sunglasses. Jordan was in his recalcitrant stage. He insisted on watching the grainy television every afternoon and refused to budge when I urged him to head to the beach or take a walk with me. I left him a couple of times, but returned always to him sitting there, zombie like, playing video games and watching reruns of bad television shows.

"Ty, you have to help me. Make him go hiking with you. You're gone and out the door every day!"

Ty turned to his son with equanimity while stuffing his granola. "Jordan, come hiking with me. You're driving your mother crazy."

Jordan didn't even roll his eyes, but left the room in a huff. "C'mon Annie. Take me down to the Napali Trail. I can get it right from the beach. I'll meet you back at the parking lot at five!"

"And what am I supposed to do all day? Babysit your hormonally challenged son?"

"I have to make that hike, Annie. I promised myself." Ty looked at me straight. Right to the back of my eyeballs. He had always played full court basketball and believed himself fit and thriving, except that in the year before our trip, he had had a few episodes of arrhythmia that sent him to the emergency room. His friend from college was a Beverly Hills doctor and suggested heart ablations. "It's just an electrical problem," Mick, the doctor said. "Great new Chinese technology. We zap the nerves and he's good as new."

Ty was eager to get zapped if it meant he didn't have to slow down or be hindered in his basketball or hiking schedule. I sat back. It was his decision and he had made it. And made it and made it, as every ablation led to a month or two of calm and then another emergency. I just couldn't see it, but then I couldn't see a lot of things.

"I want to make that hike." I knew he did.

"Well, I want to go, too. We can all go." And I knew we couldn't.

"No, Annie. I want this one by myself. I promise I'll make Jordan stop being an asshole tomorrow but it's a perfect day. C'mon. Take me to the beach."

When I dropped him at the beach he was out the door in a flash and bounding up to the trailhead. He loved going places that no one else did. On our honeymoon I swear we saw no one for weeks because he always chose the restaurant that was empty or the room on the balcony that overlooked or interacted with no human being. It was his idea of glamour, I guess. And when he hiked, he insisted on going to the farthest lookout, the off the trail cranny, the spot where no one else dared show their face. In a minute, I could only see the red of his backpack, the bundling of water and sandwich and chocolate bar. I insisted he take a towel at the last minute that he hung around his neck as a tribute to me. Just because I wanted some input into this solo journey. He smiled, the way he did, and took me with him as best he could.

Stopping by the village on the way back to the house, I grabbed a couple of sandwiches and a Frisbee. Maybe I could get Jordan to at least toss that around with me.

Back at the house, I called out to him and he dragged his sorry self back into the kitchen. "Lunch," I said cheerily.

"I just finished breakfast."

"I know. We're going to toss the Frisbee for an hour. How's that?"

Jordan was literally speechless. Then. "No, Mom. I'm gonna watch the tube."

There was something in the dismissal, the refusal to go along to get along, to dig his heels in and not give me an inch that infuriated me. He walked toward the couch and I stormed over to the television and yanked the chord out.

"No television. Outside now!"

I rarely raised my voice and Jordan was surprised. Then, he went into action, "Fuck you!" he said. And headed toward me to grab the cord.

"Oh no, you don't. Stop it!" I raised my hand high and knocked over a lamp on the table. Danny heard the commotion and came running. He started barking and running around in circles.

"Get outta here, you fuckin' dog! Get away from me!" Danny turned and starting barking in Jordan's direction, "I hate dogs. I hate this place! I hate you! Leave me alone!"

Jordan stormed out through the sliding doors and strode down through the trees. I watched him as he felt my eyes on his back, he went into a jog and disappeared among the trees.

Good, I thought. *At least he's moving.*

Danny sat down and looked up at me, wondering how in the world this craziness had started.

"I don't know!" I said to him. "I lost it, okay? I lost it!" Danny turned his head to one side. "He's a thirteen-year-old boy! He's been shrinking away from more and more, ever since Ty started having health problems. Every time there's another heart thing, and there's another bottle of pills in the bathroom cabinet, every time, that boy shrinks further and further away. I don't know what to do about it! About any of it. Ty is his own master. He wants to hike! Die on the damn Napali Trail for all I care! All by himself! What am I supposed to do?"

I sat on the bar chair behind me, exhausted, the cord from the TV hooking around my leg and tripping me, tipping the chair into the breakfast bar.

"I just don't know what to do, Danny!" I looked into his muzzle. "What would you do?"

Danny barked just once. He then sat down at my feet. He sat there still and quiet. And I wished I could have cried but I couldn't. I put my head into my hands and tried to gather perspective. Maybe I sat there for an hour, I don't know. Then I picked up the lamp and made sure it wasn't broken. I straightened the television on its stand and slowly walked over to the sliding doors to see if there was a sign of Jordan. There wasn't. Okay. At least he was on an adventure. He'd find his way home at some time. Sometime.

Another hour went by. And then another. I brought lemonade from the kitchen to the picnic table as the slant of the sun found another angle. And brought the sandwiches, and opened mine and took a bite of the ham and swiss. It was good. I knew that Jordy would like it. And the chips too. And I had a bottle of Dr. Pepper for him. I finished my lunch sure he would show up soon. Danny delicately picked up the Frisbee from where it lay on the floor near the breakfast bar. He brought it outside to me.

I grabbed it and tossed it a few feet but of course, could not get it into a proper spin. That was Jordy's expertise, or even Ty. It was something they were both good at. That they could share, compete, laugh, bond over. Isn't that what was needed for a growing boy and a fading father? Danny was kind and went to fetch and bring it back but he had no interest in getting me to play with it. He knew what certain people were good for and what they had no need of mastering.

Taking advantage of the quiet and the solitude, I grabbed one of my neglected books, and the perfect sunhat I had dreamily shopped for, and a chaise folded by the door. I carefully took my beach towel and spread it along the plastic. There was no view of the roiling ocean, no blue to gray sound of the rush and promise of a wave, soon wasted on the sand. But it was my version of haven and I settled into it, pretending I was not looking for Jordan, waiting to hear his desultory foot pads, or that I would not react when he returned.

My eyes closed the minute I relaxed. I don't know how long I slept but the sun was low and my legs were pink.

"Jordan," I called when I went back inside, "Jordy, are you back?"

No answer and the clock read 5:00 p.m. I had to go pick up Ty. Danny walked quietly into the kitchen and looked up at me. I gave him a treat and he chewed it hungrily. Then, went to the door to the garage and sat with a paw scratching the wood.

"You want to go for a ride, Danny?"

It was time to find Ty, so I opened the garage door and was surprised at how loud and cranky it was. I threw a couple of beach towels in the back. Maybe Jordan went to the beach to find his dad and needed one to dry off. It was 5:30 now and the angle of the sun sloping toward the sea was no longer subtle.

"Keep a look out for Jordan, Danny. See if we can find him? Yes?"

I pulled into an almost empty parking lot. Folks cleared beaches early as the tide came in swiftly at the end of the day. I didn't see Ty waiting on his usual bench and so parked and headed out to see if I could find him.

I took a few steps onto the sand and saw a figure lying on the beach, a red back pack tossed down next to it.

"Ty? Ty? You okay?" He rolled slightly when he heard my voice and I could see that his face was almost as grey as the sand. I came closer. He was sweating profusely. Panting, slowly, but panting.

"Oh Jesus! Ty! How long have you been lying here?"

He looked up at me with his chocolate eyes, now red rimmed. "Hi, Annie. I'll be fine. I'm fine. Don't worry."

I came over to him and wiped his forehead. Got out the water bottle and gave him what was left of the water.

"Can you stand up? Will you stand up?"

He rolled to his side and then to his knees and stopped there for a moment.

"C'mon, sweetheart. Let me try to get you in the car. Maybe I should call an ambulance?"

That got him moving. Ty hated to be made a fuss over. And he got real nasty when I actually wanted to address health situations with the proper remedies.

"No, goddammit. Where's Jordan? He can help."

"He ran off." Ty looked at me. "Don't ask. Can you get up?"

Ty took a deep breath as best he could and smoothed his hair back from his forehead.

"Here we go," he said. "I just need to rest."

Between the two of us, we managed to get him into the car and I put the front side seat down so he could lie back.

"Hey, Danny. Hey, Danny dog, you coming out to the beach with my girl?"

Danny just looked from Ty to me to Ty to me. "It's okay, Danny. Ty will be just fine."

Ty lay back and I jammed the car into gear and headed out and onto the road for the main hospital in Lihue, thirty miles away.

"Where's Jordy? We can't go anywhere without Jordy!" Ty said with his eyes closed.

"He'll be fine. He'll be fine." I repeated the mantra for both my men.

Danny sat quietly in the backseat pacing my breathing. Ty closed his eyes and moved his hand over to my leg. "Don't worry, Annie girl. I'm fine. Really. No need for the hospital,"

"Shut up, darling."

We drove the curves by the ocean and passed back by the side road to the house. Danny sat up and stuck his head out the window and barked. I looked in my rear-view mirror and saw Jordan sitting on the rock at the driveway entrance. I made a quick U-turn and headed back up to the road.

"Get in, "I said. "Dad's sick. Get in, please."

Jordan dropped the cape of disdain as soon as he saw Ty's grey face and jumped in the back seat next to Danny. I swerved the car around. "Jeez, Mom, what the fuck?"

Ty smiled, his eyes still closed. "I'm okay, Jordy. Watch your mouth."

"Jesus, Dad." Is all the boy could muster. But, I noticed as we moved along the road that he moved his hand to the side of his dad's cheek and Ty took his hand from my thigh and put it over the long bony fingers of his only child.

We made it in an hour. The ER guys came out and put Ty on a gurney and oxygen.

Jordan and I watched as they rolled him into the treatment room. And there we were.

I looked at our son. "You okay, sweetheart? You okay?"

Jordan shook his head. "Yeah."

The nurse came out of the treatment room and came over to us. "We're going to get him stabilized and let him rest for a bit. There's one chair in there and one of you at a time can sit with him. Okay?"

I shook my head and Jordan stood up. He was already taller than me. "I'll go," he said and then turned to me, "Okay, Mom?" His eyes swept my face. "I'm sorry I've been a jerk. I'm sorry. I'm gonna sit with Dad, okay? Is that okay?"

"Of course, sweetheart. Yes, yes, Jordan, of course."

I watched as he disappeared through the double doors. For the first time I took a deep breath and grasped my hands together. "Oh, please God. I need some help here," I muttered.

The admitting nurse heard my prayer. "Oh, we're great with heart stuff. Mostly all we treat are fat old guys who play too much golf at Princeville."

"He was hiking. The Napali Trail. He's not a fat old . . ."

"Oh, sorry, right, right. Of course not. I didn't mean . . . Never mind, dear. Just know your husband is in good hands."

"Right." And she busied herself with some papers that did not look important. I could see how she berated herself for saying the wrong thing. The best I could do is walk away.

I wandered through the sliding doors into the edge of purple twilight and found a bench in front of the ER. At least it was gorgeous in Hawaii. The frangipani and birds of paradise were standing watch with the easy confidence of the beautiful.

That's how I'd always felt about Ty. He was a handsome man, He was beautiful, even, and I loved him anyway, almost in spite of it. But his beauty gave him standing in a rough world and there were days I ached to see him, his chin and hair and the weight of him in our house. When he was sick I was always quietly happy when a young nurse would catch his eye and give him an extra flirt. They wanted to take care of him. That was a good thing. And I knew we had made a good life.

Jordan was our only child. We had tried again but it didn't work and Ty was okay with that. And ultimately I was, too. We were a good trio. Three against the world. Sitting in front of that ER in Lihue I floated a ring of white light around our trio and prayed we were magnetized and would not leave each other, could not leave each other. We would somehow stay connected and full of juice through long lives. "Ah, the growing old together, fantasy," I heard the voice of my writing teacher again. "And they all lived happily ever after." Such contempt he had for happy endings.

Looking out into the parking lot, I saw Danny's face in the back window. I went back inside and found a Dixie cup and filled it with water. Set it by the bench. Went and retrieved the dog. He sipped the water with his long tongue and sat quietly by my feet. We sat outside for another two hours.

Jordan sat inside, quietly, by his father. Ty held Jordan's fingers, eyes closed and sipping oxygen. Every now and then he squeezed the pad of Jordan's fingers, a Morse code of love.

When the stars covered the dome of sky, I took them all home, quietly. I fed Ty the pills from the new bottle of medicine. I fed Jordy his ham and cheese and wanted to tuck him in. See him safely to bed. Instead I managed to rub his back for a moment while he finished a glass of milk. I thought I felt him relax just a little into my outstretched hand.

When the lights were out, I sat in the rocker by our bed measuring the breaths Ty took in and I exhaled, slowly. Ty slept and slept and slept and slept.

Chapter 11

The Last Day in Kauai

Our last morning in Kauai was uneventful. Everyone found their way to the airport or to the hotels they were retreating to for more time on the island. Amanda had rented a room in Kilauea for the month and was paying for it with babysitting duties.

"I love kids. I have always loved kids. And I am very careful with them. I take good care of them," she said to me when I asked her if she was up to the childcare challenge. She didn't blink when she spoke. She didn't smile either. There was something torn in this girl. I wanted to reach out and hold her but she felt too much like spun glass.

"They are lucky to have you, Amanda. I am sure of that." I said, trying to surround her with my confidence in her. She plowed ahead with more information.

"I got a good reference from a friend of the family." Amanda stated that clearly, then stopped, embarrassed. Over compensating? "They don't actually come in 'til tomorrow, so I'll have to find a room tonight," she said, quietly.

"I'm staying here through the week. Feel free to stay. I believe David is staying as well tonight. We made that arrangement before he came. We can all have dinner together." I wasn't sure if she would be too shy to be with just the two of us but it was worth a try.

"Oh. That would be great. I really appreciate it." She smiled desperately. I don't think she had really thought through where or how she would spend the night.

"Please stay. Relax before heading into a week with little ones." I tried to cheer her, offer an anchor. She looked grateful but I was wary of overstepping.

"I'll take a beach walk, now. I'll be back in time for dinner. Thank you, Annie."

I watched as she scurried off to find her sun hat, and Kelley and Cesar made their farewells and assured me they would be back to check on me and make sure everything was in order.

"Eddie," I called. "Thank you for coming this week and being such a help." He stepped into my arms. I was always surprised when Eddie embraced me, which he did fiercely whenever we were together. Maybe it was because he had lost his own mom early on, but he had clearly adopted me and every time I felt his stubbly cheek against mine I couldn't help but grin.

"I'm sorry I can't stay, Aunt Annie. I had a great week. It's gorgeous here, and I got some writing done, but, you know, I met this girl before I came and I'm really crazy about her."

"That's great news. What's her name?"

"Shamana. She's half African. I met her in school. She's amazingly talented. She even wanted to come and write with me this week but I told her you guys would have to meet."

"Okay. Great." He actually grinned at me. "Oh boy. You have it bad, Eddie." I teased him, and he laughed. "Did you have a good time, really?"

"Yeah. Yeah, I did. I just miss her like hell. You know?"

"Yeah, I know."

"Speaking of missing. I have to ask you. You heard from Jordan? He okay?" I loved Eddie when he was being fierce. His big eyes behind horn rimmed glasses got clear and direct. Like weaponizing chocolate pudding.

"I imagine he's just fine. He's been in Japan, I think. I don't hear from him much."

"That really sucks." Eddie snorted a little and looked away.

"I got an email from a friend of his in Japan before Christmas. Says Jordan is out in the country and no Wi-Fi and that he wanted to say hello. I thought that was good."

"Unnecessarily mysterious, if you ask me." He shook his head. "Sorry, but Jordy can be a real jerk." Eddie shook his head. It was so sweet how he had adopted me, made sure I was okay.

"Not much I can do about that, my nephew." He reached out and hugged me again.

"Sorry." He stepped back and looked at me with the pudding eyes again.

"Yes. Me, too," I said. "I love you. Say hi to your dad for me." His dad, my big brother, has always watched out for me as well, I remembered.

"Yep," he said, and watched as he climbed into the last van of the day. I think I saw Amanda watching him leave as well, from a distance and with a shy smile. Cesar and Kelley waved. Danny came out and watched them drive off. I turned to find that Amanda had already disappeared.

It was quiet again. God, the air was thick with times past. I looked around, standing time out of time, and it could have been the quiet afternoon before we took Ty to the hospital ten years ago. It could have been. I found myself wondering what anchored us in time. People we love. Moments we slice in the tarpaulin that falls around us, the backdrop against which we act out those turning points that prod us to the next moment.

My head started to throb. It was the first time I was actually beginning to viscerally feel all the changes. In the country, in the life I had led for the last ten years. I felt like I could have been in a film landscape with soaring mountains and a sound track that predicted danger, and immediately felt the need to ground myself. Pierce the earth with some red infrared rays and get myself located in 2017, in Kauai. A teacher, solo, an estranged mother, a friend. Yes, rooting into the earth would be a good thing. I realized that the electric attraction I had felt to David at the beginning of the week was the beginning of some kind of thaw. Unsettling and lodged in a bay I had yet to fully secure.

"He's a nice boy." David said. He had come out and placed a chair near the table.

"Who?" I said. "Who's a nice boy?" I jumped at his voice, revealed in my reverie.

"Your nephew. He is a nice boy." David looked over at me, feeling my privacy. "He treats you nicely. With respect."

"Oh yes. Eddie. He's kind. Yes." I looked away and realized there was no need to exclude his kindness. But it took me a moment to decide.

"I saw Ed say goodbye to you from the window and thought you might like some company?" This was a question. "I don't want to intrude."

"Not at all," I said. "My apologies. This place has that effect on me. I feel like I'm in a time warp."

The memories I had stirred would not quiet. I saw my recalcitrant son run off toward the rock, heard Ty call me to take him to the beach.

"I came for a couple of weeks with my family. Husband and son. About ten years ago."

"Oh," said David. "I didn't realize you were married."

"My husband died a year or two after our visit here. But he was sick here. So, the memories are vivid."

"I can see that." He thought a moment and then turned to go back inside. "I'll leave you to it."

"Oh, don't go. Please. I appreciate the company." He turned and carefully settled into his chair.

I changed the subject, "Did you have a successful week, David?"

David smiled slightly and reached for his headphones. "I don't usually attend things in person. I'm a Great Courses man. But you're very smart. That's good."

"Good," I said. "Not sure how I should take that remark." I smiled. He took up his iPad. Put in his earphones and began to listen.

As the week played out, I had avoided the sparks between David and me. But now I did appreciate the company. Company had not been part of my daily routine for a while. I decided to sit with him and just see what I would feel. Ty and Jordan lurked in the creeping sound of the surf, slipping over the farm now and then. In the skitter of a squirrel or the landing of an errant crow. They had been shaken loose, and now hovered, witnessing.

It felt like David knew about such ghosts. He had his own, I was sure. And he sat there with his head phones as they flapped around trying to get his attention. There was the residue of Barb's departure that lingered through the week. And he had told me about his stepson in Georgia. He had written about him this week. And there must have been a wife. But he did not seem bothered by them at this moment. I liked that about him. A function of age, perhaps. Or coming to terms with his own baggage.

I got up from my seat, not wanting to disturb him, but really testing if I felt a pull towards being there with him. I was so off kilter I needed to test the new feelings and see if they were real. As I stood to leave, I felt David's energy come up and surround me. He didn't want me to leave and that easy embrace assured my ghostly visitors that I did not need them present.

David smiled and looked up, I stretched and took a breath, feeling the encroaching presence of Ty and Jordan recede. I sat again. Buried myself in my book, and felt at ease in simple companionship. It surprised me.

We fell into our own worlds. Every so often, I would look up from my book and glance towards David. His eyes were closed and he was sitting straight up, listening intently to his book. As I glanced, he opened his eyes, acknowledged me easily with a smile. Surrounded with kind regard, the breeze affirmed the change. Danny raised his head once and madly raced after a squirrel in the underbrush and then quieted.

Around five, I went into the kitchen and took out a platter of poached salmon that Kelley had left for us.

"I'll set the table," David said, appearing. He touched my hand, reaching for the plates. "You relax."

Setting the table became a demonstration of energetic give and take. Just moving together, in random, tandem, alerted us both. It had been that long since either of us had had an intimate other with which to share a space. We recognized that we could harmonize. It made the conversation pale, the awkward stumble over well-built barriers less painful. In that simple task, we recognized that we could be human together.

How to explain that kind of intimacy to people with full houses, busy lives.

Amanda came in from a walk.

"Here," she said gently. "I brought a bottle of white wine. And there's some fruit in there. I made a salad before." She opened the refrigerator and set the salad next to a set of candlesticks. I placed two tapers in the brass holders. We all went to wash our hands, our faces. Let the water flow over our respective memories for a moment.

We gathered for dinner and said little. We drank the whole bottle of wine and at the end, Amanda sighed. "This is wonderful."

David, who had said nothing. got up from the table and returned with two dark chocolate bars. "I've been saving these."

He set them on the plate and used his large thumb to break them in pieces, then offered them around like communion wafers.

It was so quiet, like a hushed church, really. We all sat in relief. I wonder if that is how Danny observed us as we heard the tink of forks on plates, the whoosh of water sealing our silent satisfactions, and the way the moon whispered promises in the hidden places in our brains.

The candles burned down. Amanda excused herself with a smile. David and I sat quietly. He cleared the table, motioning for me to stay still, the moonlight angling through the open door and giving the room an ambient glow.

The sound of the water against the plates. I sat very still, eyes closed, and just listened.

I could feel him come back to the table and take my hand. We walked out under the moonlight.

"I'm not one for astrology but surely there's a wish worth making, yes?" he said.

We both looked up, closed our eyes and sent a message.

Then he put his arm around me, hugged me to him for a moment, rocking me a little. I took it as a shared shaking off of those pesky ghosts. I stepped back and smiled.

"Good night," he said.

"Good night." I turned back to my bungalow. He watched me the whole way. I know that because I turned a time or two to see if he was still there. If there was a magnet drawing me one way or the other. I had no idea, but just as I decided I should turn and go back to him, I could feel him withdraw his invitation. And I, all of a sudden, felt like a colossal fool.

Chapter 12

India

The calm of Hawaii lasted about as long as the flight back home. I was lucky with my Kauai workshop, but I had spent three months on the campaign away from work and I needed to get myself back into business.

So, practicality kicked in. I needed to plan my next retreats, get some classes up and into the world. Flyers, Facebook, Twitter, LinkedIn. All the platforms swam in front of me. I needed to get things in order. And my computer skills were from another era. I remembered that Sylvia, my assistant from the campaign, was a computer whiz.

"Sylvia, its Annie." I left word on her cell phone. "You said you might be looking for some extra work. Can you help get me set up for classes and stuff? Call me?"

I missed Sylvia. She had been my war buddy and no one really understood what we saw in Michigan in 2016. She and I had taken alternate routes from late night phone banks to avoid pickup trucks idling next to gas stations. Her husband's cousin, Mo, insisted that she avoid voter registration assignments where she had to close up alone. Each of their family owned 7-Elevens in the small farming communities now had a handgun in the cash drawer.

"I told them my cousin was killed in the Mexican gangs back in Texas. No guns for me. And no guns around my babies!"

I heard reports of her family when she came to work. Her parents were both gone but she had cousins that had told her they wanted to come to the States. Sylvia tried to call her cousins in Mexico to tell them to wait for awhile. Their own towns were overrun with drug gangsters and they were afraid to stay put. Sylvia didn't want them paying some "coyote" to get them here to America illegally. She was afraid she couldn't help them to become citizens then. And then, her husband's family was not the most open. They tried hard to control her and keep her out of the spotlight but Sylvia stood her ground.

"I told Fareed I'd leave him if he didn't let me have a life!" she said one day as we drove out to another gathering.

"And?" I said.

She took a dramatic breath and then looked over to me. "I am *very* good in bed!" she said and giggled. And so, she had made her way.

Within a couple of weeks, she had my website updated, my social media humming, and even made me start a blog. I was never sure if anyone read those things, but she insisted and so I committed to trying to make sense of my journal thoughts and make them into blog posts. She even contacted all my old students and did her best to get one piece of their work up somewhere on the web. I was quickly becoming a hero and it was all due to her efforts.

Registrations started coming in for online classes and I could fall back into a routine.

I had taken up a meditation practice since returning from the campaign. I thought that maybe some stillness could help me digest this feeling of dread I carried at the change in the American dream. And I was looking for the return of that spark I had felt from David. Sylvia just laughed when I told her my plan to meditate.

"Well, maybe it will help, Annie. But I come from a place where having a gun in the drawer and a sharp retort ready for an asshole serves me better."

"Maybe I'm too exhausted for all that anger, Sylvia. Maybe I'll try some compassion."

"Suit yourself, Annie. But what is it that writing teacher of yours told you? It's the thing that made me instantly like you."

I thought for a moment. "Oh. Right. He was a thorny old bastard."

Sylvia asked, 'What did he ask you again?"

"How have you managed to live so long and remain so pure?" I answered.

"A good question. Good luck with your meditation. I'll be keeping an eye on the business."

I wasn't deterred by Sylvia's cynicism. Maybe just because I just didn't; see the world as us and them. I smiled when Stephen Colbert nailed people like me with our understanding that "reality had a left wing bias." I believed Michelle Obama when she counseled us with "when they go low, we go high." In the end, it was my clarion call. Generational? Or naive? Or foolhardy? I didn't know. My brain was not giving me the answer. I had to look elsewhere.

I went to weekly gatherings at a meditation spot called The Center. The relief was palpable, showered as we were by the blessings being beamed at us, the dharma lessons clanging against our metal brains like cast iron cathedral bells. I began to feel an inkling of light between my tightly crowded monkey brain and the far end of the tunnel. Sometimes. When my brain didn't crawl over itself with *if, why, how, now* and *yikes.*

"How is it working?" my meditation teacher, Brian, asked me as he watched the group disperse and me sit there a little longer than the others, with wrinkled brow.

"Well, I start with the breath and it just makes me anxious. Then, I go to the image of white light and calm and it makes me hot all over. Then, I start to snooze and get guilty all over again."

"Sounds perfect," he said with a smile.

"What world do you live in?"

"Same as you." Maybe if I shared some of what I was feeling it would help.

"You know, Brian. I worked the election. It blew my brains out. Every fantasy of kindness and people doing the right thing was shattered. There were swastikas smeared on campaign signs. It was like an earthquake, and the tectonic plates don't want to settle back down into place. I guess the best way to describe it is . . . rocky. I feel so rocky inside."

He listened politely. "That's samsara for you." And gave me a smile. "Maybe if you spent some more time. Deeper time with yourself and what you learned, then things will become more clear." Before I could move the muscles on my face he said, "Just hear me out."

He proceeded to tell me about the three-week meditation retreats that the group offers in India with the Guru. Immersion in dharma (daily chores), meditation, ritual, more meditation and more work leading up to a visit with the Guru and time in the magical temple.

"It's a big movement there. And there's an enormous palace made of marble! Made stone by stone with local labor. It's otherworldly. Over there is a good place to sort out the world we're all living in over here. And I even have a friend who is looking for a sublet for the dates in India. The rent will be paid!"

I had gone to a few hometown initiations and meditation weekends. I had seen the videos of the groups chanting, eating, smiling, crying, and emerging happy and changed. I was still dreaming of Nazis banging at the doors and Dixie pickup trucks with rifles out the front window chasing me down country roads.

And there was the obvious connection with Jordan. Maybe time at an ashram would connect me with what he was experiencing half a world away. I didn't dare intrude on him in Asia, I could feel the flamethrowers beating me back at just the thought of it. But, there was a pull.

I signed up for a three-week course at the home temple outside of Chennai, India. I would be immersed in the energy of healing and change. I would be elsewhere and maybe the dreams and rock throwing would find a way to be heard and melt away. The young girl who wanted to sublet had great references. I was set. I booked my ticket to India.

Landing in Chennai, my entire time clock was upside down. They told us to just live at the local time but my internal gauges were blown and though I tried to ease myself into the assault of the airport and finding my driver to the temple, I was lucky to not turn to stone and stay put on the runway until my body could catch up from where ever its ruling mechanisms were functioning.

My driver greeted me with the same indulgent twinkle I came to expect from those offering service to American tourists. A mix of pity, disdain, and obsequious behavior. I was unceremoniously and mysteriously deposited at a cavernous hotel on a dusty street.

"Is this the temple?" I asked the bemused man.

"Oh, ho ho ho. No temple. We wait for two days. I take you on Wednesday."

He slid my bag into the air-conditioned, thank God, cement lobby. The street outside seemed to be in suspended construction. The metal beams on the site were rusty and lie in puddles of odd liquid, like discarded bodies with oozing bedsores. There were murals from the local agricultural cooperative painted on the plywood across the highway and bare-backed men and sari-clad women labored equally, mixing cement and hauling it in buckets to a wall half alive with rebar crying out against its imprisonment. And it was hot. And it was dusty. And it was loud. And there were cows roaming the highway, which motor scooters zipped around. I wondered if they were gathered up for milking but then, no, cows are sacred. Yes, I remembered that.

"I will pick you up in two days, madam. Yes?" He checked to see if I had heard him. "The hotel management will inform as to the time. Thank you." He nodded and bowed slightly with the Namaste salute and disappeared back into the construction before I had a chance to protest.

There were very few people at the hotel. A face or two peeked out from an outsized cement balcony and the clink of one coffee cup on a saucer echoed through the atrium. No one was in the lobby. We had been told not to reveal our location to anyone from home as there was some political problem that the Guru and his followers were handling. The local government was happy to detain devotees to squeeze a few more tax dollars out of the temple and its organization. That was probably the reason for the two-day delay in Chennai. This had not seemed like a big obstacle back in the States. Now I regretted not telling my nephew Eddie where I was heading. He was so in love with this woman, though. What was her name, Shama? Oh no. Shamana, like manna from heaven, surely. I doubt his thoughts were including me.

As I stood in front of the empty desk waiting for someone to check me in I heard the rumbly elevator door open and a tall woman in perfect white pants and top, an embroidered white scarf around her neck and a haircut rendered with exquisite precision, stepped out.

"Well, it's not the Taj Mahal. Let's get that straight," She said to no one in particular with a faux clipped accent. She was not a Brit but affected the rhythm. Her blonde bangs and piercing blue eyes reminded me of cornfields and white bread. "Where the hell is the management?"

She stepped up to the desk and rang the little bell. "Yoo-hoo." She said. "I have a towel smaller than a breadbox and a body longer than a python. This will not work! Yoo-hoo!"

At this point, a young man greeted me and grabbed my bags. "Ms. Annie. Your room is ready." He whisked me off, leaving my unhappy companion negotiating with a seriously disgruntled older woman in a red, wrinkled sari. She had clearly been interrupted at her meal and was in no mood to deal with the tall demands of this skinny lady.

The river of poured concrete followed me to my room with a stone desk and whitewashed shower and bedroom walls. There was a bed with a thin mattress. It did have a very small hand towel placed at its foot. And a wrinkled, red cotton blanket. And there was a silk screen print of a goddess with many arms. I lay down gingerly upon the red coverlet, flipped off my shoes and shoved off to a dreamless cavern.

It was dark when I woke. I had no idea what time it was, except that no one was working outside my window. The traffic went on unabated. A shower helped a bit. I found my yoga pants and tee shirt, my face cream and toothpaste. I located my book and notebook and pen and with these essentials assured, I felt more present. I wandered out of the room and down a few flights to the breakfast/dining room area on a balcony with a few kitchen tables and chairs. There were three people there. And a barman. That was promising. A young man approached me.

"Dinner, madame?"

"What time is it?" I squinted my eyes at him.

"It's 2:00 a.m., madame, but we find our arriving guests from the US often need food before they can adjust their time clock."

He was so unfailingly lovely. He brought me a curry soup. Made sure to remind me that the vegetables here were okay to eat. And I ordered a bottle of beer.

And in what was becoming a new rhythm for me, I sat quietly and watched as a couple left the dining room and headed back to their room. They were not kittenish. I didn't think they would rest deeply. Instead, they seemed disgruntled and sad, clammy at the level of the air conditioner, turned low for the time of night. The barman excused himself with a discreet nod after asking for my room number. The older Indian man got up unceremoniously and headed downstairs. He was the night watchman.

I could feel my gears changing, assessing an internal and external distance that had been colliding inside me for several months. I was catching up with something but not really certain what that was. Of course, the sickening travel ban against Muslims coming to the US was already in the news. And it was clear that there was a Teflon aspect to our new leader and the fascist choices he was leaning into. Maybe it was the slash in our collective psyche from which our moral and personal power seemed to be draining. We, I, could not get my hands around the neck of the snake as the snake was still unfurling. Disaster was clearly in the room, but nobody knew what cudgel to grab.

I needed to catch my breath, my balance. Allow things to slow down so I could begin to understand what was happening. I hoped the retreat would give me a launching pad into what was certainly a new and unfamiliar world for me; privileged, white, spiritually skeptical. I wanted so very much to be teachable. And the spark that David had offered seemed far away and foolish fantasy.

There was a rattle of chairs scraping across the floor behind me. The tall woman I had encountered in the lobby was looking forlornly in my direction.

"I can't sleep. I'm too tall for the bed, too long for the towels. I was too fat for the middle seat they squeezed me into and now I feel like my head is bursting. I need to be at that meditation retreat!" She looked at me helplessly. "I'm Mallory and I am a complainer."

"I'm Annie," I smiled and adjusted my annoyance at her loud, all too American presence. "Me, too, probably. I'm probably a complainer, too." Why not try to be gracious?

"I won't bother you. I can't sit. I've been warned not to wander the streets of Chennai at these hours. I should have brought my pearl handled pistol." She said dramatically, adjusting her long white scarf around her neck.

I looked blankly at her. "Sorry?" The beer had put lead weights at the bottom of my skull and the souls of my feet. I crunched at a papadum chip the young man had left in a graceless basket.

"Never mind, dearie. Never mind." She turned abruptly, scraped another chair against the floor and into a neighboring table and left. In a minute I saw her cross the dimly lit lobby below the dining balcony. She went to the front door and tried to open it but the guard there would not let her leave.

"Not good for walk, Madame. Not good for walk."

Mallory turned on her heel and went to the staircase. I heard footsteps clatter on stair after stair until the sound finally faded and I was alone.

If we were in Boston, our teacher would have told us it was time to 'hit the mat' for some balance and clarity but when I returned to my room determined to be open and ready for change, the idea of sitting cross legged on the floors of this place was not appealing. There was a strange coating, a mix of dust and maybe mold, that lingered in corners and encouraged me to grab the small towel from the bed and use it for a rug. I was happy to discover two extra bath towels in my luggage. Feeling the intrepid traveler, I spread the bath sheet across the dubious red coverlet, folded myself up on the bed, tried for a twenty minute meditation and fell asleep maybe half way through.

My new acquaintance, Mallory, met me at breakfast.

"Mallory? That's the right name?"

"Yep."

"I have an extra bath towel. Full-size. I thought of you. Want a gift?" Practice kindness, especially to those you might want to slap. I think Brian, our meditation teacher, taught me that.

"You're kidding! Yes. Are you sure?!"

"Sure," I laughed.

"Oh great! I'll drink the Nescafe, take a full body shower and be a new person! I promise. Thank you!"

We slurped the warm brown liquid served, grabbed the faux croissants and headed back to my room. I handed her the towel.

"Once I'm decent, I'll take you shopping. I got a discount from the barman."

Forty minutes later, I marveled at the skill with which Mallory bargained for a beautiful white sari, which she told me was for her home boudoir in Connecticut.

"Now," she said. "I know you are the stand offish type, but you have to get white clothes or you will die of heat. Here, these are gorgeous. And look, 100-percent cotton, loose as a goose, embroidered and very sexy. Don't you think?" I was amused that she actually asked my opinion, but had to agree, so I bought two sets of whites.

"Did you get that discount card from Barry, the barman?" she whispered. "This shop belongs to his cousin, Sandritha." A young woman in jeans and a tee shirt came out from the back of the shop. "Sandy! Hello, I'm back and I brought my friend. She needs whites, whites, whites! We're both staying at the hotel."

I realized it was a pleasure to have Mallory in charge. I had no decisions to make and lots of fun to have. Maybe the Indian adventure would be best known for great shopping and a perfect afternoon tea at a small colonial teahouse that Sandy directed us to. The world changed as we entered the room. The dusty heat of the day fell away and we were in a cool Victorian parlor, circa 1898. Albeit with a TV off the kitchen tuned to CNN.

"Oh, perfect," I sighed. My literary colonial roots kicked right in.

"Never mind that England might have done a better job with the whole India–Pakistan split thing. And the way they expected everyone to love their 'memsahib'." I looked up surprised to hear her familiarity with local history and injustice. "Sorry, I can't bear it. Hope they have a good sherry."

Tea and scones. Sherry and port. Tarts and pudding made their way to our table. We quickly fell into a sugar and sherry stupor.

"I think it was the last mango tart," Mallory said as she stared contentedly toward the TV. "What a way to go!" Her eyes moved and she pointed a finger at the screen. "Jews will not replace us. It says so on CNN."

I jerked my head around and there was a banner on the screen announcing to the world that there was a march of white supremacists in Charlottesville. I called to the waiter who ran the shop, "Would you mind turning the news up?" I asked. There was no one else in the tea room and he moved leisurely to the screen and turned up the volume. There was a pan up to crowds marching with torches. And CNN scrolled the message *White Supremacists Clash with Crowd in Charlottesville. Crowd chants "Jews Will Not Replace Us."* And a clip from the president saying there were good people on both sides. There was a picture of a young woman, Heather Heyer, who had been rammed by a car and was dead. The image of the swastika I had seen on the campaign jabbed at me.

"Oh my God, Mallory. Oh my God!" I said

"Well, that's a pretty sight for two travelers seeking enlightenment!" she said.

I started trembling. It surprised me.

"You okay? Annie, you're trembling!"

"I guess I am more affected than I thought. I worked the election. There were swastikas everywhere. I mean, I was followed at night by guys in pickups. I thought it was a bad dream. It is a bad dream."

"Calm down honey," Mallory waved to the waiter to bring more sherry. "Drink this. My God, you're a wreck."

"There were swastikas on the signs during the election but I didn't think it would."

"It's a set up. Small groups with big mouths," she said to me.

"Mallory, can't you see? How can this be rampant again?"

"More things change, more they stay the same."

"Enough, Madame?" the waiter chimed in, noting my upset.

"No. We'd like to see this. I'm sorry, I don't know your name."

"My name is Barry. I got it when I studied in America. At Texas A&M." He grinned broadly. His hair was slicked back and he stood at attention in his clean white shirt and shiny shoes.

"Oh. Well, hello, Barry," Mallory rolled her eyes. "Your mama know that's your name?"

Barry looked solemnly at the screen ignoring Mallory. "People do not like the Jews." He said simply. And looked at me.

"Well, yes." I realized that I should not make the assumption Barry was with me. Or Mallory either for that matter.

"Americans don't like anyone of color." Barry said.

"And anyone who is different." Mallory added, alert but not willing to get into a fight.

"And the Jews are different. We have them here, too. They are usually very successful," he said solemnly.

"That so?" I said to Barry, getting smaller, cautious. "I am sorry that we are seeing such anger again, in my country." I said to him.

"I like your president. He will take care of business. Not to worry, Madame. You will see, he will change things," another broad smile, authoritatively clicking off the TV.

"Okay. Enough for today!" Mallory said with a firm shove back from the table. "Let's get the check."

We hailed a cab outside in silence. Mallory kept her eye on me.

"At least you've stopped shaking," she said. "The guy is a jerk. People love a strongman. But, they don't know men like I do."

"We're not talking about dating here, Mallory."

Mallory offered a rare smile. "It's all about getting off . . . or um . . . shall we say power . . . in the end."

"I've got to get to that Temple. I definitely need a time out!"

We waited for a moment in silence. Then, I said, "Did you leave a tip?"

"Hell, no," she said.

"Neither did I."

Chapter 13

The Retreat Center

The Dasa, dressed in white robes, Nikes, and horned-rim glasses, greeted us in the dining room. It was lunchtime. We had all been gathered from our various locations and found our way to this ashram campus in the countryside about ninety minutes out of the city.

The air was humid and thick with cooking oil. The dorms were simple and clean and had sufficient air conditioning in the sleeping quarters. And the short road from the dorm to the meeting and eating rooms split into rivulets of muddy water that pooled outside the latrine.

There was a sad red dog that sat in that murky puddle, covered with mange, his eyes like silver marbles. He referred to me coolly, either stoned or dying. Then, I heard Mallory screaming behind me, screeching down the road flapping her hands and bashing her hat back over her shoulder at her back pack. "Get him off me! My God, get him off me!"

"Mallory! Are you okay?"

"The monkeys! The goddamned monkeys jumped me! Are they off?" She kept whacking at her backpack with her big white hat.

The Dasa approached us and spoke calmly with a smile. "A good reminder to keep bananas out of your backpack. The monkeys are voracious!"

"The damn monkeys! They're rabid. They carry all sorts of diseases. The goddamn monkey jumped all over me!"

"Yes. They forage for food." Again, the calming response of the Dasa.

"They can go forage in the forest! I'm an American!"

"Maybe your friend can bring you some tea. And all will be well. Welcome to India."

I went and found a pitcher of filtered tea and poured a glass for Mallory as the young woman with the Nikes welcomed the others entering the eating hall and, despite the heat and the dust and mangy red dog and the voracious monkeys, we all started to relax. Melt a little. We settled and were reminded why we made this journey. At the very least, we were reminded that the planet was changing, and we needed to be able to carry more light to help with the changes coming up.

"How's that?" Mallory asked to no one in particular.

"Light," she said. "We need to carry more light to combat the darkness."

"Like *Star Wars*?" She turned to me.

"Sure," I said. "Something's up. I think that's why I came. I can't figure out why nothing fits, and weird changes are happening everywhere."

"Oh you mean the Nazis in Charlottesville? Fascism never dies?"

"It's that and more than that. The rules are changing. I wish I could put my finger on it, besides being afraid of the change, but secrets are being unearthed."

As we broke and shuffled to assemble for our first meditation class, Mallory waited for me while I braved the latrine.

"How was it?" she asked seriously.

"Not the Taj Mahal, as I believe you stated well, back in Chennai."

Mallory laughed, caught off guard. "I brought my own TP and

sanitizing wipes. And a barrel of antibiotics. Stay close by. I'm a treasure trove." She rolled her eyes with an added twinkle.

"Thanks," I laughed. "I feel better already."

"Do you believe all that? All that, we better clean up our act because the planet is going to explode?" she asked.

"I don't know, "I said. "But, the fucking monkey on your back might indeed be telling us something."

Mallory grinned. "Point taken."

As we walked into the Assembly Hall, the Dasa, looking like the graduate teaching fellow that she was, was standing there grinning and chatting with one of her counterparts. They were looking at some photographs. Snapshots. And they were oohing and aahing. "Amazing," I heard our dasa say. "Look at that!"

Mallory edged us closer to the exclaiming teachers. "What you got there?" she asked.

Our dasa turned openly. "It's our guru. Look in the night sky. It's a photo of our guru flying in the night sky!" She handed the photo to Mallory who was prepared for a jaundiced remark and I watched as her face changed. "Oh my," she said.

"What?" I said to her as she moved away.

"What do I know? Think happy thoughts and *away* we'll go." She spread her long arms in front of her, Batwoman on the rise.

Maybe it was the tension of the journey, the exhaustion of the time change, the heat, the food, the embrace of the community that assembled together trying to find quiet, to open to changes, to heal secret or public wounds, but that first night of meditation, as we listened to the chants, it was like we were all lifted a little higher. I mean, I could actually feel a physical change. The rumble of the chanting buzzed behind my eyes, the scent of the incense softened the scent of mosquito repellent, the coolness of the floor crept up my spine and softened the way it held the rest of me erect.

Mallory fell silent. I could feel her rangy frame of bones, usually so alert and assembled for presentation, begin to relax into itself. She just let her bones go and, sitting beside her, I could feel the distance between the top of her shoulder and the top of her head extend. She was growing taller.

I spent the first few minutes scanning the room, trying to ignore the physical changes that were sneaking in and around me. One side of a room was filled with a battalion of dancing Brazilians who created a samba for every chant. The Chinese attendees sitting in the front, one after the other burst into wails. Actual gulping wails as they slowed down and felt the whoosh of freedom. Buffeted by the weeping of the one group and the dancing of the other, I fell to my own inner castle, where there was water, so much water, overflowing its moat and sweeping through every room. And it came up through me and out my eyes, like a fire hose. Water streaming from my eyes trying to cool and set my insides to right.

Mallory told me I sat there like that for the whole session. I had no idea except that I slept deeply and woke at six to do dharma chores, embracing silence and more meditation with ease.

The first week passed with the regularity of our schedules. I continued to "water the clouds", as my dasa described it to me, weeping upward. Tears fell from an inner well of the many few months past and the gaping holes over which I had thrown flapping drapes.

A windy hallway kept appearing in my meditations. At the end of it was the parking lot with the swastika in Michigan. And if I turned another way, I would catch a glimpse of the angry boy from Sturgis spitting at the street, and wonder if he would lead me back to my son. Once there was a throne room, and a flying guru floating across the mountain landscape that was the Napali Trail, the beach on Kauai, Ty lying on the sand.

Rise at six, meditation at seven, dharma work, classes, walks, meditation, blessings, ritual pujas where the senior spiritual leaders of the community offered prayers and burned incense and took us to deeper and higher states of consciousness. There was little idle chatter. Mallory and I tended to keep track of each other with a nod of the head, a twinkle of an eye, or a robust laugh heard across the room. And I tried to stay away from the repetition of painful memories, but the images came and went on their own, perching on yantras, hiding in the tone of a chant, sliding into a yoga pose at dawn.

Our dasa watched over us as we all tumbled through the layers of consciousness, buried throne rooms, tombs and landscapes where images and guides sprung up, pushed us forward and then gently led us back to our routines. Rise at six, dharma work at seven, classes, walks, meditation.

It was stifling outside. No matter how much tea I drank, or how many chapatis and bowls of rice I ate, my stomach would not settle. I tried to ignore it. Then, there was the second week puja ritual, where the older dasas burned incense over fires. We sat, chanted and ate in the smoky silence. I was exhausted inside and out and when my lungs took in the smoke, to clean out whatever was there, they turned to fire. I could not stop myself from coughing.

As I made my way, coughing, back to the dorms, the Dasa found me.

"Annie. How is the course going for you?" I had not spoken for a few days so it was startling to recover words and put them to feelings.

"I don't know. I'm not feeling so great tonight."

"It will pass. Happens to a lot of folks as they go through this change. Body and mind work together you know."

I coughed again and took my last sip of filtered water. She ignored my cough and asked again. "So, how is it going?"

Okay. I didn't need her sympathy. I'd meet her on her own turf.

"I am getting lost in the meditations. I love the daily meditation where you play music while we listen and then, the music stops and we are charged with having to replay the music note by note in our minds. A symphonic silence." Cough, cough.

"Giving you a chance to decide what to hear. What to listen for." She took a moment and then said. "I see you as changed a bit since you came. Lighter. Leaving some things behind."

"Maybe. At the moment I feel rotten. Like there's a huge garbage dump burning up stuff inside."

"Sounds apt. You take the changes in our world personally."

"Kids in cages, Nazis marching again, kids being gunned down at schools. Families falling away. How are we not all a part of that?" As was my habit the water started flowing from my eyes and nose once again.

"What do you do when you aren't at the temple?" she asked of me.

"I help people write their stories."

"The more people know their own stories, the more they can revise them!" she smiled.

All of a sudden I was seized with an enormous stoppage in my throat and chest and I started to cough and could not stop. The Dasa patted my back.

"Go in and get some water. Don't be afraid. You'll get rid of all the old stuff and start building the new world. It's what we're here to do."

"Jesus! What the hell?" It was Mallory puffing up behind me. "Jesus. Here's some water. You're going to break a blood vessel."

"It was the smoke from the puja!"

"Good night" smiled the dasa. "See you in the morning." And she moved away calmly.

Mallory pulled out a ziploc plastic bag from one of her voluminous pockets. She shoved a cough drop at me. "Here. And let's get you to bed."

My temperature was 103 when Mallory checked and she went into Nurse mode. Since I would keep everyone else in dorm up all night, she managed to wrangle a separate room, actually two, as she swore she designated herself my personal health assistant. Putti, the German woman who was in charge of foreign pilgrims like us, did not see the need for such a special arrangement, especially at ten at night. When Mallory brought out the phone number for her cousin at the American embassy, she managed to get us into a vacant air-conditioned bungalow that was usually reserved for VIPs. She made me take a cold shower, toweled me down, got me antibiotics and cough medicine from her stash, and put me to bed.

Oh, the dreams! Yes, there were smoky fires burning and dasas in white floating around me. There were the beating drums, drumming at my temples, even a monkey made an appearance. Mallory woke me a couple of times and made me swallow more pills and drink more water, and more water, and then some more water. The VIP bungalow had its own bathroom and as I floated in and out of it, I felt like someone in an angel hospital, followed by smoky forms and yet guided easily into and out of my bed. There were book pages, I remember, and a view of a circle of us sitting in meditation. I looked round the circle and there were folks from the retreat, there was the candidate I had worked so hard for, and a pile of Confederate flags being burned in the small fire, a pit where automatic rifles were being tossed. There was Ty, my husband, and even Jordan, my son. We all just sat together listening to a cooling rain that seemed to wash us all down, put out the fire, take our voices, our prayers upward.

The smoke cleared, there were no walls. The expanse was enormous and each person rose, separate, distinct, balanced and only slightly smoky.

"Did they all get what they wanted?" asked Mallory the next morning when my fever broke and I was sitting up in bed telling her my dream.

"I'm not sure they all knew. But they were able to speak. They were a choir, they were like choristers, and as I smiled at each of them, they sang—even though I couldn't hear them."

"Hallelujah, sister. I stole some oranges from Putti's private stash. Want some?" She was quiet for a moment.

"I didn't know you had a son." Mallory said as she went to get the fruit.

"Oh," I said, my heart somehow taking that statement in more deeply than usual. "Yes. His name is Jordan. We're not in touch. He left for Asia a year after Ty died. Almost two years now."

"And . . . ?"

"Nothing really." I looked at her. "He left to find himself. He left to find his dad? Or another one? Or another family? Or? I don't know. I haven't received any word except he's no longer at the monastery where he went to study. I get an email now and then."

Mallory did not crack a joke. "That's rough."

"Yes," I thought for the first time in a couple of years. "Yes, that is very rough."

"That sounds practiced," Mallory said. "Bet you've said that a few times."

"He was in the dream. That was good. He looked good."

"Maybe that's why you came to this monastery. Maybe you were looking for your kid."

I thought about that for a minute and it just made me tired and sad and started the waterworks again.

"Maybe," I said, closing my eyes, and I drifted back to dreamless sleep.

When I finally rose from my bed, I didn't trust the feeling of lightness. Somehow, the days of water and dreams had dug out a tunnel into which new light was flooding. I felt strong and only a bit more vulnerable. Mallory filled me with her stash of protein drinks and filtered water and I was ready to return and participate in the culmination of our retreat, an overnight at the great marble Temple.

The night session before we went to the temple, we did a yantra meditation where we sat in meditation in front of a geometric form that began to have dimension and rhythm as we entered it in a meditative state. By this time in the retreat, I had gotten used to the feeling of new states of being and I didn't need to narrate every experience with something with which I was more familiar. Yes, the yantra seemed like a labyrinth to explore, but it was a hologram as well, in which I realized I was the actual hologram. I wasn't separate from it, or making a journey through it, I was the same as that geometric shape/no shape expanding as the form before me.

"Your eyes are like saucers," Mallory said, as we toddled back to the dorms, having been kicked out of our luxury quarters with my recovery.

"How was it for you?" I asked.

"Um. Fine." She was the worst liar. Instead she looked much more like the cat who swallowed the canary. "I . . . uh . . . I slipped out. Needed a night walk."

"Oh," I said. "I suppose taking care of me has been tough. A break seems right."

"Thank you, Annie, for your blessing. But I didn't know I was entitled to your opinion, dearest?"

"Mallory! I didn't mean . . ."

"I know. I know. Go to bed. See you tomorrow."

She fluffed her hair and took another path off to the side of the dorms while I headed in, tranquil in my expanded state, and happy to cement it with sleep.

Chapter 14

The Temple

The next day we woke early. Showered and ate breakfast in silence. Then, in groups of twos and threes, we were shuttled to the temple. Up until this time, we had only seen pictures. I was in one of the first groups to arrive and it was difficult to take in the scale of the marble castle in front of me.

It was as wide as a football field, glistening white in the sunlight, and intricately carved with lattice windows and gleaming spires of white stone. We were encouraged to walk through and do silent meditation as we passed from room to room, from altar to altar. This place had been built by hand by the people in the surrounding countryside. The Guru, pre-Guruhood, had been in business, someone told me, and he won the favor of the local government by employing the local population in the building of this castle equal to any of Disney's efforts.

I walked a side stairway to a corner outlook spot where the jungle spread around us. Birdcalls, hoots and cackles filled the trees, monkeys swung from vine to vine. The inside of the building was unadorned except for the area where we were to meet and receive our final blessings as a culmination of our time together. I found a corner in the marble hall and sat on the ledge to watch the others arriving and shaking their heads in wonder.

My dasa found me. "I'm glad you are feeling better, Annie."

In front of me, three monkeys jumped from the ceiling rafters, screeching, unimpressed and playing tag.

"I guess they're not impressed with this gathering of light workers, right? I mean that is what you've been calling us these last weeks."

"By participating in these sessions you had been given the task of holding more and more Light on the planet. It is needed for the great change happening all around and within us. You already understand this, Annie. It is why you are here."

"I do know that things are changing, crumbling, refusing to right themselves."

"There is more change coming. We are moving into a real shift. There is nothing to fear but we are all being called to wake up and do what we can to transform our fear into light."

"I'm afraid I'm not really sure what that means. How that works."

"That's okay," she smiled. "Willingness and quiet are needed. If humanity, I mean everyone, does not understand this, they will be given an opportunity to slow down and connect."

"Well, I'm not so sure how that will happen."

"No need. Just be present. Practice compassion. Patience."

She bowed to me with namaste and left me to sit and think, and then not think, but absorb whatever seemed to be swirling around the high ceilings and cornices of this storybook cauldron.

I shifted and looked down to the buses arriving again and there was my friend, Mallory, chatting away with Puran, the bus driver, who may not have gotten the memo that we were here for spiritual rather than fleshly delights. Puran ran the work crews of beautiful, sari wrapped women who every morning at six, when we left the dormitories, were crouched on their knees in a colorful line of black heads, bright colored saris and brown arms and fingers moving along the lawn of the dormitories removing weeds and bugs. They were a solemn bunch and Puran stood silently watching them work and providing a bin for the small green and black bits they combed out of the grass in their morning work. Mallory had asked him cheekily if she could join the girls and he answered her without humor.

"You haven't the strength and grace of an Indian woman. I am sorry, madame." And then he grinned, shooting his chin dimple straight to her heart.

That was all Mallory needed to be smitten by this handsome young Indian man. His disdain and wide smile was a perfect tease for her. Looking at her leaning into the bus now, like a teenager, made me smile, despite my feminist, spiritual awakenings. Comfort was still comfort and she was seeking some. The cavorting monkeys bared their toxic teeth at me in mocking parody and were scooted away by a passing dasa who motioned me to my place on the floor.

As the ceremony began, we were seated in rows several feet from the altar, strewn with flowers and a throne. I had no idea how I was going to get through this entire day on the hard, cold, marble floors of the temple but I soon fell into the chanting that rose from us like breath. One voice, One breath. One large sound that left us, did not come from us but was delivered through us. Time did fade away. At one point, the older dasas brought in two other monks who had been meditating day and night for the last six months. Their bodies were frail and they leaned on the younger dasas who carried them like ancient light coming through cracked pottery.

Once these two holy beings were installed on the altar and supported by pillows and flowing gowns that warmed them and gathered their energy, it was hard to avoid the heat and light that came from the altar. We were instructed to close our eyes. To breathe in sync with the holy men and stay connected to that energy. True to form, the Brazilian delegation rose from their seats in ones and twos and began to dance quietly in mad turns like the Sufi dancers that spent their dervish times connecting to Spirit. The Chinese sat erect for the first time and one by one they began to wail, let the sound of their internal imprisonments leak from them and rise above the altar. Even the monkeys took notice and stopped their rascalry. We sat that way, swayed, chanted, sipped in the air, roasted in the light, shifted by the ascended masters, for an hour, two hours, maybe three.

I lost any sense of self-awareness, any need to check relative notices of time and progress, ascent or descent. The energy was inexorable and we disappeared or rather we reappeared as part of the whole, as part of the One. We had no awareness of this at the time. But it was what was happening. We were in a thick frenzy of silent action swirling around us and preparing us to see and feel and shift in a new way.

The Guru walked in simply. He was an older, round, and brown man with a goatee. He looked like a kind doorman who held the door for you when you had too many packages. Simple, and kind, and deeply aware.

Again, he was doing it again, opening the door for us, and asking us to just to set down whatever we might be carrying, and walk through. We had no choice. We were in a pure state of reception and attunement.

The Guru smiled as he mounted the altar and sat in his robes on the throne. He had the most benevolent look on his face. He shifted his gaze from one to the other of us and we were personally welcomed and surrounded with acceptance and light. I didn't even have the inclination to separate myself, comment on the experience, or be an observer.

He lifted his palms to face the group and closed his eyes. I immediately felt a buzzing in my head and neck. Through my crown chakra, the top of my head, down through the third eye, the front of the forehead, through my throat and my heart and my belly and sit bones and then all around me. I was in a profound state of reception and transmission.

Somehow the day passed. I had flashes of walking throughout the marble halls with others and pausing at open vistas to feel the sun, take in the green from the surrounding jungle, sip a bowl of broth. When the sun was gone, we sat beneath the stars and counted the points of light and were given direct pathways to the planets. At some point, we lay each by the other on the stone floors, and found them soft and warm and welcoming and slept deeply until the sun returned the next morning.

I sat up early and looked out over the sea of sleeping bodies. It was a bumpy carpet of contentment. Last night, the bodies seemed all white and part of one flowing whole fabric, but this morning, the individuality was beginning to emerge. Arms flung in dreams fought for their own space, bodies that had all lain flat the night before were moving slightly like worms finding their way back up to the surface.

I took the opportunity to find a bathroom and sit quietly on the steps of the temple where the sunrise was completing itself. I was alone on the temple steps. Rested. Lifted. Keeping thought at bay. I had been elsewhere and I was not certain I wanted to return.

Soon, the group began filtering down the stairs to the shuttle buses waiting for us. We got on silently and went back to the meditation room at the campus and sat together in silence for one last gathering.

The sensation was that of finding balance after returning from space. There was internal debriefing in each person and the dasas suggested that we not speak until breakfast in two hours. We could walk the campus. We could pack. We could change and rest. But we were urged to not overanalyze what we had just experienced.

After breakfast, the group returned to the dorms to pack their things and pretend that they had somewhere to go. It was noticeable who gathered their cloak of business around them in order to ready themselves for the outside world.

I was not at all sure what I had experienced, but my body was moving about three beats ahead of my brain and I decided it best to just sit for a bit before I fought for a shower stall or heaved my bag down the stairs to the buses. I took a seat in the downstairs lounge where I could observe the people coming and going, the dasas smiling secretly at how we each dealt with the adjustment that we had experienced. My dasa saw me sitting to the side and came to sit next to me. She handed me a bar of chocolate.

"A gift, Annie. A celebration of change!" I looked at the bar and smiled at her.

"What happened? What happened to us?"

"Time will tell. But as we discussed before, it is about preparing ourselves for the next steps. We cannot live in the darkness of what has come before. We need to grow and be prepared for a world, a planet, a universe that is asking more of us."

I looked over at her not sure if I understood what she meant.

"You will come to this yourself, Annie. But you will come to it, because you have come here. You will be needed to help others understand what is to come. What we are creating with our consciousness."

She understood my silence, and that words had not returned to me enough to respond. So she continued, "My parents live in North Carolina and they can't understand what I am doing here. And you will agree it is difficult to describe, yes?"

"Yes. I guess so."

"It is our job. Like artists do. We bring down energy and open new pathways." She smiled again and got up from her chair. "Now, I must go do the laundry for the next group. They arrive tomorrow morning. It has been a pleasure to meet you, Annie. Thank you for being part of the change."

Somewhere inside of me I held the faces of those holy men who had been meditating and taking in the light for the planet. How they were barely in their bodies but radiant with light which I had held for a deep and expanding moment. I had no answer for any of it.

Chapter 15

The Re-Entry

On the school bus into Chennai, I was with the Brazilians and, as always, oblivious of heat and dust, they were singing and dancing their way up and down the aisle, and then right into the hotel lobby at the airport.

I had spoken to Mallory after breakfast and she told me she was going down to the Indian Ocean with Puran for a weekend before she returned home. I couldn't seem to picture her in the temple at all.

"Were you at the temple?"

Mallory looked out across the grass. "I was there and then, poof, I wasn't. And now Puran and I will go to the beach to continue our in and out of the body experience."

She looked like the cat who swallowed the canary. Literally.

"You missed it?" I asked.

"Um, I was on my own planetary journey."

I focused on Mallory's face, which was certainly more relaxed. I supposed everything could be part of the transformation.

My flight was the next day. The Chennai airport hotel had one computer with internet in the lobby, and a patch of dusty grass behind chain link fence that shone bright hot light through the dirty lobby windows. There was a plastic bench there and someone had brought out a metal chair that stood unevenly next to a trash can. I think this was the haven for the kitchen staff, but after I dropped my bag in my dark room, I bought a bottle of water and chips at the lobby counter, and two post-cards. I sat in the chair where the afternoon shadow was beginning to angle in. Where the other people who had arrived when I had arrived disappeared to, I cannot say. But once again, it was dusty and dirty and brilliant white all at the same time.

"My dearest Eddie," I wrote. "I have just spent three weeks at a mon-astery here in India and I am not at all sure what I am feeling or how I have changed except to say everything is moving a lot more slowly. And in the blink of an eye, too. Love, Annie."

The next card I wrote to myself. I like the practice of sending myself a postcard from wherever I was traveling and have it arrive months later when the moment of its launch was past and forgotten.

"Dear Annie," I wrote myself. "What in the world is going on? Any clarity yet?"

As I finished these cards, I looked up to see the tall unmistakable figure of Mallory tugging her bag into the lobby. She had her hat pulled down over her face but I could feel her glance my way and turn away in dread. Something bad had happened.

"Mallory? Are you okay? Plans not work out?"

"Oh, hello. Fancy meeting you here."

She wasn't ready to talk. "Dinner?" I said.

"As long as it isn't Fanta and papadum chips."

We took a cab to a side street in the city. The young man at the desk had recommended the restaurant to us. "Good for Americans! You won't get sick!" And he called a driver who after tipping his hat to us both, "Madame, and madame," drove us in an air conditioned quiet black sedan to Maharajah, a bright tourist spot with faux golden columns and two large elephant ears on the doors. We had both showered and put on makeup and were aware that we had taken the first step in washing away what our three weeks had embedded in us.

Mallory ordered a rum and Coke. "You?" she asked me. "Those grasshoppers look good." She gestured to a table where two men sat with a woman, relaxing and enjoying cocktails, airline attendants on their night off.

"I don't think I'm ready to jump from green tea to crème de menthe."

"Suit yourself."

It wasn't 'til after the vegetable curry and the second beer that Mallory began to sing out her disappointment. "I should have known, of course. I should have known. Tra la."

"You mean, Puran? The beach? Ecstasy?"

"Very funny. But of course. Puran's wife had the beach house. And his two teenaged sons had the local house. And we apparently couldn't go back to the wing where you and I were planted. New folks arriving, so that's that."

"Ah. I see." I said, averting my eyes, and really trying to just listen. Be in the moment with this woman. I had actually learned something from the time at the temple.

"Please don't be wise. I have had enough wisdom to fill me and leave my bowels for the rest of my life. I am afraid my Indian experiment is a bust."

"I'm sorry. Truly. I bet it was fun."

Mallory looked at me with new eyes. "Actually, it was fun. All that chanting and monkey bashing and forceful mystic energy was creeping me out. I don't think I could have made it through the temple." She took a swig of her beer. "I just can't find it. Whatever it is I am looking for. It's like God has put me on a vicious scavenger hunt and is watching as I make a complete jackass of myself."

I sat forward ready to respond quietly and all of a sudden was buoyed by a bubble of laughter that started under my arms and made them float high in the air and fell to the back of my throat and down my gullet into my belly and started to laugh and laugh and laugh and laugh. And Mallory did, too.

Chapter 16

Making Contact

The flight to Boston stopped in London. The weather was looming and ominous and we were given vouchers for another airport hotel and a dinner at the hotel pub. It was actually fine with me. The time in India was not so easy to shake off and I relished another night in transition in an anonymous hard bed with tin cans flying in the air above me.

Who knows? I thought. *Maybe the Guru is up there saying funny things to the stars?* Pushing tin was what air traffic control people called managing all those flights in the sky.

I had an old friend here in London. He had lived here since the 1980s when he managed the equivalent of a green card marriage with a Londoner who had long gone. That's what he did. He pushed tin. When I found his number and called him, he actually picked up the phone and said he'd come out to the pub to meet me. His present girlfriend was off in the countryside with her mother, the same age as he was, I believe, and he was happy to have some adult company.

Jerry and I had gone to school in Boston together. I remember an evening strolling under snowflakes down Commonwealth Avenue, where he and another guy, Jay, smoked dope and we walked and walked and ended up at Schraffts for hot chocolate at midnight. Their eyes were enormous. That's what I remember. I never smoked much dope but managed to feel stoned a lot of my twenties anyway, just trying to figure out how life made sense.

Looking at myself in the mirror, wondering how he might see me after all these years, I noticed that my eyes were large and glassy, too. Kind of like that red mud dog I saw in India. Yes, I was definitely not back to normal.

"We've aged pretty well," he said, when we sat down for a beer. "I mean you look good."

"Thanks, Jer. You, too."

We exchanged pleasantries but I could not focus much.

"What's with you, Annie? How you been?"

"It's hard to tell. My time in India was like a psychedelic trip. And you might remember I've never been good at those out of body experiences."

"I don't know. I seem to remember getting you stoned yielded some pretty hot sex in the dorm room."

"Oh my God, I just had a flash of that disgusting dog of yours. It was at your apartment and the sheets hadn't been changed in years, and the dog wouldn't get off the bed. Ooh." I shuddered in memory. "Actually, there was a stoned red dog in India that kept an eye on things there as well. Maybe he was a spirit guide or something."

"Probably not. My dog just liked to eat the hash brownies."

"Right," I said, not moving as quickly to be clever as I would have liked.

"So, again, really. How you been?"

"Honestly, I can't tell you. I've started to work again. Am teaching and getting some good responses, but ever since I worked the election I feel like my head is screwed on backwards. Something terrible is going on, coming on. It's not good."

"Oh for crap's sake. You're not going all gooey liberal on me are you?

I flashed back to a long ago fight I had had with Jerry about a woman's right to abortion. It actually happened right after we slept together at college and after a drink or two too many, he said to me. "It's a good goddamned thing the rubber didn't break, Annie. I don't believe in abortion you know. You carry my seed, you carry my seed!"

We had just rolled off his roommate's bed with questionable sheets and I started to laugh and he stood up and grumbled. "Don't laugh, Annie. I'm serious about that shit." And he slammed the bathroom door. I remember hearing the beginning of his pee flow into the toilet and that I was gone before he flushed it down. That ended that romantic interlude.

"Jer! You're not stupid and I tell you things are shifting. The world is in for some real trouble. And he didn't even win the damn election!"

"Of course, he didn't win. The Russians put him in. But so what? You think that makes a difference? You think you and me could make a fucking difference in the world, and if that cunt, that woman, was the president, that would be different?"

Why had I not remembered this part of my old friend? "You know, I just got laid off my job at this airport after twenty years and I've been laid off for a 'diversity' hire! What the fuck is that? A 'diversity hire?' A Black guy who has half my experience and a quarter of my intelligence. I'm telling you, this new leadership may just indeed have the right idea. Balance the ship a little bit."

"I forgot about this part of you, Jerry. Sorry to be reminded."

"Oh, for fuck's sake, Annie. Grow up. You've got no power and when some Jew-hating bastard comes after you, you'll be lucky to have a militia on your side."

"I don't think the militia movement in the states are exactly on my side!"

"Jews will never replace us, honey!" Jerry said with a grin. I stood up and threw what was left of my beer in his face.

I can't be certain that is what happened. I had not yet returned enough to a state of corporal certainty to be assured that certain actions happened in real time and certain actions occurred in my head. But whichever way we parted that night, it was not with a howl but with a whimper. I wanted back in my cocoon, my meditation mat, and the understanding of the screeching monkeys playing their roles as planet provocateurs.

I was not ready for a return to "normalcy" but I wasn't sure how to stay in the belly of the whale that had swallowed me in India. I remember reading Simone Weil, the Jewish-Catholic mystic when I was a kid. I thought I looked like her and was desperately searching for role models. She spoke often about being swallowed by God.

I plugged in my phone for the first time in a couple of weeks. A message came up on the screen. From David Diamond, from Kauai.

Dear Annie. I hope this finds you well. I have been thinking about Kauai. And how we seemed to connect. I remember holding you, rocking you back and forth. It made me feel better. Coffee? Have you received my gift?

A jolt ran through me. The embrace had made me feel better, too.

It was so intimate, surprising, I had thought about not returning to him that night. How he withdrew his invitation as he watched me walk away. How foolish playing the push me pull you game.

Thinking about that moment of walking away I looked around the hotel room. Shiny pink bed spread, green pea walls, rough grey carpeting. I felt like I was in a bullet. There in London, having slid into a holding zone, in this nether land neither in the city nor out. A room not provided for pleasure but rather for function or for some sleazy rendezvous between slaking desperation or funk. A place that was meant to propel someone from one place to another but not a place for full and satisfying embrace, I thought of their bare feet on the carpet beneath me—the fantasy couple—as I pulled off my shoes to spend another moment with David and my walking away.

He would be uncomfortable in this room. Not enough footage in which to pace or even to rest at a contemplative and pleasant distance. Oh, how we force ourselves to live bereft, eschewing embrace, fleeing a smile, fearing an interaction. This is what was now codified. We had all become lizard-skinned and protected. Since AIDS, sleeping with the wrong person could kill you. Since pierced bodies represented the way we loved ourselves, since we grew out of the indiscriminate sleeping around of the seventies that proved more lonely than sexy in the end.

The experience of my recent single years had been varied. A lot of damage in the men I met—divorced, estranged, and angry—with few tools to figure out what they really wanted or needed besides getting laid. I had backed off. Safer. We all had and now here we all were in our separate camps of bluster and bellows.

David's face came up again. He felt hollow in the places I felt full.

I reached for the remote and tried to turn on CNN. Local news flashed on the screen and then, Al Jazeera. They were talking about the Nazi march in Charlottesville. I recognized an anchor who used to work for a major US network. He blasted his independence on the international broadcast. I don't think he even blinked his eyes.

Dear David. It is so nice to hear from you. I will be back in Boston and around by next week. Gift? How thoughtful. I'll look forward to receiving it. And yes, I'd love to have coffee. Thanks.

David reached out. I reached back. Simple as that. Hello, out there. Human calling human.

Chapter 17

Coffee with David

"So, it was like that. The repetition of silence. The rhythm of breathing. The assault of heat. It made me start to believe. See things in the clouds. Leave off language."

"Hmm?" he asked, with his eyebrows lifted, gazing intently at the correct spot to place the fork on his Danish.

"Sounds funny. But it got to the point that I wasn't sure if I was actually saying things out loud or just thinking them and getting an appropriate response."

David used the side of his fork to cut into his apple Danish pastry. He carefully cut it once, and again, then picked it up on the edge of the tines and placed it in his mouth. He chewed almost delicately for a man with such large features and I felt myself drawn to the way he moved, the flexibility of his hands and the smooth manicure of his cuticles. I felt self-conscious as he listened to me. And he did listen to me. Simply and deeply. I went silent.

"Go on," he said. "I am listening."

"Yes, I know you are. Thank you." He smiled and I went on. "It's like everything has shifted, is shifting. I can feel it. We need less words to connect with people, and more heart to really hear what they have to say."

"I appreciate that. My former friend, Barb, who you met in Kauai, she was too busy all the time. Always moving things from one place to another. The fight we had in Kauai, it started with the newspaper. I kept putting the newspaper down in a specific place, by my special lamp, the one with the magnifier, and she would move it. Must have happened four times in the space of an hour. I finally told her she should get her own room."

"Sounds like she was nervous." I said.

David shifted and shook his head. "Do I make you nervous? And you and I just met."

I smiled at that. "No. You don't make me nervous. Not yet."

"Romance is not my strong suit. I'm far too odd I'm afraid."

"Are you?"

"Time will tell, I suppose." He looked at me with his grey eyes and I confess to feeling very exposed. He was an odd fellow, intense certainly, but carrying an understanding of himself with which he warned people. He laughed and said, "But I'm bright. I'm very bright. And in case you are wondering, moving the newspaper was not the only problem that Barb and I had to navigate."

"Not my business." I said, waving my hands as if to push away my inquiry. "We've all had friendships that work and then don't."

"Yes. But you had a marriage. I admire that. How many years?"

"Almost thirty."

"Impressive."

"You ever give it a try?"

"I tried once. It was a disaster. She's in Georgia now. Better on my own. With friendships, I hope. Friendships are hard enough." He carefully moved the fork from its upright position on the right of his plate to the upright position on the left of his plate.

"I think the way we connect with people is shifting." I said carefully. "Words are only part of the message."

In a surprisingly raucous move, David threw back his head and laughed. Loudly. "Ha!", he said. "Now you're talking my language! It's like alien speak. Surely you know about all those UFOs floating around. Some of those guys have already come down and settled in and are trying to help us out. They speak a whole other lingo. That's what I hear."

"You believe it?"

There was a slight shift. "Seeing is believing, right? I don't see so well, so I wouldn't count on anything that comes through me." He smiled and then looked at my face, all its contours, taking me in. I felt a little discovered. The first time someone had looked at me deeply since I had returned from India. "Your face is different," he said. "Yes. I'd say you are changed."

Not sure why I was embarrassed by that, but it felt so intimate. I felt so attended to for no reason except for the pleasure of the person taking me in.

"You are a pretty interesting person, David. I'm glad you asked me for coffee."

"You're very kind".

"Thank you," I said. "I value kindness."

"Yes," he said, almost to himself. "Kindness." He looked up at me and then shifted his newspaper on the table. I thought of Barb trying so hard to find the exact spot it should rest. Once it was set he said, "We often find ourselves talking to the wrong people." He picked up his coffee and held it ready for a sip. "I mean, I do. I often find myself nattering away to someone who has not the slightest interest or capability of understanding whatever in the world I may be saying."

"So, India and all that hocus-pocus conjuring stuff. You don't find it . . . silly? Frivolous?"

David looked over at me with an annoyed look. "Why in the world would you say that? Did you think it was frivolous or hocus-pocus?"

I settled in and I became more earnest. "Actually, no. Not at all. It was time out of time. We need to come back to ourselves." I took another sip. "I was so unsettled by the Charlottesville march. It hearkened back to every book I ever read about World War II. How people did not see the signs. How people waited too late to react. How old loyalties eventually killed them."

"History buff?" He looked up with interest.

"Well, no, it's just . . ."

"That's good. That's smart. Maybe a bit naive, that you think you can stop history, but worthy."

I pulled back feeling my own intensity out of control. "Sorry but I am not at all myself these days. I don't think we, our country, are at all ourselves."

"It will get worse before it gets better."

"You think so?"

"I read history, too. Remember I told you I like the Great Courses." David raised his face to mine and looked straight through my eyes. "I have often felt out of place and out of control. It seems to have been part of my experience to date. Someone once told me they thought I was an alien, come to earth to torture them specifically. That I should live in a cell on Elba, and leave everyone else alone."

I laughed. "Well, that's quite a job description."

He smiled. "I don't usually do well with women." He looked searchingly at me again. "I like you, Annie. I appreciate the company. I, too, value kindness."

"Yes," I said. "Me, too."

"You're right, of course." He said, his tone getting less introspective. "Something is up. There are changes happening. At some point we'll all get our marching orders."

"Signs of the apocalypse." As I looked over at him, I suddenly remembered the package I had on my desk, that I had just recently opened. "Oh David! Forgive me. I received your gift. I love Willa Cather! I have never read those essays. *Not Under Forty*. It was so lovely of you."

David smiled almost sheepishly. "I'm glad you got it. I was going to ask."

"I should have mentioned right off. But then, I am just home and still not fully back to normal."

"Oh. Normal. *Pfft*." David nodded a couple of times and lifted his coffee cup for a slurp and put it down.

He was such a strange man. Maybe he was an alien. He certainly was not comfortable in his skin. But then, these days, neither was I.

"Thanks for coffee."

"Gardner Museum next week? Seniors free Thursday afternoons. I think they show a movie."

"David, I'm not really . . ."

"What? Reliable? God knows I'm not." He looked around and his gaze came back around. "Let's give it a try. It's fifty percent off at the cafeteria. You can eat for free. We'll talk about the book."

"Senior discount? Sounds enticing." I said, not sure how to put sexual content into a senior discount discussion.

He smiled faintly, leaving me to figure that out on my own. "Please excuse me. Due at the dentist at five."

He assembled the many sections of his body, one after the other, and rose from the chair. I smiled as he left and he looked back. I do believe he was flirting with me, but he may have just been checking to see if he left his newspaper.

Chapter 18

A Date with Isabella Instead

I did go to meet him that next Thursday afternoon. And brought my Cather essays for easy reference. The Isabella Gardner Museum, the perfect mix of elegance and alternate reality.

I waited half an hour in the lobby, too nervous for my own good. He did say he was unreliable, and I was a little relieved he didn't show.

I was not retracting after the expansion of India, and I was getting used to the new ground under my feet. It gave me more room to see things and feel them internally, though no tools with which to digest them. Better to stroll the Gardner on my own and see if I could feel some balance again, The quiet enveloped me. I felt secure and familiar. Better.

I walked the galleries and sat happily in the garden. It was like the opening of the Cather book that conjured that elegant world of the late 1930s where elegant women visited elegant spas to take the cure and attend elegant musicales. I had loved being transported to that time in the slim volume and wanted to thank David for the thoughtful trip he had given me, but now that seemed foolish. I cautioned myself against fantasy infatuation.

I tucked the book into my purse. And as I started to leave, I read a plaque that explained that Isabella had started the museum, at the suggestion of her husband, as a way to handle the death of her son.

Along a shadowed gallery was a painting by Whistler. A figure on the beach looks out at a vast expanse of water. The figure is steadfast, the beach wide, the water unyielding.

I sat for a moment. And then it came back in full force. Tomales Bay years before. On the other coast.

Jordan was eleven and his dad asleep on the beach, carefully gathering his own strength for what would be his inevitable end. I had given up framing days around Ty and instead let him rest when he needed it. He would lie on the beach, on a hammock, on a couch, like a man who had suckers on his back. His body needed the rest that deeply, and I would watch as he would bow into gravity and I would sometimes pray that the life force would flow back into him rather out of him, dribbled and wasted on the surfaces from which he sought succor.

The dinghy floated up and scraped the sand. I looked up. "Where's Jordan?" I asked Ty. "Have you seen Jordan?"

Ty stirred and turned toward me. "He's fine, Annie. He's off exploring."

I jumped to the water.

"Annie, he's fine. I promise you." I heard Ty's voice as I hit the water heading to the lighthouse. I jumped into the water, pulled the dinghy behind me, and began to swim across to the point.

"I want to live there," he had said yesterday, when we floated by it on our way back from a beach picnic. Just Jordan and I.

But today, with dinghy behind me, I floated and swirled over the bay to the lighthouse and saw the boy, my boy, huddled on the rocks. Had he let the dinghy go? The one that had floated free at the dock across the bay, and the one, when I saw it, that emptied me of all blood and human fluids and filled me with vacuum and desire and swallow. I wanted to swallow the dinghy, like Jonah's whale, and somehow find Jordan kneeling at the bottom of its rippled interior, hiding from me, grinning and making fun of me. Him safe at home, in side of my body once again, only this time, I was in control. I did not feel the invasion of hormones in every gland nor did I rise from a chair as an inflated dough boy.

But, Jordan was not in the dinghy.

I could see him huddled on the rocks. His hair was long and he was hunched into his knees, shivering, chattering. I could see even from this distance.

"What happened?" I yelled, treading water after a speedy swim.

"I let it go," he said, "I wanted to see how far it would float and if I could catch it."

"And?" I said.

"It floated far. Fast. The current was strong."

"And what was the plan exactly?" I asked, reassuming my legs, my arms, the Speedo bathing suit securing my belly and breasts. I shoved the dinghy onto the small beach and came in off the rocks. "What was the plan? To stay on the rocks through the night?"

He looked at me with wide eyes. "I thought Dad would rescue me." His eyes grew wider. He knew his dad could not rescue him. Would not rescue him. Could not swim this far.

"It's me."

"Yeah," he said, looking away. His teeth began to chatter again.

"You've gone blue," I said to him. He was eleven. It was before he had given up on following Ty, depending on Ty, leaning on Ty to make him strong.

"I like the color, I bet. I mean I would like it if I could see it," he said.

I looked at my odd boy. Sad and suffering. Dancing with a shadow on the horizon that he knew would swallow him soon enough.

"Get in the dinghy. I'll push you across."

"Like you did when I floated out on that inner tube and you pushed me back in."

"Yes," I said. "Like that. You keep me busy rescuing you."

"You are a *Baywatch* person."

"No, I'm a mother person."

"You're not supposed to rescue me. I'm supposed to be a hero."

"Maybe in time, my son. But may I help you now? Not rescue just help."

"Maybe." He was thinking about it.

Jordan stood straight up and picked his way away from me. Across the rocks, his feet adhering like fins to the sides of the outcroppings.

He got to the little beach and walked forward into the water toward the dinghy. Then he jumped into the water. He jumped forward like a flying fish posed above the surface of the water and then crashed deeply into the slight waves. It went deep quickly out here. And there were treacherous rocks. Hence the light from the lighthouse which no longer swung over the water, modernity deciding that radar could save mariners better than light.

Jordan knew that. He foundered. He flittered and fluffed and went under. The first time he held his nose and I thought, he must be playing a bad joke. And then he came up for a big gasp of air and his eyes met mine. Like a red laser beam right into my eye and it burned out the sockets. It burned out the sockets of my salty eyes.

Because he was saying, *Don't catch me. Leave me founder. Let me flutter and kick and fight and let me go. Don't come after me. Don't ever come after me. I will never forgive you if you come after me. How could you ever love me? Stop.*

And I looked across the water and wondered at what I knew. Wondered at leaving him to his own devices, to the cave that he was already carving far, far away from me.

Don't save me! I will never forgive you for being alive when he is dying, dead already. That was radar not light.

And he went under again.

I stood there and felt the words go across the screen of my brain like on a chyron feed. Like information at a sports match. *Perhaps it is better to let him drown,* the mother thought. I read this on the chyron going across my brain. *Perhaps he will never be happy for himself, let alone for the love I had hoped to share with him. Maybe I should let him drown.*

The split second was enormously long. It included a flash of an injured friend whose son had committed suicide and who calmly stated, "It was better. It was better for him. He was in such pain. He would never be through with it. How could he ever be over it?"

And then I saw Jordan float. He floated out into the bay. He would not go under. I did not have to decide to let him drown. I went to him as a mother goes to a child. But it was different now.

It was the moment after I saw that he played me for my love. I could not help it bleeding from me, as it always would. But he would sniff it on the water, like a shark, and blame me for it, I suppose. Until he grew up. And found something that mattered more to him, that he recognized more deeply, than loss.

* * *

Maybe I was meant to have a date with Isabella instead. To think about how she honored her lost son.

A week later I received an email from David.

"I'm afraid I got caught and couldn't meet you. I refer you to the poetry of Robert Frost and hope we can discuss next time we meet. Snowy woods in an evening. It reminds me of you."

I pondered being pissed.

"Should I be angry with you? I think so," I wrote.

"Don't bother. You can save it for our next post recuperation meeting. I have had a medical issue to attend to. It will keep me busy for a few months. Thanks for understanding."

"Should I be worried?" I wrote and then crossed it out. "Thanks for being in touch." And sent back a link to a Mary Oliver poem.

"Good one," he wrote. And that was that.

Chapter 19

Winter into Spring

BLOG POST

Eddie, my nephew, called me for Christmas and insisted he wanted me to come to meet his new girlfriend (Shamana), but since an invite was not forthcoming, I assumed the invitation was for after the time they got out of bed. Which did not seem to be anytime soon.

Hattie, my landlord, visits now and then. She told me she danced with a man named Walter Steinberg at the Waldorf on New Years Eve 1970. He was a lousy lover and he wasn't sending checks so she got rid of him. But she pulled back the wrinkled skin on her neck to show me where he liked to kiss her, and put the skin back after the story to keep the memory to herself.

Love, a partridge in a pear tree.

Season's Greetings.

The next day, a copy of *Great Expectations* was delivered to my mailbox. "Hope springs eternal," the card read. "Yours sincerely, David Diamond."

I spent the next few days with the gift of the gift.

BLOG POST

Mass shooting in Las Vegas. Gunman killed 58 people with his automatic rifle who were attending a rock concert. A tax bill was signed and the President announced to his high finance business pals, "you all just got a lot richer." A Leonardo Da Vinci painting sold for 450 million dollars. God Bless America..

BLOG POST

A shooter rampaged through Marjory Stoneman Douglas High School and the wounded children take to the streets. They meet with lawmakers, march, give speeches. I study their soft faces on television, and see how jaw lines will harden and teeth begin to gnaw inside cheeks as they meet the world. Happy New Year.

I sent these snippets off to Sylvia for the blog and wondered if Jordan was wearing a beard these days.

Chapter 20

May Springs Again

In May I received a note from David again.

Dear Annie,

I suppose I should apologize for never meeting you at the museum but I have had some health issues that have been a bit daunting. And I believe you told me you may not be reliable either. Did you go? I am getting in touch now to let you know that the volcano in Hawaii, the Big Island, has erupted. Another sign of your apocalypse perhaps. I hope we meet again before our planet blows up.

Here are things I would like to do in your company. Walk the historic sites the night before July 4 with a history geek I know. Visit the Athenaeum to delve more deeply into libraries. Find an Italian restaurant that I have not visited in twenty years. Discuss T. S. Eliot, my favorite poet, though I imagine you will never forgive him for jailing his wife.

Sincerely,
David Diamond.

Dear David.

Yes, you should apologize for not being in touch, but I hope you are feeling better. Ill health is such an obstacle at our age. A struggle to keep it from becoming the only conversation. And yes, you are right. I am the kind of person who would appreciate adventures such as you outline. And, also correct, I find no excuse for Eliot's cruelty. His wife was not crazy but outspoken, and even these days, that seems to be a major annoyance most men prefer to excise. Not to seem too confrontational. Meanwhile, I am gathering strength for I'm not sure what. Perhaps we can discuss the mysteries. I will be on the Cape for July.
Annie.

Yes. Okay. I need to go to the grocery store first and gird my loins, D.

Good luck, A.

Maya Angelou cautioned us "that if a man tells you who he is, believe him." That went for our president, certainly. And David, too. But today, in the spring, the thought of David reaching out to me again made me smile. And I noticed that.

Chapter 21

Amanda's Story

In June, things got worse with pictures in the nightly news of young children being separated from their parents at the border. The images were numbing. The outrage was allowed to progress with no response. The architect of the plan was the grandchild of Holocaust survivors.

I heard from Sylvia.

"Remember I told you my cousins were trying to come up from Mexico? Their five-year-old was taken from them. I am talking to the ACLU. It's a nightmare. Send love."

"Oh, Sylvia." I wrote back.

"Send love. And maybe money in a few months."

I tried to concentrate on the work but I felt unmoored. Knocked off balance, berating myself for my idealistic adolescence. Then, I heard from Amanda. The young woman who had been at the Kauai retreat.

"Annie. Can you help me?"

"It's so great to see you, Amanda!" I said as I opened the door to her.

"So this is the belly of the beast," she said, with an awkward grin.

"It's where I live, yes. I like to think of it as a bit more welcoming."

"Oh. It's a book. *In the Belly of the Beast.* I read it." Her grin completely fell to the floor. She had planned that opening remark, and it did not go well.

"Right. Wasn't it about prison or something?" I said, gamely.

"Oh. Oh, I don't know. I'm so sorry. Never mind. Nice to see you. I'm not myself."

She in truth did not look good. It was a warm day but she had on a long sleeve white shirt and heavy jeans. She had just come from the library, where she told me she spent a great deal of time. Her hair was straggly and her face sweaty.

"Could I have something cold to drink? I mean would you mind? I'm really hot. Is it okay I came by? I have been meaning to visit." She had yet to find a spot to sit down and her pacing was making me dizzy.

"Yes, it's fine. Here," I said pointing to the kitchen table, "Take a seat."

I was happy to remember I had some mint tea in a pitcher, ready for summer. I poured her a tall glass.

"It's a pretty glass." She gazed at the light moving through the glass onto the table.

"I love that blue bottle glass, too." I said. "It reminds me of summer."

Amanda brought a prickly and slightly nauseous energy to the room. She drank the glass hungrily and then, her thirst slaked, she examined the surface of the table in front of her finding the toast crumbs from the morning meal. She fingered one or two, popping them onto her tongue. She looked twelve, daring a scolding from her mother.

"I have this story to tell. I have to tell it, Annie." She looked straight at me.

"Okay," I said, "What's it about?"

"The kids. I can't bear these children looking at me with their eyes every night."

"The kids on the border?"

"Yes, the kids." She looked at me, caged. "I want to do something to help. To get back to helping kids."

"I just talked to a friend whose cousins are caught up in that mess. Their five-year-old taken from them. Living in some kind of makeshift prison."

She was gathering her thoughts and I waited to catch them. She was sitting on a long tube of terror. I could feel her struggle to let things seep out rather than explode and drown us both.

"So, before I was a librarian, I worked with children. I love children. I would never hurt them. The pictures on the television are excruciating." She looked away from me.

"Well, you know." I tried to come up with something comforting but she went on.

"People don't understand what it does to children. Taking them away from people they love."

I just waited.

"I have to start my book. I have to start writing about that. It's why I came to Kauai, which was amazing by the way, and I did well with those kids I babysat for after you left."

"I'm glad, Amanda." But, I was beginning to swim in her upset. She caught on.

"Okay, I am going to stop acting weird. I don't like to be in rooms with the doors closed and no windows, so school is out. I want to ask you to help me. Can you help me to write this story?"

"You mean, we meet privately and I help you to write what you want to say?"

"Yes. I have done a lot of thinking about things. About children and loving them, and being one and not being one and fear of loving them and fear of losing them. All those things. They crowd my brain every night and I have to start writing this story."

"Where does it start?" I asked.

Amanda shuffled then looked up, strong. "Remember how you asked me about books when we were in Hawaii? Remember I told you I had read every book written by Willa Cather and how it saved my life? How books saved my life?"

"Yes, I do remember."

"I did all that reading in prison. I was in prison." She said that like she needed to hear it out loud. "I was in prison for two whole years and I was in solitary confinement because I had been accused of terrible things, so terrible, that they had to keep me away from the other inmates. From criminals who would have attacked me, if they were allowed to." Amanda looked up at me her eyes wide and spoke in that long sentence that flowed out of her like a long green snake. She wanted to see if the snake would choke me or I would make friends with it. She wanted to see if I could help her hold that long green snake.

"I am a felon." Again, a phrase I felt she practiced, and spoke carefully, reminding herself. "Or I was. I was finally exonerated. It has to be scrubbed from my record. But it takes about a year. It's almost gone now. Almost gone. But the story still has to be claimed and told by me."

She looked down at the small change purse she carried with her. I could see her fingers click the clasp and take out a small picture that she showed me.

"How old are you here, Amanda?" I asked.

"It's my college grad picture. I was twenty-two. Look at my hair! My mom paid for me to go to Stephanie Jablonksi, her friend, to do the color and curl it!"

"It looks great."

"Yeah," Amanda said. "I don't know if she tells the story or I tell the story. You know?"

"Who?"

"Me or the girl in the picture. Because I'm not that girl anymore. I don't think I can be that girl anymore."

I shifted in my chair. "I sometimes feel like that. Like I have no clue who set me out on my own journey. Even though it was me. With another hair style."

Amanda brightened. "That's funny," she said. "You're funny."

"Um, maybe when pushed. And only with a bouffant."

Amanda giggled in response.

"That's better, my dear. Easy does it." I wanted to calm us both, so we could hear what we were saying as loudly as what we were feeling.

"You're pretty nice." Amanda was talking to herself, almost. "I mean, sorry. I guess I shouldn't say that."

"I'm flattered." I said.

"I thought you were a hard ass when I was in Hawaii. It was the first trip I had made, you know, after."

"I'm glad you came."

"Are you a mom? I mean do you have any kids?"

I adjusted. Was it on my face, the way that Amanda's fierce fluttering reminded me of Jordan?

"I have a son. But, I haven't see him for a while."

"Oh," said Amanda. "You miss him, I guess. My mom missed me terribly. So much she couldn't handle it. After a while she stopped coming to see me in prison. She had nothing to say to me. We weren't good at small talk and it killed her that we couldn't touch, or hug."

"That's rough." I said.

"When I came home, after my brother Richie found a friend who went to law school and they got the charges dropped, it was impossible. I mean, I didn't bring myself home. The girl in the photograph. The one who used to like Justin Bieber and Fresh Prince. She didn't come home."

I wondered what I would say, what I would feel if I ever met my son again after so long.

"I had served for two years and maybe she had to believe there was something there. Where there's smoke there's fire. I think she was confused, my mom. I scared her. I was still quiet, read all the time and I was a felon. I even heard her say it a couple of times to someone on the phone. Like, 'Evelyn, she's a felon. No one will ever hire her, or talk to her again.'"

Amanda transformed herself. Her eyes wide and her small hands pretending to cover a phone, looking over her shoulder so no one could hear. I thought that she probably had her mother down pat.

"What did you do when you got home?"

"I cleaned the kitchen a lot." She looked around. "Would you mind if I had some more iced tea?"

I got up quickly, relieved to have a moment to process some of this information. I grabbed my phone for some reason. Old habit, and it made me trip a little, appear off balance. She grabbed the blue glass and lifted it from the table. Then, looked up at my eyes as I steadied myself.

"Here's your glass."

"Thanks," I said.

"I won't steal your phone when you turn your back, if you're worried. People tend to get up quickly around me. Pick up things. Keep track. Don't worry," she said. "I'm used to it."

I put the phone down by the sink and took a moment to rinse the glass. Wipe it down. Get out the pitcher, pour the tea. Put the glass down while I closed the fridge. I reached up to get another small plate from the shelf above the sink and found some ginger snaps in my cookie tin.

I placed them on the plate. I was gathering myself. And the room was very silent while she waited.

"Here we go," I said, putting the glass and the plate on the table. "These cookies are good."

"Thanks," she said leveling her eyes at me again. Her look was almost dangerous. It was a learned look. Fierce and protective. Her elbows were on the tablecloth. She lifted one of them and brushed it off. She had found the toast crumbs once again.

"Come next week," I said. "We can start working together next week." I smiled.

Amanda smiled too. But without her eyes. They didn't blink as she gulped the last of the tea, grabbed two cookies to take with her. She gathered her reddish hair into her left hand and twisted it, making a bun that somehow knotted into itself. And she, and the knot, headed out the door.

The room got a little bigger when she left.

Chapter 22

The Truth and Nothing but the Truth

The next week Amanda showed up at our agreed upon time. She had a notebook and a pencil in a pencil case. And her small change purse. Her hair was brushed and pulled back into a low pony tail. She was poised and bespectacled, much more the picture of an aspiring librarian.

"I wrote something. I wrote like, a letter, but I don't think it's right. I think that the Amanda before prison is telling the story, but I can't always get her to show up."

She was very businesslike and contained, like if she rehearsed the meeting and dressed for success, she would get the job done. It made it easier for me to go into teacher mode.

"Well, maybe she isn't ready to show up. Maybe the first voice is the one that needs to tell the story." I said.

Amanda went to the table and pulled out the kitchen chair, finding her spot.

"Want some lemonade? I made lemonade,"

She looked up at me, expectant. Looking at the blue glasses I had set on the table. I got the pitcher from the fridge and put it on the table. I left my cell phone in clear view.

"All the time I kept praying to God. When I was in prison. To help me out. To help people see reason, but there was no logic, the whole thing was random poison."

"What happened, Amanda? "

"I went to prison." It was the phrase that stopped her.

"What happened before? You worked with children."

"I was a preschool teacher. I was a great one. I loved those kids and man they loved me. Came running at me every day when they came into the room and we'd hug and cuddle and get ready for the day." This brought her back. This is what she understood.

"Sounds like fun."

"But I wasn't a pushover, you know. I put plenty of them in time out. I mean when they wouldn't listen. I would put them in time out and just ask them to try to sit there. It helped sometimes but the wiggle worms, forget it. Still, it was a good way to help them get hold of themselves. I should have put a few of the parents in time out. They were crazy. They all got so crazy." She looked at me helplessly. Her eyes again, like saucers being flooded in a riptide.

"What did the classroom look like? Can you describe it? Could we start there?"

"It was just a crappy little place in Jersey. But . . . maybe I should write some of this down."

She carefully opened her pencil case and her hands trembled as she reached for a mechanical pencil, a talisman.

We talked through more details of the school, or her days, why she liked her job or hated it. She wrote every question down thoughtfully in ordered rows. Each question numbered. Then she looked up, put her pencil down and spoke quietly.

"I just want to scream, but I think if I start, I won't stop."

"Write that sentence down too, okay?" And she did.

As the afternoon progressed, I got the following information. Amanda had been a crack preschool teacher. She was good with the little ones. They loved her and ran to her when she called and even when she didn't. She would scoop them up and put them on her lap, feel for wet diapers and got so good at the switch that she could change at least two sets of diapers while still singing "The Wheels on the Bus" at full volume. She had been known to wave a baby leg in rhythm to the sound to keep her other toddlers amused.

Amanda loved her job. She loved the babies and the way that they smelled. And she cleaned them, and patted them and changed their clothes when they needed it. They all took walks, and made picnics, and had nap time.

That's where the problem started. They were all in nap time but a few of the kids had left their little cots and had climbed up on her as she took a few winks as well. And when Linda Hensel, mother to Bobby . . .

"She was pretty preoccupied with her three-year-old son's penis if you ask me!" Amanda said, clearly arguing this out with herself as she probably had done in her cell, when she couldn't read another word, or dream another dream.

. . . came into the room during nap time, she found Bobby and two other boys laying on top of Amanda.

"We were all snoozing but one of the boys rested his head on my stomach. I was a little rounder then."

She looked at me for understanding.

"And his body fell between my open legs. I mean, we were all asleep. And the two other little ones used my breasts as pillows. I told you I was rounder in those days! And Linda didn't know what she was talking about, or what she *saw*! Christ!"

No matter, her presence caused a stir in the room.

"All the kids were jolted awake when Linda threw on the overhead lights. Babies crying, three little boys tumbling to the ground as I sat bolt upright. Linda even knocked over the apple juice and cups and cookies all ready for snack time when we woke up!" She shoved back her chair and started to pace.

"I navigated that disaster. I mean, Linda was a crazy person and her kid was a little clingy. I was forever helping him to remember where his hands belonged." She shook her head in disbelief. "I mean if that was the only thing, that would have been the end of it. And I told Linda Hensel. I told her she was overreacting and please to warn us when she is going to storm in like that. Scaring all the kids. Making a mess!"

Parents started dropping in at all hours. Teachers were on alert to make sure they did no extraneous touching. That they kept their doors open so the head of school could jump in whenever she wanted a visit. One teacher was so distracted taking care of visiting parents that she let a little one get away from her with no diaper on and he wandered into the play yard and there were parents there and all hell broke loose.

And then, there was the ultimate craziness when someone left a Satanic letter in the school yard and head of school was accused of being part of a cult. Any cult would do, as far as she knew. The school was consumed in a sex scandal. All the teachers accused of sexually abusing the little ones. Taking their pants off! Wiping their bottoms! Kissing their bellies! Scandal! Sex! Rape!

It would have been funny if it wasn't real, but it was real and Amanda at age twenty-six was caught up and accused of molesting her little students. And she was convicted. And she ended up in the state prison in solitary confinement for two years until she was finally cleared by the same Linda Hensel who admitted she cooked up the story to protect her son.

Amanda had circumnavigated my kitchen table at least fifteen times. Finally, she sat again. She spoke very quietly telling me the rest of the story.

"I read every day when I was in prison. It was how to survive. I got a job in the library and hid books under my mattress. I never looked up. I never spoke to anyone especially when that older woman came over and told me she would protect me. It was worse than a movie.

"That girl with the Stephanie Jablonski hairdo, and the bright green eyes, she went through the doors but didn't come out. That sounds so cliché!" She looked up at me, with such sadness. "How can it sound so cliché when I can hardly breathe when someone closes a door or I get worried some cop is going to say I was a convicted sex offender and I can't be alone with a kid? I can't live near a schoolyard. I can't have a story hour in the Children's Room without supervision."

"But, that's not going to happen. You got cleared."

"Sure."

"Start slow, Amanda. Start slow." This was counsel to myself as well. I looked around the room and saw how the couch and curtains, the blue bottle glasses and the rag rug near the door all held this story in themselves. They were full to the brim. Sharing the burden, artfully easing our way on down the road, was the best answer I could come up with for these times.

"I'll be back from the Cape in a few weeks. Let's see how far you can get with those questions by then."

Amanda left. I tried to shift into dinner preparations. Make a salad, sweep the floor. The room and I were now partners in her tale, we were swollen with it. I sat on my kitchen chair, dish towel still in hand and felt the images that Amanda had conjured and the rape of everything she held dear. Everything that she had believed about the world crushed.

And the only thing that eased that horror was the light that still snuck through the window, the breeze that wanted to help us blow the debris gone.

The hours in the Temple in India helped. My eyes stayed closed 'til they popped open and it was enough.

Maybe even the rag rug by the door took a sigh of relief when the breeze murmured blessings and the light shimmered new shadows. All I knew was I couldn't move this grief alone. And knew there was something bigger. And I was grateful.

Chapter 23

Waves and Coves

I slowed with the traffic along the slithery one lane road. The Cape and the long vistas of ocean to islands was soothing. I was moving toward time with my nephew, my son surrogate, leaning into humility, praying the ocean would be kind.

By the time I made it to the house, the mosquitoes were out and Eddie was rocking on the front porch with a haze of weed surrounding him. He didn't rise when I pulled up.

"Hi, Annie. I'm wrecked and it sure is great to see you!"

"Hello, my nephew. Stand up. I need a hug," and he complied.

"Shamana took a beach walk. She'll be back soon."

I headed to the back bedroom that overlooked the sand and sat on the springy bed that had been my solace for several summers. I had found this house through a teacher at the state college. It had belonged to her uncle and there were no more relatives to use it. It was not in the greatest of shape and she just wanted to be done with it. On a whim, I bought it with the left over money from Ty's life insurance, with the promise that she could come whenever she needed a weekend.

Mostly, it was rented during the year, but I kept a few weeks for me and Eddie. It was good that Eddie came. I hoped that he didn't feel obligated but he said he enjoyed the break, and his own family was in California.

"Annie. C'mere. I want you to meet Shamana!" Eddie interrupted my reverie. I checked my reflection in the mirror before stepping out to meet Eddie's love goddess.

She was plain in the most beautiful of ways. Clean, clear, high forehead, hair drawn back in a curly peacock spray, caramel skin, and delicate features. She had a slight smile on her face, not coy really, but not open either. This child was used to being the queen.

"Well, how lovely to finally meet you."

"You're welcome," she said and Eddie blanched. "I mean, I made some food, a salad, gazpacho. Would you like to eat? There's fresh bread."

We sat at the little tiled table in the knotty pine kitchen and she lit a candle I had used for years to head off mosquitoes. Shamana moved gracefully from the fridge where she retrieved cold bottles of Chablis and Pinot Grigio. I could see why he was crazy about her. Just enough disdain to keep him begging for more. And her elegance, even in a beach print sarong and green flip-flops, was mesmerizing, and practiced.

"Do you have a preference?" she asked.

I didn't, and Eddie started in, like the boisterous puppy that he was, about how great their week had been and how he has taken her to all the local spots and how mostly they've been home and how Shamana loved to cook.

"Is that what you do, Shamana? I mean when you are not at your leisure with Eddie."

"I'm a writer. Well, I was a writer, but not really now. I left the workshop." She shook her head, affirming that it was not right for her.

"We met at Iowa. The Writers' Workshop." Eddie grinned with his glassy eyes.

"But it wasn't for me. I don't think I have that kind of dedication. Maybe I will cook for a little while. I'm pretty good at it."

Eddie grinned. "Yes," I said. "Dinner's great."

"We've been talking about Shamana becoming a private chef, actually. And maybe starting a cooking blog on the net."

"Eddie. No need to sell my wares to your Auntie."

She spoke with a slight smile but was clearly uncomfortable in the introductory mode. "Let's have some dessert," she said.

Shamana brought out a perfect flan with fresh peaches and thin butter cookies. It was divine.

"How did you learn to cook like this? Mom a good cook?"

Shamana looked up. "My mother does not cook like this," she smiled.

"Where are you from? Did Eddie say Burundi?"

Shamana smiled again, demure. "No. I studied in Burundi. Have connections there."

"Then, I met her in Iowa. After Burundi!" Eddie said.

"Oh," I nodded, noting no information shared. She was very crafty, this beautiful young woman, and carefully presented. Was her cadence Caribbean? She definitely had me going. I suspected that was the idea.

"You and Eddie should catch up. Much more interesting. I'm not an easy sentence, you know." She said this with a grin. And Eddie was charmed. "No, you are not!" he declared as he tackled her and squeezed her tight. She was disarmed, truly, and I felt a bit better. She did have feelings for my nephew, even though she was definitely setting the tone.

"Eddie. Cut it out! We're in the presence of elders!" she squealed.

Again she flashed a disarming smile at me. I had no choice but to defend her.

"That's right, Eddie! Stop mauling your friend! Everyone is enjoying themselves way too much!" We all laughed and Shamana stood and headed to the sink. She straightened her hair and adjusted the sarong, rubbing her toes against the cabinet for a minute to itch an errant scratch. The running water set the tone for a friendly family conversation.

Eddie and I dug down into the catch up game. I got the update on his writing projects, on his family, on his job working with kids and getting them to write stories about their lives. He held her hand when she rejoined us and she kept pouring wine and nibbling a cookie now and then. Then it was late and later and our voices seemed to hover above us, bounce against the walls like bubbles and pop into silence. The little red table candle hissed out, gone after witnessing many meals, but probably never appreciated as much as this last week. The one lamp left on in the living room seemed to be dreaming too as it gave up the fight against the dark night.

"I hope you can sleep," Shamana said. "No moon." Eddie looked over at her. "I hate a dark sky," she said.

"There's always the stars," Eddie offered.

"The moon's still there somewhere," I said. "It's always watching."

"I guess so." She looked up, surprised.

They were already entwined in each other's arms. I floated into my bedroom, clearly in another realm from the young lovers and dropped into my own sweet sleep, buoyed by the kind knowledge that love anywhere helps those who strive to love, everywhere.

Chapter 24

Cape Goings and Comings Again

I opened my eyes, early. The fog was still rolling off the water and this back room was swallowed in the wet cloud. From the kitchen I could hear scraping of a chair and a careful closing of the front screen door. The wooden floorboards creaked, and then a resolute set of padding feet across the front room to the door, and then a second scuffled scrape of sandals. A jingle of keys, the car door opened and closed, the engine started and the soft purr of Eddie's station wagon as it pulled out across the pebbles in the drive and headed back onto the main road. I didn't investigate. My comfort was too seductive.

The landline rung more than once. I woke from a doze and thought maybe Eddie was trying to reach me. Cell phones could be unreliable out here.

"Hello. Hello, Eddie?" I was sleepy and hoped to be able to jump back into that comfy envelope after the call.

The voice on the other line was of an older woman. A Midwestern accent. Broad and with authority.

"Hello?" she said. "Hello, this is Dolores Goldstein. I am looking for my daughter, Shana? I spoke with her at this number earlier today. I hope it's not too early to call."

"Shana? Do you mean Shamana?"

There was a slight hesitation. "Oh yes, sure. Shamana Goldstein? Or maybe it's Gold now?"

"Yes, just a minute. Let me check?"

"Thanks," said Dolores. I moved away to check in the other bedroom and could hear Dolores on the line say to someone else on her side, "Yes, I am trying to reach her now."

The bedroom was empty. And it looked like there was only Eddie's bag there. Toiletries were gone from the bathroom and I noticed the dishes were done in the sink.

"I'm sorry. It looks like she's gone. I heard them drive out early this morning?"

"Oh, he took her to the ferry? Or the other way, to the bus?"

"I'm sorry. I just don't know."

"There's been a death in our family."

"I'm sorry for your loss. Will let Shamana know to be in touch."

"Sorry to bother you." She mumbled and hung up.

The sound of Eddie's station wagon didn't displace the occasional yelp of a kid rushing into the waves or a mom calling them back for more sunblock. There was a firm slam of a car door and then another. I guessed they were both back.

"Well, you called them," I heard Eddie say. "You let them know."

"I can't believe I missed the damn bus!" This argument had some steam behind it. They were not happy.

"I could have left you there for the next one."

"It would be too late! You can't wait for funerals in my family. They need to happen right away."

"Well, I get that. I understand that. I mean it's the same for Jews." Eddie was losing his battle with patience.

There was a jaundiced pause if such a thing is possible. "Yes, it is the same for Jews, everywhere," Shamana said, standing her ground.

There was a longer silence. Eddie stopped in his tracks. Just the floorboards creaked as the two stood their ground.

"Wait." I heard him say. "Are there Jews in Burundi?" An even longer pause. "I mean, I thought you told me you were from Burundi."

"How the hell am I supposed to know if there are Jews in Burundi. I never said I was from Burundi. I studied there. You're so goddamned gullible!"

I could hear him cross back to the doorway of their bedroom. It was a tiny wooden cottage and I thought maybe I should spill some iced tea or something to let them know I was there.

"What the hell are you talking about?" He was pissed, not like Eddie at all. "I woke up at the crack of fucking dawn. You say not a goddamned thing on the whole ride down to the main bus station, you won't tell me anything about your grandmother, your mother who texted you at all hours last night, who I thought was in Africa! And again this morning! What is up with you?"

I heard a mumble from Shamana.

"What? What did you say?"

"Things are seldom what they seem! Skim milk masquerades as cream!" she yelled at him. "Get it!"

Then she stormed out past him and back out to the deck where I was sorry that she found me.

"Oh good! So glad you could hear the whole torrid tale!" She was so angry.

"Um. Your mother called. Looking for you." I tried to stay as neutral as possible.

"Yes! Yes, thank you. I contacted my mother! And no, I am not from Burundi! Goddamn it!"

Shamana stormed off the deck and headed out past the dunes, barefoot and steaming from head to toe. It took Eddie a minute or two, but he shuffled out to the sliding door behind me and looked out at the beach.

"I think she needed a break," I said quietly.

"Yeah, right! Goddamn it." And I heard him shuffle back into the house, and through the front door and slam it, hard.

"The course of true love ne'er does run smoothe." I sighed with the memory of this line floating back into my head. Lysander to Hermia? *Midsummer Night's Dream*? I heard a ping on my cell phone.

"*Dear Annie*," it read.

It's now summer and we have missed the opportunity to walk through the Gardens and smell spring. Perhaps that is better as "April is the cruelest month . . ." a statement with which you might agree. I have no favorites. Here is another one which may give you an insight into my exciting life. "Television is a medium of entertainment which permits millions of people to listen to the same joke at the same time, and yet remain lonesome." TS Eliot.

I would like to invite you to a social event in September because, if we plan now, I will have something to look forward to. I hope you will accept my invitation. David Diamond.

"Curious and curiouser," I murmured, but it made me smile anyway. We wouldn't be young lovers like Eddie and Shamana but maybe our age would allow us an easier time of it My eighteen-year-old brain kept wondering what it would feel like to kiss him.

Dear David. A nice thought and I would be honored. Let's check in next month and see how our paths can cross. Sincerely, Annie.

The idea that this bright, curious man thought of me gave me comfort. But, this time I would make sure he paid the lunch bill. That made me laugh.

I headed to the kitchen. Eddie was at the dining table, poking away at his computer.

"Ooh, sorry to interrupt," I said.

"What are you chortling about?"

"Not chortling, not chortling."

Eddie looked up at me none too happy. "I have a suitor, my nephew. I have an odd suitor and it makes me smile."

Eddie watched as I rumbled around to find some cans of tuna for sandwiches.

"Tuna okay?" I said.

"I hope you find someone, Aunt Annie. I mean. We all deserve to have someone good in your life."

I continued my mundane mayo, celery, pickle, salt and pepper combo. "Okay," I said. "I'll introduce you to this strange fellow if we ever get that far."

"Where'd you meet him?"

"He was a student at the retreat. Wait! Wait! You met him! He said you were very respectful!"

Eddie paused a minute. "Wait! Oh no! Not that guy! The one who ditched the woman he came with?"

"He's just a friend. He's just a friend." I backpedaled immediately.

"You really know how to pick 'em!" Eddie ripped off. "Are you that desperate?" Eddie needed to draw blood close by and I was in his direct line of fire.

"Hey! Watch it!" I slung back. "Go after your girlfriend and make peace. Rather not be on the receiving end of your misfortune!"

Eddie and I were both surprised with my sharp retort. The room felt the slap, an unwanted interruption.

"I'm sorry, Eddie." I said. "You touched a nerve."

"Aw, it's okay, Aunt Annie. It's okay."

Eddie let his head fall into his hands and closed his eyes. "I feel like an idiot."

I reached out and put my hands on Eddie's shoulders and they immediately relaxed.

"Here's the thing, Eddie. We're not always in charge of the folks that fascinate us."

He rolled his head in his hands a couple more times. "I fell for her so hard. Swallowed all the princess shit. All the rest . . ."

"You guys obviously have a connection."

Eddie straightened up.

"How many times have you seen him? This guy."

I straightened up, too. "Well, one official coffee date. And then he was ill."

"Ah, sounds serious." Eddie said, mocking me.

"Smart ass," I said and served us both our sandwiches. I found the chips I had brought in my groceries and plopped them on the table.

Eddie ate without a word and with a familiarity that I hoped comforted him. Every bite I could feel him tussle with the ease of just being himself and the crushing desire to be as magical as this girl who he realized might actually not be as magical as he thought.

"I'm gonna take a walk, Annie. I gotta think about stuff."

And off he walked.

It had been a hard worn friendship, the one between me, myself and I, and I was happy enough to enjoy the accomplishment. But David was a fellow traveler, somehow. Bruised and battered like the rest of us. But he made me laugh with his straightforward comments on the world, and he did send me links to books and articles that I would never think to review, even when he was out of commission. He was passionate about everything from astronomy to the *Katzenjammer Kids* comics. I thought how Eddie had probably never even heard about that comic strip from the thirties. Maybe the fatigue and burn out I had been feeling, coping with the world we were living in, would benefit from an easy friendship.

The wall phone rang and interrupted my reverie.

"Hello. I am so sorry to call you again." It was Dolores Goldstein.

"She seems to be off at the beach," I said. "

"We just finished the funeral and we're taking a little rest 'til the shiva starts."

"I'm sorry for . . ."

"You think Shana may come in? She won't call me on her own." She jumped in.

"She's been a very lovely guest, Dolores." I was just trying to make her feel better.

"Well, I hope so. We raised her well. The best we could. Like you, I'm sure."

"I did the best I could. As I'm sure we all do."

"Your son seems to be good to Shana. At least, it seems that's her only location these last few months. Since she left college."

"Oh, Eddie is my nephew. Not my son."

"Oh, did he finish college?"

"My son actually didn't go to college. Well not yet, actually. He's traveling. But Eddie is college-educated. Very good catch really!" I hoped she heard the irony I was going for.

Dolores snuffled a bit into the phone. "You making a *shiddach*?!"

I answered immediately, "No! Of course, not. It's none of my business. Certainly."

"Oh, you understand Yiddish, that's good," Dolores sighed.

"Dolores, I'll tell Shamana . . ."

Dolores wasn't listening, crowded as she was with all her brand new ghost. "You want a daughter near you. Especially when you are no longer a daughter."

"Aren't we always children of our parents?" I asked, drawn in despite myself.

"I do know that pretending your parents, whoever they are, don't exist feels annihilating. I mean when's the last time you heard from your son?"

"I'm not sure that's relevant to . . ."

"My mother adored Shana. She was the light of her life." She wasn't really interested in my responses. This wasn't a conversation but maybe more like lancing a painful boil. "At first she wasn't happy about us adopting a mixed race child. She was a sociologist. So many problems, she told me. Racial identity. Abandonment issues from the adoption. At some point she will realize she does not look like you, my mother said, and then what? I guarantee you there will be problems."

"Well, it's always hard to."

"You don't have to make me feel better. The thing was, we always thought she was okay with being Black and Jewish. It wasn't weird, it was who she was. And there was another girl at the synagogue who was adopted and was Black, too. All the way Black, not a mulatto like Shana. I'm sure that's politically incorrect for me to say! It's difficult to get it right as a plain old mother, but add race and adoption into the mix. Oy."

I had no response and I don't think one was warranted.

"We adore her, of course." Dolores was into her own painful rapture. "She is so beautiful. So elegant and exotic. I'm short and stubby and so is Fred, my husband. He's a dentist. Well, he's a dentist but he does Botox on the side. Can you imagine that? I asked him if it made him feel special to be able to shoot up Lisa Brunetti's six necks for a few hundred dollars, instead of drilling holes in her teeth. You know what he said?"

"No, I don't."

"He said, he felt ambushed by my 'sociological superiority.' You mean to tell me I do a bad thing by making extra money to provide for her? By loving this kid and taking her to Cubs games? 'It's not Cubs games, Barry!' I'd say. And he'd say, 'Love is love and at some point Shana will get that. She just has to work it out. Me, I'm clear,' he says. 'I love her.' 'Yes, but . . .' I would say, and he'd say, 'If that makes me a patronizing racist then so be it.' That's what he said.' And I would argue with him and tell him 'It's a complex issue, Fred. You can't dismiss it!' 'I can do what I can do.' He says. 'I get to keep the great memories of being a dad. If she's ashamed of me. What can I say?' And his eyes would always look so hurt."

"Mrs. Gold, really . . ."

"It's more likely for an adopted kid to fail to bond, or want to get away . . . but it happens with biological kids, too. Trauma, they say. Do you suffer not hearing from him? Your son. I suffer terribly."

There was no way to escape the conversation now. I took a breath. I had a litany of defended responses. I tried this, "I look on the bright side, and try not to beat myself up too terribly."

"You don't have to worry. It's nice to hear I am not the only mother to have failed my child!" She chuckled to herself. "I eat cake every Friday night, an extra piece when I don't hear from her. Fills me up. Are you overweight?"

She must have heard me stretch the phone cord to the refrigerator so I could get some lemonade.

"Seasonably. I try to exercise in summer. Really, I should go now. Beach date," I said, gaily.

"You don't have a date but I'll let you go."

"Yes, I think that's best."

It was quiet on the phone line but I could feel the emptiness yearning for Shamana to walk into the cabin and tell her mother she loved her.

"Will you tell Shana-le her mama loves her and would love to speak to her?"

"Yes, I will."

"Thanks. Goodbye. I'll go rest now."

"Yes, me too."

My little kitchen felt almost embarrassed after I put down the phone. Too much information to digest for a room used to Scrabble arguments and games of gin rummy. I wasn't sure where I could go with all this. The beaches were full of lovers finding each other, the beds full of dreams, and the sound of grinding stones into reluctant surfaces.

Chapter 25

Starlight Stories

It wasn't 'til almost nine that the two of them came back in. They were together. They were wan, drained from tears, loving each other and fearing the final loss of the other. All those things I could see on their faces, but they held hands like ten-year-olds and came in the front door and plopped down on the couch.

I shuffled out from my bedroom.

"Hungry?" I said, as I came into the room.

"Nope," Eddie said. "We stopped for a clam roll."

"It was great!" giggled Shamana with a big grin. And I suspect there was a beer or two in their feast. "I'm covered in 'skito bites!" She started running her nails along her arms.

"Stop!" said Eddie. "I'll get the calamine." And he got up and went to the bathroom.

Shamana just lay back on the couch, she was finished. Eddie came back and made her sit up. He sat behind her, putting his legs around her and started daubing her shoulders and back with big white globs of the lotion.

"Maybe you should just give me that cotton and I can swab it all over my face," she said. "White face on the cape, we can call it." She closed her eyes.

"You'd need zinc oxide for that, besides I love how you look, with or without mosquito bites."

Shamana sighed and lay back against Eddie.

"Ooh!" he said as he held her at bay. "I don't want all that white stuff on me," and they started to giggle together, play like kids. Then, Eddie looked up.

"What have you been doing, Annie?" Eddie said with a sweet control of the situation.

"I've been watching the stars. That's enough."

The two of them leaned into their tasks of caretaker and cared for, and I sat and watched them contentedly. Finally, Shamana said, "Did my mom call again?"

"Yes," I said. "She asked me tell you that she loves you. And she's sad about losing her own mama."

Shamana smiled again wistfully. "Gramma was a trip. She was the one who really got me. She'd rescue me at Christmas when my mom would make me lead Kwanzaa celebrations at the synagogue. Me and another Black girl. We were the ones to make them all feel better about themselves."

"What do you mean?" Eddie said.

"Oh, you know, they worked so hard at me not being an outcast, that they made me a freak. I was rotten though. I used to scream 'whitey' at her when I was fifteen. It gave me an extra tool in my toolkit of torture."

"Make you feel better?" I asked.

"Not really. It's just I was Black and they weren't. It was important to me that they saw me not as some love doll, but as a separate person."

"What did your mom do?" Eddie asked as he kept daubing.

"She felt guilty and rotten. But I guess she could have just said yes, I am white and you are Black and it's weird but I'm still your mama and I love you."

I smiled, hearing what an easy solution Shamana imagined for all the things that ailed her.

"What are you smiling about, Annie?" Shamana caught the look.

"Nothing, really. It's not always easy to come up with the right thing at the right time. It's hard to even know what the other person is asking for in fights like that."

"I guess," Shamana said, too tired to contest.

"When's the last time you saw her?" I asked. "Your mom?"

"A few months. Maybe winter time. But she calls me constantly. There's always a text or a picture or something! She drives me crazy."

Eddie was watching me pretty closely. It was sweet how protective he was of me. I wondered if he felt too much of a pressure to be the good son with the absence of my wayward boy.

"Well," I said. "I guess I'll say . . . I'm sorry for her loving you so much. And in a way that doesn't communicate with you these days. I guess I get that. It's complicated."

Eddie shifted, not comfortable with the subtext of the conversation. I decided to let him off the hook.

"I have a son I haven't talked to in a long time. Maybe three years. It's been hard on me, but then, maybe it's harder on him."

Shamana startled, electric up her spine. "I mean, is it really his job? I mean, is it my job to take care of her? And her messy needs? I just have to grow up. I have to be my own person. She and my dad decided they were going to solve the world's racial problems on my back. I'd rather not, thanks."

"You have a point, of course." I smiled at her.

"Well, Jordan was different, Aunt Annie. When Uncle Ty died he never did get over it. And he was weird and mad before that. I think its fucked up he doesn't call you. It's not fair. You didn't do anything to make him punish you that way!"

"I've come to terms." I said my mantra. "I hope he has. And he may show up one day, the prodigal son."

"It is weird he hasn't been in touch at all. I hope he's okay." Eddie put down the calamine lotion and was now massaging Shamana's neck and shoulders. "He went to Japan, right?"

"He went to study at a monastery in Japan but he seems to have left there. They said he was on retreat with no forwarding address. Maybe he's writing a great novel about his awakening and he'll return all bright and shiny and take me to the National Book Awards!"

That left the two of them staring at me. Not sure if pity or outrage should be offered.

"Good night you two. I'm glad you're back and holding hands."

They both gave a goofy grin and snuggled back on the couch, all arms and legs entwined.

"We're going for a swim! Then to bed!" Eddie said.

"Noooo," said Shamana. "too many 'skitos!"

"Come on," he said, pulling her off the couch. While she screamed happily, he grabbed their beach towels and playfully pulled her out the door and down onto the sand.

I went back to my room, the sound of their protests and joy, my buoy.

Chapter 26

David on the Bridge

We were sitting on a bench outside the Athenaeum, the wonderful old library in Boston, the repository of great literary and historical treasures. It's long been a favorite haunt of mine and David had arranged a visit to explore some special collections. It was late afternoon, the musky warmth of late August surrounding us. He had planned this outing carefully. And cleared the air when I arrived on time for our date.

"Thank you, Annie, for showing up. I realize that my not being in touch after we made our Gardner date was inexcusable," he said. I believe he had thought about that sentence before he offered it. He had such a pride of accomplishment every time he managed to communicate something well. It made me smile.

"But, you did tell me you were sick. Right?" Trying to stay concerned rather than amused. "And you sent me things, links to the Katzenjammers. And I loved the Nina Simone music."

"Yes. But Aretha is still the Queen," he said with certainty.

"Are you feeling better? Are you okay?"

"I had a stay in the hospital. Had to recuperate and rest."

"May I ask what happened?"

"Heart," he said mournfully. "I had a broken heart." He looked at me like a sad dog and then laughed. "I mean, really broken. The surgeons went in and made some repairs." His hang dog face disappeared and I couldn't help laughing now.

"Glad you are better now." I said. "That must have been scary."

"It was fine. I kept thinking that my stepson showed up to try to help me. I would see him, when over medicated. It was unpleasant. And then he disappeared when they lowered the painkillers. Maybe he reported to his mother that I was still on the planet. If she's still on the planet."

"Your ex-wife in Georgia. Right?"

"That's right. I was her project many years ago. It did not work. Still, the boy remembered me fondly. I read the newspaper to him every night before bed."

I smiled. "It's fun to think of you doing that." I think Ty read the funnies to Jordan. It reminded Ty of his grandfather doing the same for him.

David looked quizzically back. "Is it? I learned how to do an excellent subway fold." He saw me float elsewhere in my memory bank. And he did not inquire.

Let's go in. And he led the way to the Athenaeum front door leaving visions of Georgia and her son floating in his medically induced vision, behind.

Books and galleries of old prints welcomed us. David took special care to find original papers from John Singer Sargent. Prints from Audubon's *Birds of America*. And then the fascination with that burglar's book, bound in the burglar's own skin.

"Can we see that one?" he asked the rare books librarian.

"I'm sorry, sir. We only show it on special occasions."

"But, today is a special occasion." She blinked in response and he blinked back. But he gave it up, leading me over to the reference computers in the room.

In the end, we had to be satisfied with a digital copy of the front of the book. The explanation that James Allen had asked that his memoir be covered in his own tanned skin was spelled out in a few special brochures. Allen requested that the warden of his last prison have a swath of his back skin tanned and then used to bind the story of his life when he died. David was fascinated with this. It seems this was a custom in the French Revolution, as well.

"But why not bind the story of your life in your own skin?" he was pushing this conversation at me like a cranky child. "It is certainly authentic. And for people like me who can't always use words to their advantage, maybe being able to touch the flesh of the deceased would give one an insight into how they lived, and what they cared about."

"I think it was a bit more compelling to go over the books that Louisa May Alcott took out of the collection in 1872. I think there was Trollope's *Emma*, and a book on Dickens?"

"Yes, but there was also a book called, *Why Did He Die?* She started out writing mystery novels, real blood and guts stuff, I seem to recall."

We had finished the iced tea and strawberries in the Tea Room. "Let's walk," he said. "I think it said she lived on Beacon Street. I wonder if there's still a whiff of her over there?"

"Ghosts on your mind?" I asked.

We walked for a bit in silence. "I sometimes wonder what will be left of us after we are gone. That's what I am thinking about. If there are no bloodlines. No books bound in our own skin. No love or monuments. I sometimes wonder."

I said nothing at first. Then, "I don't know what's left. Einstein said no matter is destroyed. The dasas at the Temple in India were so radical about inhabiting the present moment that all boundaries between now and then vanished." David's linear life view went crashing into that statement. I tried again. "Some folks say we just keep coming back and back to the planet 'til we get it right."

"What's 'it'?"

We were near the Garden now and headed across, past the swan boats.

"Get it right?" he mumbled. "I never get it right but I still do try to get it!" He chuckled at his own joke. He lead me over a small bridge that went over the boats, a replica of the Bridge of Sighs, I always thought.

David grabbed my arm. I was alarmed at his touch. I wasn't sure if he was falling or if I was. His touch was firm. It had intent but I wasn't sure what it was. But then I realized he was trying to spin me around and dip me back a la a tango move from a 1940s film. I felt like I was a fish being wriggled from a net.

Then, he swooped down, and he kissed me. Lips closed. A bit of bristle. It felt like he was making a grand effort to go for a huge smackeroo but midway rethought the move to a more modest cheek to cheek embrace. I wasn't sure if he wanted to imitate a movie moment or if the effort of expressing himself with words was too much.

He looked at my surprised face as we pulled apart. "What do you think, Annie? How was that? Life affirming? Is that the 'it'?"

"A Fred and Ginger swoon? I suppose . . . yes."

He was pleased he had pleased me.

"We can't make children, Annie. We have nothing to leave but a kiss on the bridge over the swan boats at the Boston Garden!" he said with a flare.

That made me smile.

"Yes. Well, there's a worthy memory," he said, pleased with himself.

And I had to agree.

He took my arm and hooked it through his, patting my hand. Proud of himself in a roguish way.

We strolled along as if nothing happened. Not sure if it had or not. We didn't really know.

I thought he would walk me to the MTA and I would head home. But instead, he took my hand and brought me to a bench like he had planned a post-museum concert. There was a young violinist playing for coins. We sat and she was joined by a cellist and then a viola. They launched into the music, the vibration of the strings so close I could feel it in my chest. The music floated upward. David closed his eyes. I felt his breathing go regular. His head hung to the side, almost touching my shoulder. He was asleep. With post coitus depth. He was spent.

I enjoyed the music. And the odd familiarity of the feeling of a man breathing regularly, evenly, propped by the touch of my body as a touchstone. The violinist and I shared a smile when I nudged David making sure that his slight snuffle did not become a snore. He slept for half an hour, comfortable and satisfied. The breeze was easy on our skin. The music wrapped us like a cotton quilt. I liked the way it felt to rest, touching another human being, without asking or being asked for anything.

Now, it was almost seven. The trio took a break and another kid came by a few benches away and set up his music for some dance moves for coins. David opened his eyes.

"Are you going to take me for dinner?" I asked. He a bit groggy. Me, feigning familiarity.

"Oh, I'm too sleepy," he answered. "Aren't you sleepy?."

He stood and started to leave. I put a few bills in the cup for the players and the young violinist smiled at me. I turned to catch up to David, already down the block. He had his bus pass out.

He waved to me. "There's my bus, Annie." Then, he thought better of it and came back to me. He took my hand and kissed it. "Thank you for a lovely afternoon." And he grinned a sleepy, beguiling smile.

The bus stopped, he got on and sat in a window seat to wave goodbye. Leaving me standing at the bus stop, my shoulder still warm.

Chapter 27

Aretha after the Bridge of Sighs

I was watching the determined blonde Dr. Christine Blasey Ford testify in front of Congress. John McCain had died and the family asked that the president not attend the funeral. 'R-E-S-P-E-C-T!" The great Aretha Franklin had passed recently and I cranked up her music as a soundtrack to the misery on the television. Maybe they would feel it in the hearing room.

This woman was mutilating herself, putting her version of the truth in front of the committee pushing through the nomination of Brett Kavanaugh, a good ol' boy, accused of rotten behavior. Her large glasses were the only things that kept her eyeballs in her head.

David called.

"Hey, David. I'm watching the hearings. Have you been following them?"

"You're listening to Aretha. Good. I knew you would. She died a few weeks ago. And McCain died a few weeks ago. A good man, too."

"I'm hoping the guys in the hearing on TV can hear Aretha, too!"

"I doubt it. Mostly the landlord. Yes. I liked Aretha very much, I told you that. There's a concert. We should go. The kids at Boston Arts. We should go."

"Okay." My eyes couldn't peel away from the television. "These hearings are so painful!" No answer. "How are you, David?"

"Oh, I am much the same. I am walking and murmuring a great deal. That is normal for me."

"But what are you murmuring about, David? How are you feeling about our politics? What's your story?"

There was a silence on the phone. "There is no story. There is no story. Can you turn the music down?"

"I'd rather not. I'm going crazy watching these hearings. The music is helping."

"Well, I can't hear you."

"It's not me to listen to. Are you even aware of what's going on in the world?"

There was a slight pause. "Is there going to be a quiz?" I didn't answer. Surely, he had to have some awareness of what was going on in the world. Instead, he said, "I never have liked teachers, Annie. I don't like the clever questions offered to make someone spill beans. When beans are available to spill I will make my own decision about spilling them."

"Gee, David. Sorry. Didn't mean to pry."

"Actually, you did. It is what you do."

I glanced over to the television to watch the determined look on Blasey Ford's face. "The senators are letting this woman roast herself. It's torturous."

"There's a time and a place. There's a time and a place."

"Someone has to step up to tell their truth these days," I said.

"Send them a note, Annie. I'm sure they'll all straighten up and fly right at your suggestion."

"David, is there a reason you called?" He caught my tone but had no idea that the testimony on TV and the overwhelm of this woman trying to get her truth into the world might be something to address.

"About the concert. I thought you told me you liked Aretha." He was mystified at my question. "That's all. Don't scold me. I don't like to be scolded."

"I'm not scolding."

"Or teasing. I'm not good with teasing. I'm a rather straightforward fellow."

"Yes. Yes. I understand." Or did I?

The hearings went to commercial break and David was gone, too. Relief all round.

We had planned to meet for dinner before the memorial concert at Boston Arts. He was late, so I bought some sandwiches before he arrived and put them in my purse.

"We can take bites, if we get hungry," I said.

"No. No. I won't be stuffing my face like that at the concert. Like we should all sho' nuf bring baskets of fried chicken and potato salad!" He shook his head in contempt.

"Not exactly," I murmured. "Not exactly," as he moved into the crowd and found our seats.

The heat in the hall grew with each successive group of singers. David stood. He clapped and stomped with the best of them, a sense memory from another time. Never mind that his stomp was usually one beat off everyone else's, his claps singular.

"R-E-S-P-E-C-T!" he chanted. I was up and swaying and clapping, too. The passion of the music clicked us back in sync, I hoped. I patted his back trying to make amends. He blanched. He looked around. I moved back to my own rhythm. Something had gone off.

"You really got into that, David!" I said, as we were making our way up the aisle.

"I saw Aretha perform in Georgia before she died. With my stepson. His mother didn't attend." He looked for his handkerchief and mopped his forehead. "She was magnificent."

"Aretha? Or . . ."

"Of course, Aretha! My ex-wife was always telling me *respect* is what it is all about! She thought she owned that idea. Coming from Detroit, going to church and hearing Aretha sing! But it goes two ways." He pushed ahead of a group of kids taking selfies together. "Move along, will you?" he said harshly.

"How long were you together?"

"Five years," he said with a bark. "It was not good for the boy for her to demand my departure so quickly and decide she wanted out. It was not good for the boy. Or for her either."

He was on a roll now. Thinking of his almost family, of his almost fatherhood, of his almost family man days. "I did very well for her. She was impossible. She never listened to me." He kept pushing ahead, moving around the congregating groups of choir members and their families, flower bouquets being exchanged, shrieking kids and proud mamas gathering for pictures. He urgently wanted out and away from this crowd.

"Want something cool to drink?" I asked, as we emerged from the auditorium, hoping we could salvage some kind feeling between us.

"No. No. I'm too sweaty. I'm going home to take a shower. Thanks for coming with me." And he shook his head yes and said, "Goodbye for now."

He turned abruptly, as was his wont, and headed back toward the MTA train station.

"Wait," I called after him. "Wait!" I caught up to him. "Let's just walk a bit, or talk a little? The concert was so amazing, yes? And you're upset. I want to talk about it a little."

David was clearly distressed but maybe he thought surrender was easier and he motioned across the street.

"The Starbucks is air-conditioned. We can sit there," he said.

We found a seat in the crowded table area. There were young kids, overflow from the concert, streaming in, then leaving, then looking for seats, then coming back. It was chaos. David got up abruptly and returned with my iced tea.

"Didn't you get anything?"

"No," he said. "I'm hot and want to get showered. He looked at me straight and I was embarrassed that I had pushed this.

"Oh, David. Not good. Let's go."

He abruptly shoved his chair back and headed out of the coffee place.

"Good night, David. I thought we might be able to talk about the music, the people." This was falling on deaf ears. "Sorry." No response. "I enjoyed the concert. Thank you."

He started to walk away and then turned to stand his ground. "I'd rather not be patronized by you when I am with you."

"What are you talking about? Because I wanted to talk about what you were feeling? Because I patted your back?" I knew immediately that that was a wrong move.

"I'd rather you didn't touch me at all."

I took a deep breath and re-centered. "Yes, of course. No problem, I apologize if you felt invaded in anyway."

"I've been told my disagreeable nature comes from being on the spectrum, but sometimes I think it's because I actually see things too clearly."

"David. Let's not make a big deal about this. We obviously are not communicating properly. I just was enjoying you, enjoying the music."

David shifted and looked over my head. He was getting wound up in his own thoughts and I could tell something was coming. "I am going home now, Annie. I am not available for fawning over the Black man's rhythm. We're hypocrites really. Us white people thinking we are entitled to the music of a race of people who are still inconveniently present in an America that would have rather had them fall into a mass grave following slavery. We don't want them here. And all this do 'gooding' about the wonderful Black music from liberal white enthusiasts is nonsense."

The rant seemed to be taking on breadth. I tried to engage. Wrong move. "But, then, why did we come? You clearly enjoyed the concert."

"You're a white liberal, Annie. I thought you might enjoy it."

"And you're not?"

"Let's say, I have fewer delusions than you do. Read the literature. We are hopelessly caught in our own paternalism."

"That's not fair, it was your idea to come after all! It wasn't just about the music for you, obviously!"

"And I am embarrassed." He stood his ground, looked toward the milling crowd thinning and then focused back on me.

"I embarrass you?" I asked, incredulous.

"Think you are entitled to the world. To everyone's story. It supports your false world view. Not everything is yours to examine."

"David. I am sorry if I continue to fall short of your expectations."

"I have few expectations. I am just disagreeable. I am going home."

He turned and headed to the T station. I recognized this scenario. It was the feeling I imagined Barb had felt that day in Kauai when he dismissed her so easily. It did not feel good.

There was a bench at the bus stop and I slipped in and had a seat. It was a hot night for September. No hint of the calming cool of autumn.

I sipped my iced tea and heard a loud voice coming from a tall woman across the street caught in the crush of the crowd.

"Will you *kindly* move out of the way! Thank you!"

There was no mistaking that voice. There was Mallory, from India, right here on the street in Boston. She must have been at the concert.

"Mallory!" I called from the shelter of the bus stop. "Mallory! Over here!"

She squinted and then her eyes went wide. Still wrapped in white cotton, she made her way across the street.

"Oh my God, Annie!"

Chapter 28

Mallory at the Wine Bar

We hugged while Mallory sang out, "OMG, what a concert!" She grabbed my hand. Next I knew, I was seated on the back patio of a local wine bar, hearing the details of her move to Boston after India.

"My life completely changed when I got back. I took a job with the Temple Types! The Meditation Temple–North America. I'm working part time in the office!"

"Did you tell them you never got to the Temple?" I laughed.

"Never mind." We laughed, enjoying our shared experience.

"Have you heard from Puran. That guy in India?"

"Please . . ." Mallory lifted her eyebrows at least two inches from the upper rim of her big glasses. "That was folly. I've sworn off men."

I took a drink of my cool Lillet.

"You go to this concert alone?" She asked, noting my silence. "They were heartbreakingly great, yes?"

"I actually came with a friend."

"Yes?" she said, raising those eyebrows again, "a man?"

"A friend. A man. A friendly man, I thought."

"Friendly is good," she lifted the Pinot Grigio from the ice bucket and poured me a glass, my Lillet now gone.

"But?" she probed, as much for fun as for information.

"But," I continued, "he was hot and needed a shower and he took off." Mallory had been stirring the ice in the bucket with the tips of her fingers as she listened.

"And didn't invite you to join him under the spray?" She flicked some cold water at me.

"Not that kind of friend." I flinched and over reacted to the spray of water, grabbing my napkin, keeping busy.

"Oh yes, then why are you so rattled?"

"I'm not rattled. I just had a fight with this difficult person."

Mallory smiled and gave me a moment. I was surprised to be upset, and hurt and unsure. Then she said, "You think being an older woman means we're not still teenagers at heart?"

"I was just having a friendly connection, no need to make a big deal of it." I had another sip of wine.

"You're fine all by yourself, no need for comfort or soft nights and easy brunch after the crossword? God. Does that really happen?" Mallory was looking over the menu.

"I think so. I think at some point it becomes too foolish."

"Are you talking to a real person with that sentence? Jeez."

"This guy is challenging—but I have enjoyed his company. So much for the feminist in me. He's smart. Not bad looking."

"You're lonesome, dearie. It isn't a federal crime, you know."

I shook my head. "Nothing makes sense to me anymore. We have a crazy government, the world is sizzling, they're putting kids in cages, no amount of screaming gets anyone's attention, we're heaving good men along with the bad into oblivion for being guilty of stupid jokes."

"Is that what you're doing?"

"I have no idea," I said.

"To get a Harvey Weinstein you have to sacrifice an Al Franken." Mallory got the attention of the waiter. "Young man? Another bottle please? And some nachos. Stat." She turned to me. "This sounds serious."

The wine was affecting me and my head was spinning.

"He accused me of being a racist. And I probably am, everyone who's white in this country is a racist in some way. Comes right from the top!"

"We do what we can do."

"It's not enough! It's not enough to do what we can! It's what let Trump take over! It's what's making enemies of neighbors and keeping us from getting any sense of each other."

"I say it again, you're lonesome my friend."

"Is that a crime?"

"You could come back to the Temple Types for solace!" She started to laugh. "You could always get a cat. People are crazy about their cats. And they have such diffident loyalty."

I let the evening breeze find me and said nothing as she poured us both another glass and added some ice from the bucket, flinging the last cube right at my chest so it slipped conveniently down the blouse I was wearing.

Before I could protest, she said, "I'm sorry he was an asshole, darling. "We're all trying to plug in the right plug to find the right connection in that big PBX switchboard in the sky. But, the technology is outdated. We can ring up someone but if the old PBX board doesn't find their brainwave, we're out of luck, friend. No forwarding addresses offered."

Mallory looked at me simply with a smile. "I'm so wise, yes?" She ate the last bite of nachos and licked her fingers, "Lonesome, says the Guru, is a state of mind."

Her usually carefully placed white scarf was dripping off the back of her chair, her hat askew. Her hair was a faded blonde and showed her grey roots. Her long face looked so tired that when she relaxed, she let the false animation fall away. She kind of reminded me of her Maisie cat, loyal but mangy. Nobody had chosen her over the cat so far. Except me.

Chapter 29

More Murder

It was a Saturday afternoon, already late October. Restless all day, I had done my appointed rounds of grocery store, laundromat, coffee stop. Then, up the stairs with my several bags, swift placement in closets and pantry. Discomfort bedeviled me.

David's attack on me at the concert was enough for me to retreat but this Saturday, I confess to feeling the snaggy process of letting go of a habit that had become a comfort. And this autumn, there was no feeling of bounty but rather a furtive op-ed in the paper saying that the sane people had an eye on the crazy person who was leading the government. The sense of dread at owning up to ourselves fell over us all like fine silt.

The winter gourds and scraggly Indian corn on my table reminded me of trailing pick-ups with Dixie flags and shotguns in crusty fields. Campaign signs scribbled with swastikas. I swept the autumn totems into the trash, and we both sat, forlorn and cranky.

I sought refuge in my email.

"I know you must be angry with me. I apologize for not being a normal person. I hope we can still be friends." This was the third email I had received from David this week. That was after three telephone calls, which I did not pick up.

The soft afternoon light urged me to take a break in its waning comfort. I headed to the couch to close my eyes before the evening task of filling the hours without my usual Saturday night dinner with David. I flipped on the television. It always put me to sleep. The news feed on the bottom on the screen jolted through me before I could close my eyes. *Eleven people shot at Pittsburgh Tree of Life Synagogue. White Supremacist Ties.*

The phone rang and I grabbed it up without thinking.

"Are you over-identifying as usual?" It was David.

"Oh my God! Eleven people shot in the Tree of Life Synagogue. Oh my God, what is going on?" I babbled.

"The guy had posted on an internet board. Didn't like the immigration work that HIAS was doing. Thought he'd take matters into his own hands. He was not that old, but he killed a lot of Jews. I thought you'd be upset."

"Eleven people!" Then, a begrudging thank you was in order. "Thanks for thinking of me."

"They are your people after all."

"My people? Dead is dead, David."

"Your people will get well mourned. It's the Black families who lose a kid every other day from the cops or some crazy racist that don't get mourned enough."

David's tone was edgy and harsh.

"Everyone deserves mourning!" I was not going to take his bait. "Everyone deserves respect, certainly."

"Yes. That includes me?"

"Are we talking about you? I thought we were talking about racist murderers."

"I don't like calling and calling and you not picking up the phone. That is not respectful." Can a voice sound like a pout and a roar at the same time?

"David, are we really talking about you right now when this horrendous thing has just happened?"

"Horrendous things happen every day. I am a horrendous thing. I happen every day."

The world went atilt. He had just heaved himself into the disjointed trash like the gourds and Indian corn, unable to represent who he is in the world to his own satisfaction.

"A horrendous thing! Is that what you think of yourself?" I could feel him turn off his hearing and send his wailing rant into the ethers, toward me.

"If you have something to say then say it! Don't shirk your responsibility like whoever wrote that anonymous essay in the *New York Times*. 'We are watching the madman for you.' How patronizing! I expect that respect. And I expect the respect of being mourned, or being noticed, if you have deigned to spend your time with me at all."

"David, I'll talk to you some other time." I had no way to respond to him, his pain, confusion, complexity, sad, sad, sadness.

"No! No, you won't!" He was screaming at me. Furious and loud.

The television screen was filled with photos of people hugging each other outside the synagogue. The commentator was describing the way in which the shooter had planned his attack. David's voice kept scraping at me, trying to break skin.

"David! Stop! People lay murdered. I can't help you."

"Yes, murdered! Annie! Annie! Do not hang up on me," he puffed. I clicked off the call and tossed my phone onto the couch.

The faces of mystified mourners filled the screen. I looked at the bodies being carried out on stretchers and in my mind's eye, David's face filled the screen, murdered as well. Bloody and gaping.

"Mallory, have you seen the news? Could you call me? It's Annie. We're all murdering each other!"

The phone rang but it was David. And it was David again and again, every ten minutes for three hours. Finally, it stopped ringing. I sat glued to the couch, my eyes to the screen.

Fox News told us the president's reaction was that if the Jews had more guns, they wouldn't be such victims. Like he recommended for the teachers at Marjory Stoneman Douglas.

His remedy was more murder. More annihilation. I turned off the television and waited for Mallory to call.

The phone kept ringing every half hour. It was David's lifeline. His fury toward me. I finally turned it off at 2:00 a.m. with no word from Mallory.

I was not a Jew shot in the Pittsburgh basement, I knew that. But my fear wanted to keep me there, wanted me to carry the horror on a frame that was too low to the ground to get any leverage. David's rage was streaming above me, keeping me crouched in a corner. Murder was everywhere.

I got a flash of my dasa from the temple. I could see her smiling but I wasn't sure if she was pleased, laughing at or laughing with me. I kept the vision of her face with me.

Slowly I grabbed my wool coat which I had left on the back of the kitchen chair and lay under it, feeling the back of the couch against my spine.

Slashed by David, the murders, the history we were all making, my own power was seeping out of me with every passing minute. I could feel the suckers on my back drawing me deeper into seclusion, the cotton batting of the couch. The dasa's presence floated there. Slowly, slowly sleep came. The seepage slowed.

When I woke on Sunday, the news shows all featured the same story. I drank coffee, turned on the phone again and felt a bit steadier.

David did not call. Neither did Mallory. I sat without changing clothes, drinking too much coffee, and finally turning the television to a black-and-white film noir that, despite the caffeine, captured me and sent me to rest, a few hours of blackout.

"You should have come with us to the mountains. The weather was crisp and glorious and there was a very cute bar in town that I found after the campers were in bed!" It was Mallory, late Sunday afternoon, at last.

"I was dealing with David calling me every five minutes, and my overreaction to yet another racist murder rampage in the country." I put down my pen and closed my computer. A good reason to stop obsessing over articles on White Supremacy on the internet.

"Yes. Well. You have been busy. The times are too nutty to sink into every disaster, Annie. You are locked and loaded, as our fearless leader likes to say. Triggers, triggers everywhere and not a drop to drink."

I had not counted on Mallory for wisdom but she was totally correct. I was like a ticking bomb and ready to blow at every trip in our bumpy road.

"There are a lot more bumps to come," she said to me. "They were talking all about it at the retreat. The world is changing. Get ready for everything to change in the blink of an eye. Expand, breathe, get in touch with co-creation."

"You sound like you are the marketing megaphone for the Center."

"You know I am not much for following rules, rumors, or leaders. But you know and I know that the world is crumpling around us. This guy in the White House is only one part. Get rid of him there's still the disregard for nature, corporations throwing themselves back into pre-Union celebrations of worker abuse, you name it. Not to mention . . ."

"The kids in cages, putting unqualified judges on every federal court . . ." I added.

"Right. There you go. That kind of shit can get a girl down." I heard Mallory take a drink of something.

"Jesus, Mallory. I have to get a grip. Maybe I'll start spending more time at the Center."

"I'll be there and we can always skip class and smoke in the bathroom."

"Yeah, right."

"But first, has that guy stopped calling you? David? He is not a good idea."

"He has stopped for now."

"Good. What was the big draw there?" I needed a moment to answer as I really had no idea. I stood up and walked over to the sink, looking for a cookie to put in my mouth. Nothing available. So I grabbed a sponge and started compulsively wiping down the counter.

"Oh who knows? I thought his dysfunction might have actually been a key to getting through all these changes."

"You actually figured that a guy who had no emotional IQ was the one to lead you to nirvana?"

"I don't know." Now I was grabbing for the cleanser. It was time for a good scour of the sink, anyway. "Don't be cruel," I said as I scrubbed. "There obviously was something there for me."

"Well, I know you like a straightforward approach to life, but these days, those of us used to ridiculous instability may have an advantage."

"Okay, okay, enough." I rinsed the sink and grabbed a towel.

"What are you doing? Taking a bath?"

"Cleanliness is next to godliness. My sink was dirty."

I walked over to the front window with towel in hand and leaned against the large window frame. It was cool with the weather and there was a golden maple at the end of the street. It stood out like a beacon. Time to go.

"I gotta get out of here. I'm going for a walk. Talk later?"

"Eat ice cream. I love you."

I stopped when I heard that. Mallory could hear the silence on my end of the line.

"Oh don't worry. I don't love you like *that*. Goodbye now." And she hung up before I had a chance to spin that one out.

Chapter 30

The Golden Maple

Wrapped in car coat, beret and gloves, I didn't know I was heading directly to the golden maple, ablaze and fiery in the afternoon sun. It was the clear destination. The light demanded it.

The tree stood so tall. I wondered why I hadn't noticed it before. Not as the conductor of the winds above it, or the umbrella against the rain, or the sponge for the coming snow. Not as the commander of our street and now, of my fascination.

My eyes traveled to the interior of its top most branches, looking up, standing under it to understand its power. I thought about actually hugging the thing and put my hand on its smooth bark. Standing there, on the street, I pretended I was a city gardener on official business. Inspecting it for a benevolent purpose.

A young couple, full of book bags and library eyes, smiled as I rooted around, pretending to be busy, slapping its sides like a familiar horse drawn from the stable, thanking it for its sturdy presence. As they passed, I dropped the pretense and stood there, pilgrim, and I dropped my cares and foolish agitation right into the ground around it. Like recycling. The debris of my thoughts rattled down into the tree like old tuna cans and single use water bottles.

The kind wind blew an extra breeze through one ear and out the other, vacating space. I thanked the tree for just letting me touch its smooth bark and feel grounded again and then, it happened. A shift. A headache? No. A shift.

I looked around to see if there was anyone else there who could feel what I was feeling, who could recognize the angle of the afternoon light, experience the lightness of being that was moving up my body from my feet, up my spine, to my neck, my head.

I felt a distant familiarity of being in and out of time at the same time. It was like the day at the Temple, when we wandered under the blaze of those blessings from the ancient monks broadcasting grace like the old RKO radio tower. It felt like that. Like a waking dream descending and wrapping me up.

The harsh realities of murder and disconnection fell away merely by being part of larger light.

My hand stayed connected to the bark and I could feel the easy lift to the very top of the maple.

Moving like the chattering monkeys in India, I swung to my perch and settled, the vista of city around me, the harbor and ocean to the east, the woods to the west. There was a copse of tall evergreens, a small marsh where reeds rustled, hiding secrets.

My eyes belonged to a hawk, framed by feathers, rippling bony wings, spread wide. How they swelled at the wind. I swiveled my ruff, leaned into the cold breeze and dove to examine my territory. A huge rack of antlers came from the trees. Breaking branches, stripping leaves. The large buck shuffled forward, shaking his rack to rid himself of debris. He raised his head, sensing me. His eyes round and black and soft and hard, rapt, as I rose to ride the wind.

I glided closer willing to pace him. Land on his back. And at just the thought of my presence he reared and shook his antlers. Up I sailed to the familiar sky. He moved to the incline, stumbling, losing his footing. Drops of rain dripped off my beak, feathers, marbles of ice pelted the world below me.

His antlers retracted into branches of trees. His body shrunk to sturdy stumps.

I shone like the moon.

He was no longer there.

I don't know how long I was standing, pulled into the breath of the tree. But I was released at last and fit more easily into the waning day. The vision of the hawk's eyes on the stumbling buck left me. But so had the confusion of the last few days. There were predators and powerful engines of life that sailed and sank as we did every day, we frail humans. Sailed and sunk and came up to sail again if lucky.

What remained of the late afternoon was edgy, but gentle. It had deep pockets into which I could disappear. I found a bench near the community garden where a man was at work cleaning out the summer blooms.

He was a round man. Dark like the Guru in India. He smiled at me.

"Old stuff ready for the mulch pile," he said, with that same protective gaze I had felt months before.

It was a day of wonders, or maybe just a lack of sleep. I almost asked him what he thought of my vision, but it didn't make any difference. He had finished his work.

The Guru turned and smiled at me again as he left, jangling his keys, offering the tinkling of bells to seal the day.

Chapter 31

Amanda Again

Amanda showed up for her monthly meeting looking wild-eyed, but determined.

"Hi, Annie. Nice to see you."

She walked to my table and took off her jacket. Just a bit wary of the door being closed behind her, and taking in the late fall sunshine. "It's pretty out."

"Yes," I agreed. "I've made friends with that great big golden maple down the street. He's become a touchstone."

"That's nice." She looked at me with her big green eyes. "I'm not sure I know what that means."

"Me either," I said, a little embarrassed.

"What do you have for me today?" I said bringing tea and a plate of animal crackers to the table. "I love animal crackers," I said. "I used to buy them in the little box with the circus animals for my son when he was little."

"That sounds nice." She took one and put it in her mouth, the whole thing, as if it were a lozenge and it would dissolve in her mouth.

"What you get, a lion?" I asked.

"I think it was a tiger." She didn't open her mouth when she spoke. I guess the cracker was melting on her tongue as she gazed at me. "I wrote my mom and told her I was trying to write something." It was garbled but I got the gist.

"How was that? Will she work with you? Help figure things out?"

Amanda's eyes twinkled and swiveled in their sockets. She reached into her bag to produce a pink envelope and a handwritten letter.

"Behold, Mary Margaret Winston." She said, covering her mouth with her hand.

"Swallow and read me the letter."

She did and took a swig of tea. Then she started to read, as if she was at the library and introducing a great book to her circle of seven-year-olds.

"Dear Amanda. It's Mother. You know that of course." She looked up at me with an incredulous grin.

I am writing you a letter because it is hard for me to be with you and say what I feel and how my heart hurts when I see you. I know you were not responsible for the terrible things that have transpired in the last two years. I understand that. But I still live here, in a house that I have lived in for over forty years and in a town in which I was born. It has already become impossible for me to remain here. Should you decide that you will revisit the whole sordid mess, and write a book about your situation, I must tell you I can have nothing to do with it. As a matter of fact you might want to consider changing your name. I don't think you have any idea what your situation has caused the rest of your family. I need to move away to another community to find some peace of mind.

I know that is not your fault. Richie has suggested that I look into North Carolina where many seniors are retiring and where I might start again. Jane Elving's sister lives down there and I have been in touch with her. I can get a nice townhouse and still have some money to spare. Perhaps once I am settled there, and you have made a new start in Boston, we can try again to be together.

Perhaps you will even find a young man there in Boston who will keep you company. You know I wish you well but right now I cannot spend time with you. It hurts too much.

As always, I will send you money if you need it. Richie is the best way for us to be in touch. The doctor I am seeing said it was better for me to not try so hard anymore. And the pills he wants me to take make my headaches and moods even worse.

Who knows who will publish your book, but I suppose scandal always sells? Please remember that what happens to one of us happens to all of us.

I am sorry and I wish you well.
Mother

"When's the last time you talked?" I asked carefully.

"Last week. It was Richie's birthday. They had a party. I was invited by Richie but I think they were relieved when I told them I didn't have the money to go down to Jersey. I mean, I'm innocent. It's been cleared and still she treats me like I'm mentally ill or something. She'll send me a check. She makes me nauseous."

"So, what would be better?"

"Nothing. Nothing would be better. I want nothing to do with her."

She folded up the letter and slipped it back in her bag. "I prefer spending time with you," she said.

I looked up. "I'm nobody's mother, Amanda. That's for sure."

"Don't you have a son? Did you tell me that?"

It was tiring to keep dodging this story of Jordan and his estrangement and the whys and hows and what to dos. I had not become more expert in this over the years.

"I have a son. Yes."

I told her the story.

Chapter 32

Jordan's Departure

This is the story I told Amanda. This is the story that I remember and part of it is on infinite rewind in my head.

"No."

And he left the room. His legs had grown long and rangy and his black hair fell over one eye. He had had his hair over that eye for a couple of years already. I confess to watching him carefully to see how he navigated around chairs and tables and cats.

Ty had been gone for three years. He died two years after our long ago visit to Kauai, a major heart attack that was a long time coming. Jordan was only fifteen at the time. He had worn one of Ty's suits to the funeral. He stood next to the casket like a soldier, saying little, his father gone and he not at all sure where to find ballast.

I was grateful for his involvement with school. He was a good student, he liked chemistry and robotics and Mr. Schramm and Ms. Kelley were terrific at wrapping him up in activities and keeping him busy, his last years of high school. He loved his Japanese language lab and started taking up martial arts to further fill his days. One of his teachers invited him to a Zendo where he started doing Zen meditation.

He started sitting at home on his beautiful pillow. He threw out his old baseball trophies, Little League awards, music posters. His wooden floor became scrubbed, he asked for all white sheets and set up a small altar at the end of the room. There was always some kind of meditative music flowing from his iPod or computer. If a kid was going to be obsessed with something, I suppose this was a good world to embrace.

Maybe it was when I told him I was thinking of selling the house? It had been three years. I thought Jordan was heading away to college. I didn't need all the room. I frankly needed a new start. I was looking at Boston where I had some college friends and an offer of a teaching job at a community college. It was a great opportunity for me and I thought Jordan might be excited about it as well.

"Wherever I live is always your home. You know that, right?"

"Are you asking me or telling me?" he said, wary.

"I guess I am doing both. You are moving ahead and I really need to as well. Dad's death has been hard on all of us." I tried to get a look at his face but those long bangs did a good job of obscuring his thoughts.

"Thanks for letting me know, Mom. I'll throw my crap on the street so you can move on with your life," he said.

"Oh, for Chrissakes, Jordan. Let's talk about it. Would you rather I waited a few more years? I can do that. I can still teach back East and rent this house out. That's another solution."

"Frankly, Scarlett, I don't give a damn." He stood up and motioned for me to leave his room. I did. He slammed the door.

I wrote him an email. "Jordan dear, if you'd rather I didn't sell I can understand that. Let's keep that on hold. Sorry to upset you."

Since Ty's death and Jordan's obsession with all things Japanese, I dove into teaching, taking on extra assignments that left weeknights jammed and usually Sunday afternoons free for time together. I instituted a Sunday walk, usually at the Descanso Gardens or maybe the Los Angeles Arboretum. We never talked much, but he walked with me, and we would end the day in West Hollywood at El Coyote for baskets of chips, fresh guacamole and a plate of tacos.

Today was Descanso with its sumptuous rose garden and draping willows. They moved in the scant breeze and always made me feel like there was something bigger than myself. Especially when Ty first died, this was a place of solace. It felt like Ty was still around. Many a solo walk I mumbled questions to him about how he was, how to handle Jordan, what my next steps should be in a life without him at the center of it.

We found the small Japanese teahouse that we had been visiting for many years. Jordan's legs were too tall to sit at the tables front wise anymore. I liked to think his interest in all things Japanese might have started with our early visits here, and the small cookies and porcelain cups of tea carefully placed on the stone tables.

"How you doing, son? Tell me. Feeling okay?"

"You've been busy all week. Now, you want me to fill you in?"

"Too busy?"

"Never been different." I took this information in but remembered too how Jordan would barricade himself in his room most weeknights, leaving me on my own.

"Sorry. I want you to know I am sorry I upset you with talk of the house being sold."

He didn't look at me with that one. I decided I might as well continue. "Sorry that I seem so busy to you." Nothing. "I am sorry that your dad died. That you had to finish up your high school without him." Jordan just continued to stare off into the trees. Taking a sip of tea. "But I want you to know how proud I am of you. Of what you have accomplished." *At least I got it out*, I thought.

"Yeah. Thanks." He waited a minute. "I don't like to be so busy. I like to be quiet. I like to stay away from all your busyness."

"Yes. Okay. I get that."

And this next part is the part that I run over and over in my head. The recurring loop of treacherous shards.

He took a breath and then let it out. And then quietly said. "I am not going to college next year. I am going to Japan."

I took a moment. "Really? You have a plan? How will you . . ."

"Dad, left me my college money. I'm going to take it and go away. I'm going to go away and stay away for a long time."

"A long time? What's up with that?"

"We don't fit, Mom. We never have. You always wanted me to be somebody, do something, make something. You were the same way with Dad. You pushed him."

"I didn't. I never pushed Dad. Dad did what he wanted and made us all a good life."

"No. He told me. He told me he had to give up his music when he got married. He had to make money for the family. He wanted to provide for you. He even told me he wanted to make sure that if anything happened to him he wanted you to be able to take care of yourself."

"Well, is that a bad thing? He meant take care of you, too."

"You didn't need to let him do that. He could have done less. He could have been less stressed. He didn't need to travel so much. Or have new cars every year. He never wanted that. That was you. I could never stand that."

"Jordan, your father was a strong man. He made his own decisions."

"He was a young guy. He loved to hike. He loved to play basketball."

"Are you blaming me because your dad died?"

"Well, he did and he had so much on him. The house and work and going out to dinner and traveling to faraway places and all of that crap. You wore him out, Mom. You fucking wore him out and you wear me out and I'm going away. I getting out of here before you fucking kill me too."

My head began to swim. In my years of taking care of a dying man and his mysterious son, I may have been too much in a whirlwind to notice the small things. The ways in which he closed himself and what made him do that. The ways in which I would always miss the right way to handle his emotional shut downs. His furious reactions to feeling overwhelmed. His childhood temper tantrums. All these things swam before my eyes and clanged in my ears. I said nothing. I took a sip of tea. I watched a young couple with a toddler help the child negotiate the steps to the koi pond. We were quiet a long time.

"Well, I guess we should go." My eyes were tearing and I had an anvil in my chest but I was sure Jordan would not be any happier with me crying at this point. I stepped away and down the stairs past the child at the koi pond. He was a curious little one, exclaiming happily as the fish came up to eat a crumb or two. The couple scooped him up and headed off.

"Come on little one," the mom said. "Honey, could you grab the diaper bag, please?" A little frustrated that her husband wouldn't think to get the stroller ready, to make sure they didn't leave anything. "Hello? Earth to Stephen."

They were young in their marriage and he put his phone back in his pocket and grabbed the required items. She gave him a look.

"Sorry," he said. And they walked off just a little more tired of each other and this stage of their life.

I watched them walk off and then felt Jordan beside me.

"What will you do?" Jordan asked me.

"Well, I guess I will stay busy!" I couldn't help myself. Anger was my only defense. "But let me get this straight. Are you saying you want to get away from me? That we can't be friends? Can't be in touch? Have I harmed you so terribly?"

Jordan sat himself down on a rock and answered casually, cruelly.

"You can sell the house and get more money. You can leave California, you always hated it. I don't care what the fuck you do, but I'm gone." That was it. The tears were gushing now.

"Jordan. Sweetheart. My sweet boy." He stood up.

"I am not your sweet boy. I am a thing you have accomplished."

"You are a young man who I gave birth to and who holds my heart in yours."

"Oh, please, Ma. This isn't a poetry jam."

"Jordan. Jordan, please." The tears were pretty copious at this point.

"You're always so big on telling the truth. Getting out your feelings. So there they are. I've had it. Dad left me the way to get away and I'm taking it."

He strode off. Past the teahouse where we had sat and laughed as a family, past the koi pond where we he first saw the beauty of the Japanese fish. Past the lotus pond and the field of blue hydrangea. I watched him walk across the beloved landscape. Then, I called after him,

"Jordy. For God's sake wait, will you?"

He stopped. And stood still.

I walked slowly up to him. Trying to get hold of my sobs.

"Come on, let's at least walk back together," I said. And silently we walked the path back to the parking lot. A maintenance man came by in his gold cart, ready to clean up the guest areas at the end of the day. He looked over at my red face and Jordan's stony one.

"Everything okay, ma'am?" He asked.

"Sure," I smiled. Jordan strode on. He walked fast and faster.

I let him go and sat on a bench at the front of the garden to gather myself. He obviously had his set of keys and he pulled our car up to the front of the garden. I got in and we drove home in silence.

"No," he said simply.

It had been a stormy week. Both of us tiptoeing around each other to avoid contact and substantive connection. I had been watching TV solo, making coffee solo, living in the house with not only Ty's ghost but Jordan's attempt to be unseen as well. I needed to make some progress.

"Jordan." I followed him into his room.

"Take off your shoes, please," he said. "If you are coming in here."

I slipped off my sneakers and entered. I held out Ty's T-shirt. I had been searching for it all week. Something for Jordan to take with him.

"I thought you might want to take this with you. It's his Rolling Stones T-shirt. The one with that huge tongue. I just found it in the drawer and I remembered you used to like it. You used to laugh and tell Dad he should get you ice cream so he could lick it."

Jordan was surprised by that. All dressed in his pull-tie cotton pants and Indian cotton top, I wasn't sure how Mick Jagger's tongue would land. But it was all I had.

"I always hated this thing. Dad wore it to tease me." I said.

"Yeah," he said. "I remember." He turned to put it in a drawer. "Yeah. Thanks."

"Jordan. I feel badly about you leaving on your adventure with no kind of conversation. I mean, you are my boy." That was true. It was what was in my heart. My boy. He heard me.

I stood there, feeling like the boulder that I was. This was my third try, my most direct.

"I think it's a good idea for you to go to therapy, Mom. Great idea."

"And I want us to part with some kind of equanimity," I said.

"Right. The sweet memento of Dad as a stoner should really help."

"Jordan. That's not fair."

"Go for it, Mom. Knock yourself out."

"I want to understand."

Jordan shook his head from side to side. "You are not invited to every party." He shook his head, he bowed to me with his hands in a Namaste salute. His eyes were brimming.

"Jordan, please." I said.

He turned his back, walked into his room and closed his door. I could hear him walk away from the door and then his footsteps returned. I heard his voice softly, whispering through the wood.

"I don't know how to tell you what I feel. If I knew how I felt I could stay here and be a normal boy. You could bring me an ice cream cone and we could talk about Dad and chocolate would cure us. But I have never been a normal boy. I don't want to be an angry boy any more. I want to be a better man. Like Dad tried to be." He waited. "It's monastic to talk though wood, you know. The monks in Catholic monasteries counsel people through grates. Then it's the sound that floats and heals, they say. No need to bother with faces twisting and turning."

"Jordan," I whispered. "I am so sorry for all the ways I have not held you." I put my cheek against the door so he could hear me.

"I know. I forgive you."

I wondered if I wanted to be forgiven. I wondered if I was ready to accept my part of his misery enough to truly be penitent. But there was no time for this thought. I heard a sigh, an om. The sound faltered. It began to drip with stuttered inhales. He was crying. My son. From the other side of his bedroom door.

I heard the click of the lock.

I rubbed my palm against the wood, soothing it. "I love you, my son. But it can be so hard with us."

I heard some deeper breaths. And then quiet.

"I know. I love you, too."

The light went out under his door. I heard the shakuhachi flute music envelop him, smelled the incense move through him, and watched the escape of a small flicker of the candle from his altar until I felt too clumsy, until I felt the weight of Samsara jump on my back like the monkeys in India. I was too solid to remain. But the door opened.

Jordan paused and took a breath. He then looked straight at me and through me and said quietly "Not right now."

It was everything he could do to stop with that. He could not stop with that. And gently, painfully like placing shards of glass under fingernails he said, quietly, "You pounce, you don't step. You are constantly wanting to talk about everything. About Dad, about what I am feeling, about what I am doing, what I may do. I have no idea."

"Is it wrong for a mother to want to know her child?"

"You need to earn permission!" He was starting to lose it but at least he was talking. "It was Dad who understood me. It was Dad who figured it out. All you have ever done is organize me, get me from here to there, force me to move, make changes . . ."

"That's not true!" I knew I blew it. Too emotional.

"Leave me alone, Mom!" He yelled at me, Zen peace shattered. "Just fucking leave me alone!" Reverting to the thirteen-year-old again.

I guess it's the last time we ever really connected, even in conflict. He went right back there to throw me off his back.

There was nothing more. There was nothing more. I left his room. I got in the car and found myself on the top of Mulholland Drive looking out over the Valley as the evening lights came on, offering light to the big darkness falling over all of us.

Jordan left for Japan three weeks later. I took him to the airport.

Chapter 33

Amanda Pokes at the Crater

"So, he's gone to Japan and has been gone how long?"

"Almost four years now." I watched her face as she watched me. I wondered if she could imagine the compassion she clearly had for me directed towards her own mother. I wondered if she had been as cruel to her mother as Jordan had to me. If she had told her the truth, knew the truth as the world saw it.

"Have you called the American embassy? I mean, excuse me, but he could be dead?

I was surprised at this from Amanda. "Oh I doubt . . . I mean, they'd have to ship the body, wouldn't they? There's no war. No mass graves I need to fear." I had not allowed myself to dwell on these kinds of thoughts for a while. It confused me and made me hot and then cold. I must have gone grey.

"My God, Annie. You okay?" I poured another cup of tea. "Get a grip. At least try to find him. All kids want to be found. We only hide in the closet when we want to be found. This I learned from my years with the little ones."

"We're here to write your story, not mine, Amanda." I said with a lame attempt at regaining control.

"You're the one who told me, back in Kauai, told us all, 'our own stories are released by brushing against the life we live and the people we meet,'" she read from her black notebook. "It's right here. You said it." Amanda grinned first and then, looking at my face, she softened. "I'm sorry it hurts you so much, Annie. I wish I could help."

"Does it hurt you that your mother has abandoned you? Or maybe it will be easier for you to make your way, your new life."

"Maybe it will, but it's like part of me is hacked off. I mean the whole crap that happened hacked me in half. My mom at least was my mom. But, she has no guts. Not where I'm concerned. She'd rather faint away and clutch her smelling salts. It's pretty disappointing."

I smiled at Amanda trying to posit out her feelings. "Scary?"

"Sad. I'm pretty sad. My therapist says I'm going to be sad until I can find the new growth." She grinned again, grabbing a cookie. "Maybe I'll adopt you and you can adopt me. I mean, until we circle around and manage to get enough guts to reconnect."

"Why not write about how you and your mom had tea parties in the back yard? You told me you loved that and how you had a high tea for toddlers in your class once a week."

"*High Tea for Toddlers*. That's the name of my book," she said.

"For now," I said.

"For now," Amanda gathered her things up. "Thanks for the cookies."

"I'm sorry you got that letter from your mom." She looked up.

"Yeah." And then she just stood there and looked at me.

"Take some more cookies." I said.

"Sure," she said. And put a handful in the zipper pocket of her back pack. She moved to me quickly. She hugged me tight. I felt my chest heave. Then, she disappeared out the door.

Chapter 34

Postcards and Emails

I kept thinking about Amanda's suggestion to call the American embassy about Jordan. I mean maybe there was some kind of terrible problem that he was caught in. I remembered a Freud quotation that said: "After thirty, only you are responsible for the look on your face."

Jordan had a few years before he turned thirty. Maybe I had ignored this for too long.

I went to my desk and found the email from the monastery I had received in December. I had committed to sending an email to that address once a month for the years he was gone. I rarely received an answer but it made me feel like I was doing what I could do to stay connected.

I was surprised when I received a response from the monastery saying that Jordan was no longer there and had left no forwarding address. They promised to see what they could find out and I had been waiting, ignoring the information. I did nothing, because there was nothing to do.

Now, I googled the Japanese embassy in Boston and called. I left a message in the general consular mailbox. Then I wrote a note to the info email address. It felt like bobbing for apples in an enormous barrel.

Dear Sir or Madam:

My son left the US several years ago to study in Japan. The course has long ended and they say he has left no forwarding address. It had been at least two years since I have received even an email from him, and several months since the monastery informed me he had no forwarding address. I wonder if you might be able to locate him.

I finished the note with the name of the monastery, Jordan's age and passport number and the people with whom I had been corresponding. That was the most action I had taken in several years. I was ready for the mystery to be solved. But not ready to fly to Tokyo to find a search and rescue mission. I remember that day at the lighthouse when Jordan flipped and flopped in the water, begging me to never rescue him again.

At least I took another stab at connection. I had made the decision that reaching out had to be based on my concern for his safety rather than my need to be loved by him. The second goal was far off and confusing to me. The phone rang.

"Hey," said Mallory. "Come over and play?"

"Too cranky but thanks."

"Do tell," she said.

"One of my students. The one who is writing a memoir about her time in prison."

"Cheery," Mallory was deferring, as usual.

"She is pushing me to find Jordan. Says all kids who hide want to be found."

"And?"

"So, I connected with the Japanese embassy."

"And?"

"And, I am waiting. Rereading my obsessive notes about it all."

I went over the list of things that caused our estrangement including an assessment from a social worker from his high school who had told me that Jordan had tendencies toward a kind of stubbornness that could keep him caught in the same groove. He often had refused to try an alternative route to solving a problem. "He can be fanatical in his unwavering belief in his solution as the only one. I hope and suspect that this will temper as he continues his education and matures as a young man." It had not. I read this last assessment to Mallory, off my journal page.

"Annie. I want to hear, but I have to set up the next class. Can I call you later?"

I shifted in my chair. My attention now fully caught by my journal page where so much of this was worked out.

"It's okay, friend. Just shoveling things from one pile to the other. Talk later."

Turning the pages of the journal from five years ago I saw the endless scribbling. Notes to remember about self-care. About meditating, About helping others. It's probably why I ended up volunteering for the campaign and ending up with a compounded PTSD. Nothing like amplifying your personal impotence by putting it in a political construct.

I sighed and moved from the chair to the window. I saw a man walking down the street and toward my building. It was David, and I groaned in dread. He had some papers in his hand. I wasn't sure what to do but when I heard the buzzer ring, I could feel my heart jump a little.

Was he dangerous? Still holding a torch, a grudge? The buzzer rang again. I walked over and pressed the intercom.

"Hello," I said.

"It's David. I'm here to deliver some papers you might be interested in."

I stood there for a moment and made the decision to not let him upstairs. "Can you leave them for me? I'm in the shower."

"You are not in the shower. I saw you watch me come up the street."

"David, really . . ."

"I can wait but I would like to speak to you face to face. Unless you're going to call the police. An overreaction, I would say."

I waited a moment longer and pressed the intercom.

"I'll come down." I grabbed a jacket and took my purse. And in a moment of unease texted Mallory. "Mall, David is downstairs at my door and I am going down to meet him. Will you check in with me in an hour, please?"

David didn't look at me when I came through the door. He had a packet of papers and he turned and gave me the top sheet.

"Here," he said. "This should make you feel better."

He handed me a typed copy of a letter that read: "Letter from the Jewish Community of Pittsburgh to President Trump." David took a deep breath and started reading, "Dear President Trump," he looked up at me to make sure I was listening. I was listening, but more closely watching him.

"Wait. Wait a minute. No need for you to read this to me. I appreciate it. Thank you."

He looked at me again and folded the paper and put it in my hand.

"Take this. The letter does the right thing. It tells Trump to stay away and stop being an asshole. Tells him he is not welcome." That last was thrown out at me, a little dagger I managed to side step but I could see David had his own agenda here.

"Thanks, David. I'll take it upstairs and read it."

"You won't invite me up, correct?" He shifted and looked bigger and taller than I had remembered.

"No. I don't think that's a good idea."

"I am not President Trump. He's the one making you fearful and crazy. Not me. Why should you be fearful of me?"

I hadn't realized how stiff my body language was and realized that a part of me was fearful of David. He paced a little with a tight smile on his face. I had to change the direction of this encounter.

"David, thanks for dropping this by. We could go for coffee, talk a little. Would you like that? Maybe stop fighting with each other?"

That did not sit well. "I am not fighting. I am just saying that even the bastard asshole Donald Trump received a well-thought-out letter when he was told not to visit anymore. Even he got that respect."

His eyes were a little wild and sad and I didn't understand what he wanted and if I could give it to him.

"Look, it's okay. We are friends and let's just give it some time so we can figure out what didn't work, okay? I have no ill feelings toward you."

"No. You just treat me with disrespect. Patronize and categorize me and I don't like it."

"Okay," I looked at him. "Okay, guilty as charged. So let's leave it. Let's just leave it. You know how to do that. You certainly were able to leave your friendship in Kauai with that lovely woman. You know about endings!"

"I don't have any special feeeeeeelings about you, certainly." He dragged out the word feelings with a contemptuous tone. "I just am tired of the whole damn charade. People trying to find each other and brutalizing themselves and everyone else. I'm through with it. Through with it."

And David turned on his heel and left, walking briskly down the street.

That night at eleven the phone rang and I answered it. It was a subdued David and I knew he would be calling.

"Hello, Annie. I want to apologize."

"Okay," I said.

"I got myself all wound up in some kind of fantasy, some kind of idea about taking the edge off difficult things and I made up the idea that you would solve that. That is absurd and unfair. We hardly know each other and I am sorry I have been annoying or unkind."

I took a deep breath.

"It's okay, David. I admit that I too have made up ideas about you and who you might be for me in my life. You are not that fantasy. You are just you, and that's just fine."

"Spoken like two people much too familiar with psychotherapy."

"Okay," I said.

"Okay," he sighed.

"Yes. Better," I said. "Thanks for calling."

"Thanks for taking my call. First-time caller, longtime fan."

That made me laugh. "Okay. Catch you next broadcast."

"Right. Good night."

"Good night."

We hung up and I sat quietly on my couch. I looked around at the comfortable room I had made, the place that I live well and alone and full and happy enough and I was grateful for it.

I hoped that David could find that ease somewhere. Damn, it was hard getting older and even wiser, gaining every rocky inch of progress while losing another layer of skin.

Chapter 35

Fair Trade Coffee

The next day, I met Eddie at the small fair trade shop off Copley Square. Amanda worked at the library near by so I told her to meet us so I could give her some notes on her latest pages.

I gave Eddie a big, bulky hug, throwing concern about toppling coffee cups and coffee shop decorum, to the winds. It was great to see him. It was great to be welcomed by him.

Eddie had a stack of books on race relations in the US. Prominent among them were several James Baldwin titles.

"Oh, *Fire Next Time, Blues for Mr. Charlie.* What a writer!" I said as I unwound my scarf from my neck and pulled off my gloves.

"I am working on a project for a small journal my friend runs. He wants 3,000 words on biracial relationships. He actually wants to know how Shamana and I manage to stay together. And he doesn't want a love story."

"Love fogs up the frontiers, I'd say."

"Well, Baldwin's early stuff is pretty compassionate toward us white folks. He's clear he's not the problem. It's our inability to see him and the lies of our country." Eddie opens one of the books and pages through, looking for a passage.

"But, then?"

He looks up. "Well, later, he fell a little more out of love with compassion and waiting for us to get it right. He embraced the more direct path. Telling the truth and letting us white folks figure it out for ourselves."

"And Shamana is letting you figure it out for yourself?" I asked him. He smiled sheepishly.

"She just smiles and calls me White Boy. She won't engage. Says it's not her job to educate me, explain herself . . . at least in that area." Eddie smiled despite his best efforts. "I'm more concerned about how we see race in the US than she is."

"I believe she said it well at the cottage. She is not an easy sentence, right?"

Eddie grinned again. "You bet." He shook his head.

"Still in love?" I enjoyed so much being able to ask him such a question and relish his response. Over the years with Jordan, it was a minefield to say anything personal. I was treading on explosive territory just by being in the same neighborhood. Maybe there was a part of me that didn't want to find Jordan again and have to deal with our convoluted relationship.

Eddie looked up so soberly. "She is not an easy sentence. She is endlessly fascinating to me. She's smart, beautiful, confused, creative and sexy as hell! I haven't slept in two weeks." He blushed a little with that confession.

"The course of true love ne're does run smooth." Eddie looked anywhere but in my eyes. I squeezed his hand. Eddie closed up the books.

"How bout you?" he asked.

"Well . . ." I haltingly answered. "It's been interesting."

"Oh yeah?" he smiled slightly, tearing open his third pack of sugar to dump in his now tepid coffee. "Ooh. Did that guy get weird?"

"Eddie, really . . ." I said.

"I bet it got weird!" he said.

"A little," I said.

"I knew it! I told you he was weird!"

"But it's fine now." I hurriedly added. "Really! He's fine, I'm fine. The world is fine. Give me a break. There was something there. A friendship maybe."

Eddie laughed. "I love it, Aunt Annie. I'm actually getting to know your dodges!"

"Congratulations." I smiled and sipped my own lukewarm cup that he had bought for me. Time to change the subject. "And . . . I decided that it was time to find Jordan. I sent word to the Japanese embassy."

That was the first time I said that out loud. I had been so guarded about my needy wound over the years, I rarely spoke frankly about Jordan, but that was old news to Eddie. He shook his head a little and then said simply.

"Cool," he said. "That explains it."

"What?"

"I got an email from someone named Toyoshi."

"You got an email and you didn't lead with that?"

"I was waiting for the right time! He said he was a friend of Jordan's in Japan. He said they belonged to the same organization and they both taught yoga together and he wrote to say that Jordan wanted to send me word but he knew I was pissed at him. But this Toyoshi said that it was time for Jordan to leave Japan. I guess his visa ran out and he got a notice from the government. He wanted to know if Jordan could contact me."

"That's weird."

"I thought so. Toyoshi said Jordy was somewhere in the country, he had been living with a 'spiritual community', doing 'training', and there was no Wi-Fi there. Toyoshi had recently come back to the city and

so was paving the way for contact."

As this information settled in I saw movement by the door of the shop and in walked Amanda, bundled in her ski jacket and ski cap and wound up in a long blue scarf. She looked like she had been walking for a while and had no gloves on. Her cheeks were rosy and she looked happy and content. She spotted us and came over.

"Hi," she said breathless.

"Hi, Amanda! I thought you were coming from work? You look like you just walked a mile."

"Just going in! I love this weather. I count on it to blow out my brains!"

Eddie smiled. "Really?" he said.

"Oh, not really blow them out like with a gun . . . but blow them out like a great cool filtration system. Perfect. Cold from ear to ear. Love it!" She smiled easily and I could see Eddie was charmed.

"Oh wait! I know you from Kauai!" he said.

"Yep. You taught that awesome workshop on POV!" She recognized him now with visual pleasure.

Eddie grinned again. "Thanks! Yes. Glad you enjoyed it!"

"Yes," Amanda said, almost jovial. "I really did!" She smiled at him and the two saw something inside the other.

The moment extended and then I said, "Come, sit down. Want coffee? I want to give you the notes I promised." I rummaged in my bag. "Sorry, Eddie, forgot to mention Amanda works here at the library and it was an easy meet up for us as well."

"Great," said Eddie, sustaining a smile, with a quizzical look on his face. "Nice to see you again."

"I can't stay long. Shift starts at four-thirty." Amanda was business-like but with a devilish smile I hadn't seen before. She was definitely making progress.

"Eddie is just telling me that he heard from a friend of my son's in Japan. I took your advice and reached out to the Japanese embassy."

Amanda's green eyes widened. "Wow, that is really great." And she turned to Eddie.

"I told Annie that kids who hide want to be found. I used to work with little ones and I learned that early."

Eddie was a bit skeptical of that information about his cousin. I could feel his distrust.

"Well, I'll connect with his friend and we shall see."

"What has he been doing?" Amanda asked.

"Not sure. Just that he was in a monastery, and this guy says he's been living with a 'community', I got the idea it was some kind of colony or group. Spiritual and teaching yoga and getting some kind of 'training'."

"Gee," said Amanda. "It makes me think of those cult groups in Japan. You know there's a big one that's still got lots of members that has colonies like that. They recruit young folks from monasteries. They're connected to that weird group that threw the Sarin gas in the subway a long time ago."

I shifted in my seat. "I can't imagine Jordan getting involved in some cult. He has always been pretty independent."

"Oh, I just thought of it because the leaders of the subway attack were finally executed last summer. Been a lot of recruiting action." Amanda looks at Eddie to explain. "The book I'm writing is about crazy cultish behavior and how folks follow a lie blindly to punish. They think they are punishing others, but ultimately, the cultists always are punishing themselves somehow. It's weird."

"Jordy went to study at a monastery. He was very into salvation. He thought that those monks had the answers. Maybe he found he was right?" Eddie was thinking aloud and looking at Amanda. She grinned.

"It's a mystery!" she said, smiling. "I'll check through some of the research and let you know what I find, Annie. He probably just fell in love and went to get his graduate degree in the Japanese countryside. The food is great. That's for sure!"

"I know a great sushi place near Harvard Square," Eddie blurted out, and then reddened.

"Oh, I know that place! The wasabi rolls are killer!" Amanda looked straight at him. She was getting bolder and bolder as the weeks went by. "Now, they'll really blow your brains out!" she said. Amanda and Eddie laughed. Then stopped and were both immediately embarrassed.

"Okay," said Amanda. "I've got to work. Nice to see you again, Ed." Amanda said, letting her eyes catch mine.

"Amanda!" I said. "Here's the notes!" I handed her the pages and she smiled.

"Thanks, Annie. Making progress, yes?!"

"Yes," I said, "Making progress."

Amanda grabbed her hat from the table and wiggled out from between the tables deftly. I had never noticed how slim and agile she was, and neither had Eddie.

Chapter 36

Skype Truth

Hi Eddie,

I appreciate you connecting with me via Toyoshi. I wonder if we might have a Skype call sometime this week. I need to come back to the states, visa expired and want to tell you what I have been doing—Aunt Annie: Give me a call. Here's the email from Jordan. We spoke today. Give me a call.

I picked up the phone, nervous and absolutely uncertain of what I was feeling.

"Hi," I said. "did you talk to him?"

"Yes. We spoke last night." And that was all he said. I could hear him pouring a cup of coffee from across the room. He raised his voice to reach the receiver.

"What are you doing?" Then, the sound of him coming back across the room to his desk. The chair scrape, his settling in.

"How did he look?" I was attempting to approach that rocky minefield that was Jordan, again, and my boots were already stuck in the mud. I didn't think Eddie understood how much.

"He looked fine. Skinny. Older. Clean." Eddie laughed a little.

"So," I said. "I need some help here. Is he coming back? Does he need money? He shouldn't unless he gave away the money he got from Ty to the place he was living in."

"I didn't get that impression."

"Why did he call?"

"In the end, I don't really know, except he says he's going to join a few friends he met there, other Americans and they're going to find a place in the country, he had to leave Japan he said, maybe continue doing what he's been up to?"

"And that is . . . ?" I was getting impatient.

"Well," said Eddie, "It was a little weird. He started off by telling me he had lived in the first monastery and studied Zen for about a year and then grew tired of the community, or maybe they got tired of him. He met a woman who led him to more spiritual activities outside of the monastery and then he joined this other group where they've been living for the past couple of years. It seems to be kind of like what Amanda suggested. When I asked him, he said that they're offshoots of the people who gassed the subway but his group has denounced those tactics."

"You're kidding me. That can't be right."

"He said the community was strong and no one was killing anyone."

"Well, that's comforting," I said, trying to keep panic at bay.

"I guess a bunch of them were executed last summer and he said the group lost its cohesiveness."

"What?"

"Executed "

"My God, Eddie. This is a bad dream."

"Annie, he made the point that this group was not violent. It has high standards and lots of outreach to their community. Good deeds, that sort of thing. He told me it was easier to be honest about it."

"His friend said his visa was expired. Will he be coming back?"

"I don't know." Eddie could feel the vacuum that opened in my heart. "He actually looked good. Seemed pretty normal and he smiled more than I remember."

I tried to picture his face. I tried to see him in meditation and ease. Then I didn't try anymore.

"The whole thing was kind of screwy, I admit," he said. "I asked him if he was going to call you and he said, when the time was right. He told me he may have to leave Japan and I think he was sniffing around to see where he might land."

"I guess I should just say thanks and let it go, right?"

"Well, Annie, it's just that I don't think he is thinking much about any of us, really. Except as a last ditch escape plan."

"Oh." I was disappointed. I don't know what I expected. I wasn't his lover. I wasn't someone he should come running back to. But I longed for contact.

"I told him he should send an email, something to you to tell you he was okay. He said he would. But I wouldn't hold my breath."

"That's all he said, yes?"

"That was it. You okay?"

"Oh sure. I don't know what I expected."

"Call me if you want to talk or anything, okay?"

"Thanks, dear. I appreciate it." I got up from the table to put on water for tea, but I wasn't ready for Eddie to hang up. To sit alone in my room with the looming presence of my kid who is my constant silent companion. "How's your article coming along?" I said.

"Well, I'm on my own."

My brain changed direction. "Trouble in paradise?"

"Shamana decided that I shouldn't write about us. It was too personal and she didn't like that I wanted to talk about her 'identity' thing, either."

"How you doing?"

"We are taking a break. She is off doing a holiday cooking seminar for a week. She said it would give me a chance to finish my article and to give us some space."

"You, okay?"

There was a moment of quiet and then, "Yes. I am fine. And wondered if maybe you might have Amanda's number."

"Amanda, its Annie. Eddie wants your number. What do you think?"

"What?" A squeal came through the phone receiver so shrill I had to move it away from my ear.

"Well, is that a yes?" I said.

Amanda laughed. "Sure. Why not? This is my lucky week."

I had to smile. It had been a couple of dark days since my conversation with Eddie about Jordan's call and I had been surrounded by unrelenting fog. I caught Amanda up on the details.

"That's crazy," she said. "He may not be as involved as the other group members were. You can take solace in that."

"I am not at all sure what solace I can take in anything or if it's even my place to take solace at all."

"Annie, I wanted to tell you. The reason I have been so happy lately. The day I met you and Ed at the coffee place? I got the email from my lawyer. My record has been expunged. I'm free. My story is all my own now. It's been removed from all the databases. No history to follow me, bog me down. And I can apply for the official job at the library now. It's a wonderful feeling."

"Are you going to call your mom and let her know?"

Amanda stopped. "My brother can tell her the news. She said she wanted no contact."

"Oh, Amanda. She has been hurt too, you know."

"My therapist has her own ideas about that. She didn't speak to her mother her whole life, almost."

"How'd that go for her?" I asked.

"She wants to write a book about it."

"Feel free to have her call me." I sniffed. "Or email is better."

"I actually gave her your number. She said she'd reach out when I was officially out of therapy. And that's just about now," she said with a flourish.

"Well, congratulations, I guess." I said as the wounded mother, avoiding the list of things I thought Amanda might still want to consider.

Chapter 37

Knauta's Call

"Knauta Krause leaving a message. Amanda told me you are a hell of writing coach. I can't walk for shit, especially in this Arctic weather. Can we meet at my place? I live off Charles in an antique snow cave. Please call? Amanda has finished treatment with me so no conflict of interest there. Yes. Please call."

The message had been on my phone for almost a week now. Knauta, the therapist that thought it was great to be estranged from mothers. Her voice was a solicitous command. I bristled, imagining a therapy session with her and Jordan, and I was definitely the problem. *Never mind*, I thought regaining perspective, *she's a paying client.* The holidays were coming up and things would get slow again. Thinking of my bank account, I made the call, which is how I came to be seated across from a large, grey-haired woman with a thinning bun and lumpy shoes. She was installed in an ornate chair, on a dais in a high ceilinged apartment off Charles Street.

"Knauta Krause," she had said with a smile, as she opened the door to me, juggling her cane and the security chain, her eyes doing a practiced assessment of her visitor. I could see she was limping, her body at odds with her inquiring face.

"Anne Simon."

"Well, come on in, Anne Simon. Sit over there. Thanks so much for coming over." She gestured to a warn couch with a glass table in front of it. There was a box of tissues, a bowl of butterscotch candy and an ashtray.

"Amanda tells me wonderful things about her work with you, Anne."

"You can call me, Annie," I said. "Anne was my parents dream, Annie is who I turned out to be."

Knauta smiled. "Guess how it felt to be a Knauta for all these years?"

She was charming, clearly gnarled and clearly grounded. She had years in her favor.

"I'd have happily met you for coffee," she continued, "but it's tough for me to haul myself up and down the stairs these days." Knauta settled herself into her throne. Her buttocks spread beneath her like an enormous, comforting pillow.

"If life was different I'd serve tea and cookies but my helper is off today."

She was accustomed to setting the tone, the scene and the agenda.

"I asked you here to help me make a start on a book I need to write. I have a bunch of notebooks." She gestured to a filing cabinet on which stood a pile of journals. "Take a look," she said.

I glanced to the pile of notebooks across the room, well worn, coffee-stained. We were sitting in what once must have been a back porch, now winterized and sanitized for visitors. Behind glass doors to the left of the filing cabinet, were large Lautrec prints and a red sofa. Bright blue Indian indigo pillows. Reed baskets with newspapers and fresh flowers, daisies on the side table. No TV. No desk. The windows had light white sheer curtains and the room belied the spectacle of the heavy-handed woman sitting on her own specially made dais. Knauta noted my assessment of her living room.

"Nice in there, yes? I keep it just as I want it. Well, Ellie, my trusty housekeeper does. She even makes sure I have fresh flowers. It's a kind indulgence."

"I love the prints on the wall. Lautrec was a fantasy friend of mine as a young writer in love with Colette."

"The prints remind me of growing up. Paris was beautiful, even after the war. We lived above a boulangerie and the smells kept me sane. Funny."

"The room is so perfect. Almost like a stage set. Do you imagine yourself telling the story from there?"

"Hmm. Maybe so. It's a place of respite. When I was a kid I was sent to work as an au pair in the countryside to a family with seven boys. They had inherited the family home and had very little money. The Americans had taken over the house during the war and they had gotten it back and never had enough money to maintain it. The house was madness. The children were allowed to scrawl on the walls, they planted trees in huge buckets in the living room, and there were all sorts of stray animals and a large dormitory for all the children where they threw their clothes into big baskets. Every kid had his own basket and every Sunday afternoon they had to wash their clothes. I was supposed to help them in that endeavor. I lasted about ten days. But the way the parents remained sane was to have one room that had a lock on it. It was their sanctuary and it was perfect and quiet and always spotless. The rest of the place was a shambles but Dorcas, the mother, made sure her bedroom was perfect."

"So, that's Dorcas' bedroom."

Her eyes lit up. "Oh yes, perfect. That is Dorcas' bedroom. Let's make that the title of the book."

"Up to you," I said. "But I like it."

"Were you the only person there to help?"

"Ha. No, there was a cook, but she was hopeless, an aging aunt of one of the parents, I think. I remember she would stand at the back door and call out into the fields when she needed help. *'Boy!'* she would shout. Just *'Boy!'* And sooner or later one or the other of them would show up to bring in the groceries or move some table to another room to make space for the growing brood."

Knauta grinned at the memory.

"And you only lasted ten days?" I asked

She shifted a bit and went for a cigarette. "Yep." Her eyes started to twinkle again.

"What happened?"

She was reaching down for a cigarette from the leather pouch at her feet and squeezed out the response as she got herself upright once again. "Dorcas seduced me."

"The mother? Dorcas? With the seven sons?"

"Yes, the one with the beautiful bedroom."

"Yes, that Dorcas," Knauta grinned. She loved holding me in thrall. "She seduced me and I was not at all sure that I ever wanted to leave! But, sadly, her husband, Johnny, a long-time witness of Dorcas and her ambisexual adventures, explained to me that Dorcas was not to be trusted and that he wasn't interested in supporting any more children in the house. Including me. He sent me packing." Knauta laughed heartily. She smiled with the memory and I could see someone else behind the folds of skin on her neck and the gnarls and knobs of her hands.

"There's your first chapter." I said, happy to be in territory I understood.

"You think so? It's not really what I'm after."

"Oh," I said. "What are you after?"

"This story I want to tell is about my mother, about me growing up, about losing her and finding her and then finally, myself."

"Classic tale."

"What do you mean?" Knauta said. She leaned forward again and I wasn't sure if she might fall forward on to the floor but her hand found the little leather purse she kept on the floor near her seat, and took out another cigarette. "You mind if I smoke? I like to have a spare nearby. That way I can light one from the other. Another trick to ease arthritic hands!"

She didn't wait for my answer and the room was soon filled with smoke, again.

"You can open the window if you want, but I'm an addict and it's my house, so I see no reason to stop."

The room was large and the smoke rings floated up to the high ceilings. The place reminded me of the Gardner Museum, the same era. I pictured Knauta as a young woman, maybe having tea with a suitor at the Gardner, when she still had a body that worked, that moved without halt and pain.

"Knauta. That's a beautiful name. What does it mean?"

"Get up and outta bed!" she cackled. "That's what I thought it meant. Always heard it screamed from the other room when I was a kid!" She laughed again. "I have no idea. A whim of my mother's, I suppose. She was crazy. I mean certifiable, and I think my name was one of her first delusions.

"Took me years to forgive her."

"Did you?"

"What?"

"Forgive her?"

"When I thought it was time to deal with it. I could never really remember what it was that she did wrong so, I gave it up. Being mad at her. I came to understand that she was quite a woman. She and my father worked for the French resistance during World War II. He was a character too. He was a cross dresser so they loved to use him as a decoy. Anyway, Mom fell in love with him and . . ."

"As a boy or a girl?'

"Gee, I think as a girl, but then they had me so there must have been something heterosexual about it." She opened her eyes wide sharing the joy of the information. We both laughed. "Isn't life grand?" she said, as she continued to chuckle.

"Yes, I suppose it is." I agreed, wrapped in her good humor.

"Sense of humor, Annie, has soothed more of my patients than any of the drugs I pedal." She shifted her weight again and smoothed the light green fabric on her voluminous dress. "But, I couldn't wait to get away from her, from my crazy father. I suppose living what they lived through should have generated more compassion in me but I wanted a father who wore suits and a mother who was not babbling secret codes in her sleep."

She puffed a few times, businesslike, the smoke sponging off the regret she was examining now.

"I got a foreign study visa as a teenager. I kept extending my stays in the States. Finally found someone to marry me. I had pretended my parents were lost for years. Then, when I turned fifty, and being a therapist and all, I figured I had to find them. Or her. I knew he passed early."

"Did you find her? Them? Traces of them?"

"I was lead to his grave by government sources. He had been in the Resistance, of course. And she . . . she had married again and was widowed again and lived with her second husband's kids in Paris."

"What did she say when she saw you again?"

"She looked me straight in the eye and told me she had never worried a minute about me losing her. She knew there was no way that I'd escape needing her. I need to write about that. About getting over the fear of what love can do."

"Love?"

"It's pretty powerful. Can be terrifying to come to terms with who we love or loves us. How we can't bear holding that much love."

The dust motes from the perfect room, behind glass, floated lazily. They had no issues with ambivalence.

"You waited a long time. She didn't miss having you in her life?"

"She said she didn't. But then, by the time I found her again, she didn't care enough about me to make me feel bad. She had moved on and I had, too. Except I couldn't, not without figuring out why I had left myself bereft for so many years. She just found another family. I wasn't so lucky."

"You didn't stay married?"

"No," she said dismissively, waving her hand in front of her face as much to disperse the fantasy of a great marriage as to dispel the curling smoke from her cigarette. "We have a daughter. She went back to live in France, of all things, so I see her very little. Sometimes I have dreams about cartoon steam ships going over the Atlantic back and forth, carrying us to and fro, but no one is going the right direction to find anyone."

She laughed easily, knowing her own self well stood her in good stead. And I admired her, that ease.

I smiled and shook my head. "Well, I'm dealing with a bit of that myself."

Knauta looked up as she blew the last puff of her cigarette, and then crushed it in the full ashtray next to her seat. "Yes?"

"I have a son who hasn't spoken to me, avoided me for several years now. He hid out in Japan and is just now coming back to the States."

"Ah," She began to reach for another cigarette but decided against it. "I can't say that it's always so horrible a kid breaks from the parent. Sometimes survival is a better goal."

"You think so?"

"I know it. But someone always loses. It just how they lose that matters."

I wasn't sure if I could forgive Knauta her dry and realistic assessment of how things go in life.

"And did you ever find Dorcas again?" I asked.

Knauta looked up sharply. Shook her head. "No, I never found Dorcas. But I think I want to write this book as a letter to her." She looked at me waiting for my response.

"I'm a person who can help you find the threads," I said.

"I think of myself as knots and bundles, these days" she said, raising her gnarled hands and kicking out her legs, varicosity and bruises on full display. "Adding threads should be great fun."

Chapter 38

Thanksgiving

Knauta brought dessert, Mallory, wine and weed. It was a big deal for Knauta to arrive and make it up the one flight of stairs to my apartment but with patience and a big blue cane, she made it just fine. I brought one of the upholstered chairs to the table for her and she was more than happy.

The table sported a white tablecloth and a platter of turkey drumsticks, cranberry dressing and a heaping bowl of sweet potatoes that no one ate but we all insisted was a seasonal necessity. Crumpled napkins, two wine bottles, each drained, and a third of Prosecco to go with the pumpkin pie and vanilla ice cream. We had been laughing and talking all evening, especially Mallory.

"So," Mallory drawled after draining her Prosecco and inhaling a huge toke, "he called me to have phone sex."

"Oh no!" Knauta and I screamed with delight. "No more sex stories, Mallory. I challenge you to spend at least fifteen minutes not talking about your glory days in the hayloft!"

Knauta gestured with a hearty laugh. "I just met you. Charm me with your intellect!"

"You're just jealous, my new friend!"

"Well, did he get his phone sex?" I asked getting up to clear some dishes.

"A guy can dream."

"Thank God we didn't need to sit through that rendition!" Knauta took another puff on her cigarette and a long drink of wine.

"C'mon. I bet you could match me one for one!"

Knauta laughed. "You bet, but it makes me so tired to think of the applied mechanics!" And she laughed again. And so did we all.

The room was comfortably still. The smoke from the weed dancing with Knauta's Marlboro's. I sat by the open window, leaning into the cool breeze coming up from the street.

I had devised this Thanksgiving gathering after my second meeting with Knauta, realizing that she and Mallory had things in common. Absent mothers and too many affairs. And, perspective and rejuvenating, wicked humor. The evening so far had been a series of explosive discoveries of each other's secrets. I sat back and enjoyed the two of them sparring over who had more lovers in more countries.

"So, Mallory?" I asked. "What's the rest of your story? You never told me about your mother."

"Oh, it's so tedious. And treacherous," she said, pushing me away.

"Do you have any children, Mallory?" Knauta asked.

"Heavens no. But I bet I could support you for a few years with the kid's therapy if I had."

Knauta smiled demurely. She didn't like to engage with us about her work. "My daughter lives in France. In the countryside. She has a farm and sends pictures all the time. She seems to have married a pig farmer."

"You weren't able to travel?"

"No. They came to visit. He's a hearty fellow. They grow pigs and

I understand she has started a little sausage business. For the gourmet crowd. They live outside Agen, not far from Bordeaux. She actually asked me if I would travel there and live with them, which was gratifying. The medical care is free, I hear. And it's not a bad option. I'd have to learn French again."

"That sounds pretty nice," I said.

"We shall see if I can make a good start on the book and then I'd have a project for the long years in the bunkhouse."

"Where will you go, Mallory? When you're old and grey?"

"I'll never go grey, darling. Count on that." She smiled but I know she often thought about where she would land for her last chapter.

"Have a plan?" I looked over at her lovingly. She had been a good friend to me in the last months and I had begun to see the practical woman behind the facade. "And your hair looks great, by the way," I said.

"Fabian Dressler, off Cambridge Square. Cheap and trendy," she said automatically, smoothing the back of her bob.

Mallory let the smoke out slowly. "Maybe I'll go join the monastery in India. Putti can't stay forever over there. And now that I am working for the community here, they might consider it. It wouldn't be a bad place to wind up." They both looked at me.

"Well," I said. "I've always had a fantasy that I could open a full time writing retreat center. Live in the country, give workshops, invite friends to do the same, live in community. Die somewhere beautiful."

I looked around the room at my two new friends. *Here we were, women of a dying age some might say, but women so vital and having the best wisdom of our lives to offer. Perhaps the new feminism that was rising would see our value, support our frailties as we support their growth. No matter, we embody hope and wisdom*, I thought. But it's always nice to think that someone else in the society shares your vision of yourself.

"I used to hope that I could live near my son but that's uncertain at best. So, now we, us women who are strong and vital and alive, we get to make a real future in which we are the one and only focus. We are figuring out how to do it together, I think."

"So, why are you so hot on people telling their stories, Annie?" Mallory asked.

The question surprised me. I smiled at her. "I think we understand ourselves by telling our stories. We get another chance at living, by finding a new ending, changing the players, creating a new purpose. I live with all the stories of who I am but I am not always courageous enough to tell them. I learn from yours, and Knauta's and Amanda's and even David's."

Knauta leaned forward, glass of Prosecco in hand. "Who's David?"

"You'll hear soon enough. Annie's rescue project of 2018," Mallory said.

"That's unfair!" I said.

"Never mind," said Knauta. "You're on a roll, Annie. Keep going."

"Maybe that's being a voyeur," Mallory posited, truly stoned. Her eyes as big as a fishbowl.

"Maybe. But maybe I'm a fellow traveler. So there."

Knauta laughed. "This Prosecco is terrific. I feel I need lacy gloves on my fingers to drink it with the proper elan. Here, girls, have some."

Knauta poured the Prosecco in the flutes and I offered seconds on pie.

"I tell you. This is more fun than camp," Knauta cooed. "Is there such a thing as writers' camp? Sign me up!"

"Actually," Mallory said. "I have been holding out on you. An old friend of mine," she began. We both looked at her. "Don't ask, don't tell. An old friend of mine has a lodge in Vermont that is empty. His nephew Toby runs it for him and Toby called to tell me it was free all of January and February if I knew of any groups who might want to come up. He thought maybe some of the Meditation Center crew might want to do a retreat."

"It can be pretty snowy in January and February." I said.

"It has a full staff and lots of fireplaces. Toby is the cook. I hear his cocoa is pretty outrageous." Mallory said

"How many people?" Knauta wondered.

"Enough," said Mallory.

"Would you write?" I asked Mallory.

"Stranger things could happen." She smiled easily with the help of the weed. "Or I can lead meditation every day, maybe a little creaky yoga."

"Bedrooms on the first floor?" said Knauta.

"Yep, as I recall," she said.

"Ah." I said.

"Ooh," Knauta added, intrigued.

"Done," said Mallory. And a new adventure was upon us.

Chapter 39

Toby in Vermont

"*Dear Annie Simon*," the printed letter said.

Toby says that you will be coming up with a group to run a writing retreat for a week or so in late January. I've been staying with him for the winter and the following is my audition for your group. I actually want to write murder mysteries, but this piece came out when I started to think about how to explain my presence here with Toby, living in an RV, and hunkering down for the winter.

By the way, Toby is a great cook and runs the place like a top so I do hope you will finalize your plans and we will both see you in January.

Sincerely,
Ken Jackson

I sat down to read the pages.

MARY AND ME
By Ken Jackson

My son, Toby heard the phone ring in the main house just as he was coming back to the cabin to grab his favorite bread pan. Last night this place smelled like heaven, as Toby was working on perfecting his sourdough baguettes and it kept him busy for hours. He had let Betsy Blake, the hostess at the Black Diner, down the road know he had finished the six loaves he had promised her and he knew she'd love them. She already loved him. Yes, but Toby gave her bread instead.

"I just wish I loved her more. Had a little more spark," he said to me, his visiting dad.

"It's like I'm already too comfortable with her," he said. "I mean, I think I should feel this way after ten years of marriage and things are nice and secure but a little calmed down, you know?"

"Marriage is hard work. Don't skip the early years. They're hard too but you're right, there's some great fun in sex on the kitchen floor every now and then!"

Toby rolled his eyes. "Okay, Dad. Thanks. Too much information."

"Just saying," I offered.

"You might want to think about pulling your RV over more on the gravel pad. If it's going to be there for a while, you don't want it to get stuck in a rut when the mud and snow set in." And Toby headed back to the main house to grab the ringing phone.

I watched my handsome thirty-three-year-old son head out through the storm door. He was wearing the Vermont costume of checked flannel shirt over tee shirt. Hiking boots, khakis. He was a handsome kid, I thought. Looking more and more like my wife, Mary, especially when he turned to me and raised his eyebrows in alarm, or at least, disapproval. That was the look that sent me packing.

It was stupid, I knew it, but I had to breathe again. It had been a few millennia since sex on the kitchen floor had been a consideration. I had to feel there was something that would get me wound up again. What a disaster that was. I gave into my mid life crisis and started fucking the blonde secretary working at the insurance agency across from the office. I'd worked as a securities guy for twenty years, had made a good salary and had put away enough, and when that young one smiled at me at the diner a couple days in a row, I fell crazy, howling and swept away.

There was a Christmas party with the two firms, owned by brothers. There was the champagne and my own Mary refusing to go after fifteen devoted years of smiling at boring colleagues. She figured we had enough money at this point and she didn't need to support my career anymore. So, I went to the Radisson with the smiling young blonde woman. And I couldn't believe how soft her skin was, how soft her hair was, how she came so easily and rubbed me all the right ways.

I knew it was wrong but I couldn't stop. I talked to a friend. I talked to a guy at church. I talked to a bartender. No one had anything to offer except for the bartender who told me not to cock up my life. The bartender had seen plenty. But I didn't listen.

I told Mary I was leaving. I told her I still liked her very much but I didn't love her enough to give up this last chance at feeling alive. I moved out. Mary's eyes were pierced. That's what I remember. Pierced with needles that let out one tear after the other. I knew I wasn't worth it. I knew I was a shit. I knew I couldn't stay. So I moved into the Radisson for nine months.

Then, Toby called and said Mary had been diagnosed with breast cancer, stage four. She had already done one round of chemo and wasn't going to do another. She had asked Toby to call me.

"I'm sorry, Mary," I said when I saw her lying there in bed.

"You're a shit. I know you're sorry." She closed her eyes and drifted off to sleep.

I moved back in to the house. I nursed Mary night and day. I quit my job, retired from the firm, and sat by her bedside making her laugh at the memories of times we had shared.

She lost her hair, she became as small as a pea pod, and as thin, I thought. She was shriveling away right in front of my eyes. I had dreams of holding her hand and watching it disintegrate into dust. From dust to dust pile I walked thinking I could blow God's breath on her and make her reassemble. I dropped on my knees in the dream, in the smoke of her bones, and wept, asking God to forgive me, lost in a cloud of choky smoke.

When I woke to sit by her side, she moved her head and motioned me to come closer. "I forgive you," she said. "I'm sorry, too." I took her hand and sat with her as her breath got shallower and her legs started to turn a grey blue. It would not be long before she would puff herself away. Toby had been there as often as he could. He had forgiven me, too, which I really didn't deserve. But I welcomed it.

He told us he would be right back and left the room. Mary smiled at me, her husband of thirty years, puckered her lips with a kiss and left. Toby walked back in a few minutes later with a fresh bouquet of flowers he had picked from the garden. And he knew he was too late. He went to sit next to her. "Oh, Ma. Oh, Mama, you wouldn't wait for me." He looked up to the ceiling, then put his head on his mother's chest.

I rose and walked to the living room. The sound of Toby's weeping felt like rain on a wet leaf.

"Ken's story was a surprise," I said to Mallory. "He sounds pretty self aware. Do you know him? He's the brother of the owner I guess, Toby's dad."

There was a short silence, "Oh, he's the shit that left his wife to fuck around when she had cancer!"

"Well, actually, the story says he came back to hospice her, and that she forgave him."

"That's what you get when history is written by the winners."

"Is that a non-starter for you? If Ken is there and takes part?"

"Oh, no," says Mallory. "There are shits everywhere. I'll build a snowman with Knauta and we'll manage our own social life."

I spread the word to my former students and was gratified that Eddie was able to come and organize again. Though he and Shamana were only on "friendly" terms, he suggested that maybe she could cook, needing a gig.

"Well, Toby, the guy who runs it is usually the chef."

"She can help me out then, okay?"

"Separate rooms? I'll need to figure it out for the count."

"Oh, we can share," he said breezily.

"By the way, Amanda is coming, too. Will that be a problem?"

There was a slight male pause. "I don't think so."

"Just trying to make sure we don't bake problems into the cake."

I continued working out details with Eddie. With he, Shamana, Amanda, Ken, Mallory, Knauta and me, it made seven writers. Mallory had offered rooms to three monks on retreat so there would be another three rooms rented out. Mallory said that the monks would stay to themselves, rise at dawn, chant away, work in a community center nearby during the days, and come back to sleep only. Toby felt that ten was a good enough number with which to enter the house and we negotiated a good price, covered by tuitions with a little left for me to pocket. We set the start date for late January.

"It will be cold but even if there is a blizzard, the lodge has generators and emergency vehicles and all will be well!" wrote Toby, on a Post-it attached to the contract.

Sure, I thought, *why not?* and sent out emails to my mailing list that we had secured a place and deposits were due by the week between Christmas and New Year.

On Christmas Day I went with Mallory to the World Food Mission and served up some turkey dinners, sorted out bags of clean white socks, soap and towels, plastic sheeting, underwear, tee shirts and more white socks. Everyone who came to the mission was offered a bag and most took them, folding them into jacket pockets, and making sure to spend time in the bathroom of the mission, which had hot showers, sacks of free soap and toiletries. I thought of David and how he would sniff at my "one-day-a-year do-gooder effort" and it kept me humble. Still, the meal was served, a small token of survival offered while the upper middle-class turkey carvers in the kitchen talked about Jim Mattis resigning as chief of staff, the budget for Trump's wall being rejected, and the recent death of George H. W. Bush. Head shakes all around but again, this feeling that nobody was able to affect change in any meaningful way. I hated the paralysis that had gripped me at the results of election in 2016 and lingered and flared when I let it. Mostly, the country felt wound in rotten clothing, like the pile that some of the homeless guys left in the corner of the bathrooms as they stripped off six months of sweat and stink, and scrubbed for a better winter to come.

I couldn't help but realize we were continuing to bandage problems that needed lancing but leadership had deserted us, even our own. The population was so stunned, it was hard to grab a consensus to lead toward liberation. It was clear the country had to dip even lower, lose even more of the rule of law and justice, to be able to react. Surely, we could stop ourselves from ruin but the slide south was continuous. I was guilty that I was looking forward to my time in Vermont, tucked away again from the difficulty of our political reality.

After rounding up the last box of Legos and Tinker Toys in the kid's playroom, and making sure all the Barbie dolls were distributed or stored for next year, I went to hug Mallory, who was working hard in the kitchen, scrubbing the floor on her hands and knees.

I grinned at her. "You're good at that," I said.

"Very therapeutic. A skill passed from devoted housekeeper to lonely, privileged child. See you, friend," and she continued moving her bucket and sopping soapy towels over the tile floor.

It was a nice wintry night. The streets were quiet with celebrants tucked inside, already done with Christmas dinner or Chinese takeout. I walked past a couple of ground floor apartments with windows that perfectly framed the day. Though I hoped to be reminded of Dickens and the *Christmas Carol*, I saw instead super hero kids in flameproof pajamas in front of screens, boxes and gift-wrap still lingering in piles. Exhausted parents asleep in recliners. Doggies scratching at the door to be let out. The perfect fantasy of Christmas was just that, a fantasy.

We were all mindlessly disconnected, scratching at the door to be let out, but with not enough conviction to not shit where we ate.

Nobody had a clue how to move from our American adolescent fantasies of strength and manifest destiny and get a grip on what would lead us forward. These thoughts were relentless. I looked forward to putting my feet up and numbing myself with leftovers from dinner.

The landline phone was ringing when I put the key in the lock. Not many people had that number so I was sure it was a robocall. My cell was quiet. It was probably someone selling life insurance on Christmas night, another sad thought.

I took off my boots at the door, noticed the zipper was going and calculated the cost of new leather boots in my head. I counted the days 'til January when I would get another infusion of cash. I had given a couple of my students Christmas "presents" of reduced rates sessions but I had to stop that.

Knauta hadn't allowed me to give her a discounted rate. "Self-esteem, Annie. You offer a service you get paid for it. Feminism missed you on that one." I smiled at the thought of this new friend. She was wise and angry, like many of us of this age, but there was a burnished quality to her affect that cheered me, same with Mallory. I appreciated the ease of women who had had to go through a few things and knew the intricacies of survival. That was a good Christmas gift.

Eddie had sent a sweet card from California and that was lovely. Cookies from neighbors. It was fine all round. I lit a big white candle on the dining room table as I put on the kettle, found the cookies, got ready to settle in and then it rang again. The landline.

"Hello? Who's calling?" I was fairly abrupt. I didn't really want to handle a cold call from some Christmas cheer agency. It was quiet for a moment and then I heard his voice.

"Mom?" he said. "Hello. This is Jordan."

I was immediately sorry I had answered so gruffly. How could I let myself alienate him with my toughness before I had even heard him?

"Jordan. Really? Hello." I sat down in the nearest chair. My heart started beating hard.

"Yes, really." I could feel him smile. *He was happy to surprise me and be in control of the situation*, I thought.

"Yes, Eddie told me he had spoken with you. Are you back in the States?" I was thinking fast but it all felt like mush. I didn't know what was allowed in the conversation. I did not have the presence of mind to say nothing and just let him speak.

"Actually, not yet. Next week I think. I have to clear some old visa issues, immigration interviews."

Visa issues? Shall I ask about that? No. I shouldn't. "Oh," I said.

"Well, how are you?" That was safe. Hopefully not intrusive.

"I'm fine. I have grown a lot. I have a new community. The American government thinks it needs to vet me again because I have been living with this community. It's racist propaganda. Though I doubt that it will affect my ability to come back to the States." His voice was a bit deeper. Maybe it was late there. Or early. Maybe he was tired. Or older.

"Really? Was there trouble?" I said. Talk about paralysis. I had no idea where to take the conversation. If I should be angry or sad or grateful or mute. "I really don't know what to say. I am happy to hear you are well."

"Yes. I am. I just thought I would say hello before I head back to the States." *That was good*, I thought. *Saying hello.*

"May I ask where you will go? Do you need anything?"

"I'll let you know."

There was a long distance, long silence, a stillness that gripped us both. Stillness said more than words but it was jagged and tricky. We both listened to it and then he said, "I'll call again, if that's okay."

"Yes. Of course. Yes. Okay." I said. I didn't want him to hang up.

"Let you know my plans, if you want," he said.

Do I want to know his plans? Of course I do. "Yes, that will be good." How did that sound? Too eager? "Maybe let Eddie know. He always knows my teaching schedule."

"Oh. Sure. Yes. I see he has been filling in as surrogate son," Jordan said steadily.

"You are still my son." It came out fast and strong and true. Straight from the heart. That was good.

Jordan sighed. I don't think he knew what he wanted from this conversation either.

"Okay, good night. Mom. *Haha. Haha* means mother."

"*Haha.* Ah, sounds like a joke?"

"The Japanese have an interesting twist on things. Eddie can call you *Okassan.* That's someone else's mother."

"Oh."

"It's morning here, by the way."

"Good morning, then."

"*Musuko.* Oh, *shisoku.* The word for son." He said the words as if they had no bones.

"Shall I practice?"

"Sure."

And the line went quiet. Did he hang up on me? The line was dead in any case.

* * *

"Can you listen as my friend? Or shall I pay you for a session?" I said to Knauta, "Or may I bring a bottle of Prosecco?"

I was pretty distraught but had waited a full hour before I called her. We settled on a friendly chat that Knauta said was free because I was a new friend and she had permission to drink wine during the call.

"But why did you break with your mother?" I asked.

"Well, I broke for my whole adult life and I might remind you that your son just called you."

"Right. That's right."

"Here's the thing. I left my mother because I was angry. All that tumult in her head, the endless stories about the war, the way she made me memorize my address backwards so even if someone tortured me to get it, they'd never find our house. I didn't know what to do with all that pain."

"Is that true? The address backwards?"

I heard Knauta light a cigarette and blow a puff. "Oh yes. In two languages!"

"I bet that Stephen Miller kid, the one that looks like Goebbels, truly," Knauta laughed. The white wine suited her. "The Jew who is incarnating a Nazi for some delicious and psychotic reason I long to dig into. I bet he's pretty pissed off having to carry that shit with him, too. At least your kid isn't trying to live out his revenge fantasies!"

"No! No, but . . ." I paused.

"What?" Knauta said, lighting another cigarette.

"Jordan said he had visa issues or some questioning he had to go through before he came back to the States. I think he was involved with some Japanese cult. The one that threw Sarin gas in the Tokyo subway. Amanda did the research and it seems like the men responsible were all executed in August of this year. The Japanese government was keeping an eye on all the devotees."

"How involved is he? Was he?"

"I don't know."

We sat with that. And she let me hear what I didn't know.

Chapter 40

A New Year: 2019

Toby called to tell me that he had confirmed with their staff that the retreat was a go. He asked me again about any special needs diets or access, which I thought was very thorough. I told him Knauta would need a room on the first floor.

"She can have the primary suite in the house. It used to be where the owner lived. Has a big king size bed and a separate bath. She'll be happy. But no smoking in the lodge. Have any smokers?"

I realized I had better check with Knauta again about the trip.

"I am fine!" she said when I called. "The weather makes me achy but I have wine, weed, drugs and love to keep me warm!"

"No smoking in the lodge, Knauta. You okay with that?"

There was silence. "In that case, I may ask Anita to join me to get me in and out of the snow drifts. No problem."

"Will she need an extra room? We're getting pretty booked."

"That won't be necessary. We can bunk together."

Really? I thought. Another aspect of Knauta that I was getting to know.

She continued, "Anita is all excited because her home country,

Austria, has finally okayed gay marriage. She's celebrating because now she thinks she'll be rich!"

"Who will she marry?"

"Me, of course. Maybe we'll take the occasion of Vermont to officiate our own vows."

"Wow! Really? We'll have to make a party!"

It hadn't occurred to me that Anita and Knauta were lovers but a wedding in Vermont when we were all together sounded like fun.

"I'm not sure Anita will allow that!" Knauta chuckled. "She's pretty private. Mostly she's happy she can get my money, and the rights to this terrific book I am going to write under your tutelage. If I live!" She laughed again and I could hear her light up another cigarette.

"Like Simone de Beauvoir and her Sylvie. She adopted her, a grown woman, so that she would have someone with whom to leave her estate!" I said, ever the literary historian. "But Madame de Beauvoir never considered herself a lesbian, the feminists say, because she never bothered with . . . uh, huh . . . down there! *Ha!*"

"What are you talking about?" Knauta asked.

"Oh, in her biography I read that she didn't consider herself a lesbian because, she slept with, kissed and bathed with her Sylvie but there was no fondling of sexual parts! At least that's what the biography said!"

Knauta laughed. "Well, I love being a lesbian, full stop. Time and arthritis may have altered my habits but not my pleasures!"

"Good for you, Knauta!" I said. "May your pleasure sustain you if your habits cannot."

"Oh, the things I tell you, Annie!"

Knauta was already slurring her words a little and it was not even two in the afternoon.

"Anita is nattering at me. Coming my love! Coming," she called. And I could hear the voice of a woman coming closer.

"Off the phone now. What stories are you telling about us?" a prim voice chided.

They laughed with each other. There was a rustle of the phone, and a clunk, as it dropped off her bed and then it went silent.

Chapter 41

Vermont at Last

When I drove up to the white-framed house at the end of the road, I was confused. It looked like a 1950s VFW post, old white siding with black shadows in the seams. Through the window was a battered meeting room with a homemade bar. I could smell the beer and arguments from my car. Not exactly idyllic.

I pulled into the side drive and immediately was hit by the long low sling of the rest of the place, extending back and back into a large meadow of snow. There was a porch and a second floor balcony that looked out to the fields and woods behind the building. The front entrance was a ruse to disguise the welcoming spread of the farmhouse, maybe the place that brought in revenue when the crops failed. The central porch off the back was the original entrance, built when it had been a working farm at least a century earlier. Carolina rockers piled in a corner peeked out from their winter tarps, huddling for warmth in a practical, no nonsense, Vermont way.

This main part of the house was wooden and well painted, white blending into the gray trees. The bright blue sky and the fields of snow banked the house and framed its freedom. Off the back was a small cottage where I imagined Toby lived. A big RV parked there, dwarfed the dwelling.

With no response to the crackling slam of my car door, I crunched along the gravel and made my way toward a posse of trees at the end of the path, happy to stretch my legs. I could feel them buzzing, noting a new arrival, measuring changing winds. The quiet was enormous as the trees spoke volumes. I heard a door open behind me and a man stepped out of the RV.

"Annie?" he yelled. "I'm Ken."

In no time, I was ensconced in my second floor room, perched on my window seat, a promise of meeting Toby and his dad later. I begged off dinner. Time to adjust was needed. My eyes closed. Oh, what a nap it was. No dreams, just the cool breeze and the click of branches keeping track of time.

Betsy's Diner was a sweet spot supported by locals. Checked denim framed the windows and covered the tables. Matching napkins, heavy red glass water goblets and one plastic flower in a tiny vase between the plump salt and pepper shakers greeted me. I loved spaces like this. Like at the Cape, I was being welcomed into someone else's history. No way to feel lonely, though alone. The clatter of conversation cheered me, and I happily tucked into the blue plate special of meat loaf and mashed potatoes. The Craig George Trio played its Sunday night supper jazz quietly in a corner, the fold-up metal music stands fragile and superfluous as the local trio pretended they were channeling Miles and Coltrane.

I reviewed the work ahead of me, making notes and daydreaming about the stories we would all write in this beautiful spot. Thank God for Mallory. She always got me where I needed to be.

Stepping out the door, I was showered by starlight, the light traveling without impediment through the crisp night. But, then, I sensed a presence watching me. And not from the heavens. The door of a sedan opened. A big man stepped out. Backlit by the diner sign, wrapped in a muffler and unlikely ski cap. I couldn't see his face. He was clearly focused on me.

I quickly jumped into my car, hurried to lock the doors. Breathing hard now, I don't know what I imagined, but none of it was good. The man bent down and put his face against the window. I was ready to scream. But then, it was David.

"Oh my God. You scared me to death," I said without opening the window. He motioned that he couldn't hear me. Probably because of the ridiculous muffler and clownish fur hat he was wearing. I cracked the window. "David! What are you doing here?"

He pulled off his hat and began to resemble someone I had once known. But his face was thin and drawn. He didn't look as hale and hearty as I remembered him from a few months before.

"I've been waiting for you," he said, into the window.

"What? Are you stalking me?" The steam from my breath landed on the glass and I had to rub it off.

"Roll down your window," he commanded. "You're being ridiculous. I am coming to the retreat. I heard you were here for dinner. I came to meet you."

I was more than surprised. David had not registered. He had not been in touch since our last conversation in November. I didn't want to talk to him alone in this parking lot, although I knew that I was overreacting. It looked like Betsy's was going to be open for another hour. Probably better to meet with him in a public place first.

"Go inside? We can have a drink and talk. Will you do that?"

He wasn't happy about my suggestion but I had no idea what he had in mind. He turned and rumbled off, and I could see he went into the restaurant and sat at a window table. He glanced out the window after he had taken off his coat. He smiled a silly smile and waved. Then I came in.

"What were you thinking? You didn't let us know you were coming. I don't know if there's a room at the place. Have you paid your fee? Honestly, this is really too weird. How long have you been sitting in the parking lot?"

"I just pulled up. Toby told me I could find you here and said he thought you might like some company." He looked at me, straight through me as he used to do, and I once again realized that he was not threatening me at all. He had made a decision and followed through.

I could see that for David, there was nothing too unusual about him showing up for the workshop a night early and with no notice. He had attended a workshop before. Why would this be different?

"I thought I should let you know I was here. I didn't want to startle you," he said.

"David, what about a phone call or an email?"

"No reception out here, remember?"

I let out some air. "Right. Yes. Okay. You win."

"I didn't mean to create a stir. Quite the opposite."

"Is anyone else at the lodge? Anyone else arrive early?" I said trying to restore balance.

"Yes. There were some monks with a long tall woman. She seemed to know Toby. She wasn't very friendly when I told her my name."

I smiled. "Ah, that would be Mallory. And the monks are from the meditation center. They are working at a community center for the week and filling out the rooms. Mallory helped me set up this retreat."

"I see," said David. He seemed at a loss for words. A little down hearted. He looked around the room. "I apologize if I acted impetuously but I thought it would be good for you to have another tuition. I should have preregistered."

He was at a loss. He had driven all the way to Vermont, assumed he could join the band and all would be well. Well, why not? I had told him I wished him well. I might apply a little compassion. Why did he unsettle me so?

"It's fine, David. Did Toby give you a room?"

"Yes, there was one left upstairs. Bathroom down the hall. Just fine. I brought my computer."

He called for the check and paid for our coffee and the extra piece of pie that my waitress had brought as a gift when she saw me return. "See you there, yes? At the lodge," he said. "Sorry to have disturbed you."

I looked up. "Yes. Okay. See you later."

I watched as David rose and put on his coat and headed out the door. *He's lonely*, I thought. *Even David can get lonely.*

I sat for a few more minutes, watching the waitress gather her checks, listening to the last tune from the trio. Then walked out to my car with the hostess.

"Good night. Thanks, again," I said and got into the car and started up the engine. I waited for her to pull out, went to the driveway and turned left back up the road to the lodge. Behind me, I saw a car pull from a side driveway and follow at a few car lengths distance.

I noticed the presence but dismissed it. It was a main road and many cars travel it often.

Then, the car made the turn I made back to the lodge. What was going on? I pulled into the side drive and starting honking my horn. Loud, often, repeatedly.

Mallory came out on the porch. Ken and Toby opened the door of the cabin. I turned off my lights. The car stopped at the end of the driveway.

I got out and hurried toward the porch as I saw the car coming slowly up and toward the house. It stopped and turned off its lights. David got out. He came up to me and Mallory on the porch.

"I waited for you. It's dark and I wanted to make sure you got back okay."

I looked at Mallory.

"Oh, okay," I said.

"Look, David, that's creepy." Mallory was on fire. "I don't know you very well but you have shown up with no reservation, you've obviously freaked out our fearless leader, and I'm not sure at all about you hanging in with us this week."

David said nothing and his face fell again as it had in the restaurant.

"I have some work to do and I have had a friendship with your friend, Annie. Perhaps she should decide if it's appropriate for me to be here."

"It's fine, David. It's fine, Mallory. Come inside." I turned to David. "See you in the morning"

HOW WE SAW THE MOON

* * *

That night, the monks and David and Mallory and I settled into our rooms to begin the process of rearranging the energy in the house and finding a place for ourselves. Lodge's like this one had so many years of spirits and souls leaving traces of their visits. This place had been empty for a month or two before this and we now had to re-inhabit it and fall into harmony with its past and with each other. All this silent scurrying and jockeying for space!

Since my time in India, I had become much more alert to these sensations, the resonance of space and the energy that inhabit places we enter, both the energy we bring and the energy that precedes us. Since spending more time alone, since sitting quietly trying to keep myself rooted in the midst of the politics and roiling wreckage of our American life, all of this had enhanced my antennae. Just sitting still, not even admitting to meditation, allowed the granular potency of 'being' to come closer.

I could feel the many people who had come through the lodge over the years. Or so I thought, when dawn came without sleep. I managed to blame the memory of families camping in the farm fields, or the Ukrainian cleaning women who I knew were happy there was a midwinter rental. I had found a little charm bracelet in the soap dish of the bathroom and had already made up a short story about Masha and her daughter, Tatiana, and how they used to work for the railroad but found a new and happy home in snowy Vermont changing sheets and pillowcases. I blamed these stories, real or not, for my sleepless night, gazing out the window from the window seat, watching the air shift in starlight and cloud drifts.

I refused to blame the real reason. The constant knot in my chest that had been there since I had heard my son's voice on the phone. His sense of unease infused my own body. I was carrying every bit of his anger, his unresolved sadness, and I knew it wasn't mine. So, I preferred the story about the Ukrainian housecleaners and the years of other souls who had floated through these rooms.

Mallory was next door but I didn't hear anything from her room for which I was happy. I was glad she was resting. David was across the hall and he had a sleep apnea machine that whooshed quietly all through the night. At least, I told my fantastical panicky self, I can tell where he is. He has a mechanical sound tag to locate him. Finally, the quiet movement of the monks through the predawn light to their first sitting of the day jarred me out of my head and into a deep bathtub. Maybe that would help.

I don't even remember getting into bed but woke with a sleepy satisfaction when there was a knock on my bedroom door. It was 11:00 a.m. by my phone.

"Hey!" Mallory said. "I'm coming in," and she did. I had neglected to lock the door handle. I stretched and was happy to see her.

"I didn't sleep a wink 'til 5:00 a.m. But a pleasure to see you now."

"Yep, you missed breakfast but we have stuff to do so coffee in ten minutes. See you there." And she was gone.

True to his word, Toby had coffee and snacks on the counter of the kitchen and I grabbed a mug. Mallory and I sat together, looking out at the fields.

"Gee, Mallory. This spot is great. Thanks for getting us in here. Have you talked to Ken yet? Seen Toby?"

"Toby, yes. And I managed to sneer at Ken but he ignored me, and then asked if we could take a walk later."

"Really? Clear the air maybe?"

"Who knows. I need some exercise, so I said okay."

"How well did you know his brother? Were you a couple?"

Mallory smiled. "Actually, truth be told, he's just an old pal from Pittsburgh. Our moms played cards together and so we sat out back and smoked when the ladies came over for canasta.

Ken didn't hang with us. He always thought I was too . . . something or other. His brother, Paul, lives in the Bahamas in the winter. I like his kid. He did well with him."

"Sometimes apples don't fall too far from the tree . . . but then again," I said. "But then again." I shook my head.

"So have you heard from Jordan since Christmas?"

"No. Maybe Eddie has. He wasn't sure about his plans. I don't want to get any hopes up. 'Wait without hope, because hope would be hope of the wrong thing,'" I said.

"That's impressive."

"T. S. Eliot actually. *Four Quartets* and the crazy man, David, is the one who got me reading Eliot again."

"Fine. Fine. Let him read the classics far, far away from you!" she said, and we both smiled.

"You're so protective," I said.

"Self-interest," she said. "I finally have a girl friend and I don't want to lose her. "

"Not so easy to make new friends at our age!" We both said in unison and laughed.

"Amen," said Mallory as the door from the outside opened and Ken stepped in. He was sturdy and had half a head of hair, the back half. He looked like he didn't have the habit of covering it frantically with baseball or other caps, as his forehead was nicely tanned. Though his chest was a little sunken, his stomach was round and firm, and he had a good strong step.

"Ready for our walk, Mallory?" he said.

She looked up. "Sure. Let me get my coat." She grabbed her car coat and the ubiquitous long scarf—this time in blue cashmere—from the peg on the wall.

"I don't think we've walked together since I walked you home from school lo these many years ago," Ken said.

"You did not."

"I did, too. You were just too crazy about Pauly to notice me as I brought you from basketball practice straight to our house for dinner."

"Basketball practice?" I said with a smile.

"Ms. Mallory was a girls basketball star in high school. If she hasn't regaled you with her tales then she has become so very modest in her old age."

"How many crappy things can you say in one sentence, Kenny?' she said. "Familiarity does indeed breed contempt."

I looked at the two of them and had to admit they sparked each other. I rarely saw anyone best Mallory and her mouth.

"Have a good time, you two. Milk and cookies at three!" I waved as she puffed and headed out the door. Through the window I saw her sigh and pull her ski hat down over her hair. She had a serious demeanor, maybe a little nervous, I thought. They stepped into the snow-tracked drive and she lost her footing. He grabbed her arm, steadied her, and she pulled her arm away. Then, she trekked on, stumbled again and he grabbed her again. He said something clear and strong to her. She reluctantly held onto the crook of his arm as they climbed a few crusty snow hills to hit the trail off to the woods. Not sure when she let go. But I bet it was within a few steps.

Knauta and Anita arrived around one. The birdlike Anita had beautiful blue eyes and porcelain skin. She fluttered true to form around Knauta, taking charge, as if her charge was an invalid.

"I've brought her wheelchair," Anita said. "But I can see there's no place for her to use it here!"

"I'm fine, Anita. Stop fluttering, please. You're not my nurse and every one knows that we are engaged to be Austrian so, shh. There's a birdhouse out by that cabin and I'll banish you there if you don't stop."

Anita stopped, her face dropped, she ran her thin fingers through her hair and started to laugh, embarrassed. We noticed a gold band with a green gemstone on her left hand.

"Show everyone your engagement ring, Anita. It's beautiful"

And her face came back up with a grin.

"Knauta, you embarrass me!" she kept her grin, and the toss of her hair from her face. Strong and lovely, she was actually not that much younger than Knauta. Anita was a good-looking woman in her fifties, dressed in a cardigan and slacks and pearls. She wore a thin gold chain and an emerald eternity band on her finger. She spoke to Knauta in German and Knauta laughed. Knauta took her hand and showed me the band on Anita's finger.

"Look, I gave her a ring! Subtle, tasteful and real!"

Anita smiled. "Show her the ring I got you!" Knauta did and it was thicker and more solid. Had rubies running along it in a thin center line. "It belonged to my mother and now I can give it a home."

"Congratulations, you two. It's wonderful to celebrate together!"

Anita looked a little worried. "No need to call attention!"

"Are you kidding," said Knauta. "I haven't been promised in a long time and I want everyone to know." As she smiled, years and folds fell away and we saw a glimpse of the young handsome and exotic Knauta, her strength and gleam.

"Ah!" Anita waved her arms in front of her face and then blew some air through her lips and we all laughed together.

"Let me show you to your suite, you two!" I said and led the way to the back of the house. Knauta squeezed Anita's hand as they made their way down the hall. They oohed and ahhed at the big windows and the view of the sky and were soon ensconced. I showed Knauta the back porch where she could smoke and warned her again. "This place can go up in flames! So no cheating!"

"No. No. Not to worry."

Anita came in all flush faced with their overnight bag. "It's so beautiful, Knauta. I met this lovely young man who is going to shovel you a path to the car and the little gravel road there! We're going to take a walk!"

I left them to their preparations and I could hear them laugh and enjoy the fact that they had arrived.

By six everyone had arrived except Shamana who was planning to join us in a day or two. That seemed to delight Amanda, who, though a few years his senior, had taken quite a shine to Eddie, or Ed, as she called him. They sat together at the table, with David at the far end across from

Knauta and Anita. Toby was happy in the kitchen and he brought out a big tub of vegetable soup and his famous bread and we enjoyed serving ourselves family style, offering parmesan cheese one to the other, pouring wine or offering beer. Then, bringing in pre plated chicken breasts with pasta and a generous salad assisted by his dad, Ken. Plates cleared easily with Amanda bringing in coffee and cookies for dessert.

I watched with an internal sparkle. I never remembered how comforted I was by big meals with compatible company. The ease of sharing conversation and dirty dishes, sitting longer than needed to digest and bathe in companionable satisfaction was pleasure to me. None of us had lived with family for quite a while, I realized, but mostly everyone, even David, managed to melt into the communal whole and allow an easy familiarity. We talked of the weather, the open sky. We made a bit too much noise against the quiet of the woods, talking of the candidates who were starting to declare their desire to be the Democratic candidate to defeat Trump.

"You going to get involved again?" Mallory asked me.

"Not a chance," I said. "I'm still reeling from the last election."

There was some desultory talk of politics but everyone was relieved we didn't have the pressure of responding to media reports during our time together. We drank less wine than we thought we would have needed. Everyone felt the relief of not having to think or talk about themselves, since most of us had met before, we knew we had gathered to spend time together and apart and to enjoy a web for a week that would allow us to swing free with an invisible net.

Through the swinging door came Toby, back first, and turned around to reveal a little cake with a sparkler in it. He set it in front of Knauta and Anita.

"Understand there's an engagement in the house."

Everyone clapped and Ken popped open the champagne that had been cooling in the kitchen.

Knauta smiled so broadly. I was surprised to even see some tears in her eyes. Anita spoke to us, "We have waited ten years to make it official, mostly because I wanted to be married in my home country. I wanted to welcome Knauta to my home after she had held me so close in hers for so many years. Thank you for celebrating with us. We are very honored." Anita turned to Knauta and gave her a big kiss and hug.

"Okay everyone," said Ken, "I'm saving the roses for the celebrants." As he grabbed the cake to distribute. "Mallory, will you pour the champagne?"

Surprised, Mallory looked up and then moved to the sideboard to get glasses. And filled them for a toast.

It was Ken who lifted his first. "May your marriage sustain your love and your love sustain your marriage," he announced.

Mallory looked up at him. "Good advice, that's for sure," she cracked, though no one noticed, and everyone drank. David had only a little bit in his glass and sipped it gingerly, but he was trying to be congenial. He caught my eye and pretended he wasn't looking toward me and I knew I had to sit with him and figure out what was happening, but not tonight.

We sat for another half hour and then the first of us to leave was Ken. He had grown quiet watching the celebration of the women's engagement. Jealous of their new beginning, perhaps. He mumbled something about helping with the dishes and he was gone. Mallory looked up, obviously having a silent conversation with her old acquaintance and then, uncharacteristically, said she was exhausted and was going up.

Knauta and Anita were next. They thanked everyone roundly and stopped in the kitchen to thank Toby as well before heading back to their suite. That left David, me, Amanda and Eddie. David chugged whatever was left in his glass and said, "Excuse me, all." And rambled out of the room. I heard the porch door swing open so imagined him sitting in his coat under the sky.

Eddie turned to me. His manner business like all of a sudden. "I heard from Jordan just before I came up. Did he contact you?"

I was surprised. And his tone sliced at the contentment in the room just moments before.

"We spoke Christmas. I think I told you. Yes. It was a bit scratchy but okay I suppose."

Eddie adjusted in his seat. "I've been wanting to tell you but the party was so relaxed."

"Yes?" I said. Amanda looked at me too. Obviously, Eddie had told her whatever it was, already. They both sat up straight, at attention.

"Jordan told me today that he was being 'detained' in Japan for a few more weeks. An investigation, which he swore he knew nothing about. But, it seems that someone in Tokyo, someone from his 'community' just rammed a car into a crowd of people. Supposed to be in revenge for the executions of all those folks last summer who had let out Sarin gas into the subways."

He let that settle in for a moment. I was instantly transported from the quiet of Vermont trees to the busy streets of Tokyo, red lights flashing, bodies strewn on a sidewalk.

"Oh my God," I said. "Is he involved in that? Do you think he was involved in that?"

Just the thought forms created needles cutting into my heart. Maybe this was what I had intuited, bringing my heart to my throat since I had arrived. "No. That can't be. Tell me. Did he tell you?"

Amanda took a file she had put under her chair when she came in to dinner. She handed it to me. As I opened it, I saw a newspaper article about the attack and how the authorities were investigating the sect members to see if the perpetrator had acted alone. There was a photo of a busy Tokyo street, emergency vehicles, white body bags.

"Oh my God, Eddie. No. He wasn't involved in all that, was he?" I was so stunned. My heart seemed to stop beating and then pounded so hard I thought it would fall from my chest. "How could you keep it from me? We are sitting here reveling in peace and you are holding onto this information?"

"There is no evidence that he was involved, Aunt Annie. Really." He ignored my accusation of betrayal and proceeded cautiously. "According to Jordan, everyone who lived there, in their commune, is being detained for questioning. He said, he knew the guy but had nothing to do with it."

We let that information settle. Amanda could see I needed more to find balance and some way to react to this new situation.

"But then he told you the guy was driving his car, right?" Amanda said, looking straight at Eddie. "You have to tell her the whole, truth, Ed. It's not fair."

Eddie sighed and continued. "Yes. He said that he owned the car but had not driven it for over a year. It was just at the compound. Everyone used it!"

"It was Jordan's car that killed the people?" I was assembling the parts of the puzzle, at a loss for the missing pieces.

"Right!" said Amanda.

"Look, he dismissed it out of hand," said Eddie. "But, he wanted me to know that maybe he would not be back in the States for another few months. I suspect he also wanted me to know that if he disappeared again, it might be prudent to get him a lawyer through the embassy!"

"Is it time to get him a lawyer? What are we looking at here? What am I supposed to do?"

Eddie was so uncomfortable being the bearer of bad news. He just wanted it to be over. Amanda smiled at him. She clearly had more practice with these kinds of conversations.

"Anyway," Eddie sighed, "He asked me to tell you he'd been detained."

"Not enough guts to tell you himself," Amanda said as I looked around at her, surprised at her vehemence. "I'm sorry, Annie. It's just I told my mom right away. But then, I wasn't guilty."

I looked at Amanda and then Eddie and shook my head. I didn't know really what to do.

Maybe this news was what was making me so panicky, so over reactive around David. It certainly wasn't David's fault but maybe I was feeling this and maybe I was blaming him for my intuitive feelings about my kid and maybe . . .

Eddie interrupted my inner monologue. "It's weird times, Aunt Annie. Please don't be upset. I'm sure it will all be fine."

"Or not," said Amanda. Eddie looked at her. "I told you my story, Ed. Sometimes it's just not." The silence was pretty thick as I contemplated the possibilities. Somehow my head went to the koi pond in Descanso gardens, and the false freedom of the fish, at the mercy of whoever ran to the pond.

"Let's go for a star walk, Annie. What do you say? Before we all turn in." Eddie was eager to please me.

"Great!" said Amanda. "I'll check on Toby and make sure all's okay. Meet you in the kitchen with my coat. That will be nice, Annie. Get your coat. Walking will be good."

I nodded, happy to have directions. We split to the hall to retrieve our coats and meet at the kitchen door. Toby was already wiping down the counters. "Dad's gone back to the cabin. You guys going for a walk?"

"A little one. It's a nice night," Amanda said, totally in charge of the situation.

Toby smiled. "Take flashlights. They're on the porch."

We piled on to the porch and found the basket with the flashlights and prepared to step off the porch. Then, we heard the slow rock of a chair. I looked up and there was David sitting in the shadows.

"We're going for a walk, David." Amanda said. "Probably just to the end of the road. Want to come?" She was orchestrating the threads of disharmony and making them work together. I was so grateful and surprised that she had so thoroughly changed, healed, morphed since our meeting in Kauai three years before.

I could feel David unsure of his welcome. But Amanda had opened the door and he stepped through. "Yes, that would be nice."

We stepped off the porch and navigated the gravel path to the front of the house. It was dark and bright and we fell into listening to the rhythm of our steps. There was little to say. I had forgotten what had made my insides grip themselves but I knew that my ribs were holding my heart from jumping onto the road we walked on. I kept sighing to get enough breath. We walked four across the road. Then Eddie took my arm, and I shook my head.

"Let's walk, Annie. Let's just walk it off, okay?" He whispered to me. Amanda came to my other side and David fell into step with Eddie. He didn't know exactly why we were together, except I could feel his strength, I could feel his regard for the march we were making. He was in. Whatever we were walking off or into, he was willing to be in it with us, with me. We, four hapless travelers in Oz, crunching toward a wizard with no answers this night.

Chapter 42

David and Me on the Porch

Amanda and Eddie left me on the porch after our walk and my request to sit a bit before I went in. David held back and then sat in a rocker next to me. I could feel it groan as he let his weight settle into its wooden frame.

"I apologize again for my presence, Annie. I really should have given you notice."

"Really, David, it's fine. I'm a bit nervy but it has nothing to do with you. Issues with my absent son. I suppose I am not sure how the week will go."

David took a moment. "It will go fine. I won't stay for the whole week. I haven't been well, actually. I think I told you that. So, it's probably best to stay only a few days."

"It's fine, really!"

"I'll still pay for the whole week," he said.

"Oh, David. It's not that! I don't feel comfortable around you. You say and do things that don't seem to have much logic. Sometimes you actually scare me. I don't like that." I rocked a couple of times. "Oh forget all that. You're fine, I'm fine. All is fine. Just let's sit quietly, okay?"

We did. We sat quietly and rocked a bit more and I could see David's breath and he, mine. Then, he spoke.

"Yes, I am an erratic and difficult fellow. But, I appreciate being able to think about you."

I turned to him. "Really? What is it that you think about me?"

"Oh, I think that if I were a different person and you were a different person, we would have been great friends. Without our impediments, I mean."

"My impediments?"

"Language. Don't let it get in the way," he cautioned.

"Okay," I said to him. *Okay*, I thought to myself. *He is not the problem.*

"I admire that you have survived one life and have gone on to live another. I admire that you have a difficult son and yet are still standing. I admire that you have taken care of yourself and your face is strong and your body, too. I look at Knauta and I know it must be very hard for a woman that bright to be unable to move well. She has to rely on other things. But still, she has a partner that is willing to commit to her. I admire that you have found her and the others in this group and have gathered them around you and you allow me to stand with you, even when I scare you."

I looked over at him. "Oh, David," I said putting my hand on his arm. "You don't scare me. Really!"

He was quiet for a moment and then said. "I admire that you know that, deep down, but still you balance me at a distance so that if I topple, I will fall like a tree in the forest, large and witnessed by birds."

I continued to rock a few more times. I could feel tears coming down my face. I wondered if they would freeze or chap my cheeks in long zebra lines. I knew they were falling but I was not certain why. Maybe it was the prospect of David as a fallen tree in an unseen forest, unnoticed but worthy. Maybe it was that we were all lost in that forest.

"You know, you do have gifts to give," I said. "You do give gifts even though they can be misunderstood. Or kept secret."

"Like Mr. Darcy in *Pride and Prejudice*. I like to think of myself that way when I am puffed up." He sighed. "But age gives us ourselves, and our selfishness. I'll have to think about that. What gifts I give." He looked at me with his eyes wide open, thinking.

"It's not a hard assignment, David."

"Oh. Okay."

David said nothing. But his nothing was cavernous.

Chapter 43

David and His Boy

"Annie? Annie?" The voice came through my bedroom door. "Can I come in? I saw the light on. May I come in?" David was at my door. We had been in our rooms no more than forty minutes.

I wasn't sleeping. I had yet to change to pajamas. The image of Jordan, lost in fury, backing himself into trouble, kept gripping me, shaking me to my bones. I kept thinking there was something I had done. Should have done. Should do now. Waiting to find out was its own purgatory.

"Annie. I want to talk with you."

I shifted on the bed and couldn't bring myself to open the door. I turned off the light.

"Annie! Don't do that! I know you are not sleeping."

I said nothing. I could hear him pacing outside in the hall. The floorboards creaked.

"Damn," he said. Then, came closer to the door. I heard him move something, maybe it was the cane chair in the hallway. I heard it brush against the doorknob. Then, the chair sigh as his weight sunk into it.

"I have something I want to share with you. I know it is odd and makes me feel predatory, but I want to tell you something."

He paused waiting for me to move, perhaps. But I lay still. Waiting him out.

"When you asked me that. About the gifts. When I heard you say that, I was flummoxed. Stumped. I didn't remember. I don't remember any gifts I have given. I mean there was the time I took Delly out for ice cream after Charissse told me to go back to Rochester and the IT firm. I really was doing my best to be a friend, a figure of some kind to the boy. His mother and I lived together for an entire year. I felt responsible and she was a friend to me. Until it was too much for her and she told me she couldn't stand the sound of my voice and preferred that I didn't live there anymore."

He must have been sitting sideways on the chair, whispering into the crack in the door. Trying his best not wake anyone else on the floor.

"I thought that the least I could do was send the boy a present now and then. He had grown fond of me. But I couldn't think of anything."

His voice stopped. I heard the weight in the chair shift. I heard his hands against his knees, patting them rhythmically, coaxing the words with the rhythms.

"Then, there were drums. I thought he needed drums. He could bang on them and get his sadness out. Whatever sadness I saw in him because she saw nothing. She said I was the sadness in the house, how I talked and lumbered around. But it was his own sadness. It was there before I came and was there when I left."

I thought he had left but then the voice started again, a murmur, really.

"I wanted to tell you that he shot himself. When he was fifteen years old. I hadn't sent him any books in a long while. I loved to send him books. I sent him a set of art books, but Charisse told me to cut it out. Said, if I sent him another thing, then she would call the police.

"I stopped sending him things. He shot himself that summer after his fifteenth birthday. I know only because I tried to call and ask if he was okay. Tried to ask Charisse if she knew he was sad, in the way I knew he was sad. But, she screamed at me. 'He's dead, you sonofabitch.' Then I read about it in the police reports. He used the gun Charisse kept in the cabinet for protection."

It was quiet again. He took a deep breath,

"So, I know what it is to lose a boy, Annie. I wanted to tell you that I know what it is to lose a boy."

He sat there for a while longer. I lay on my bed looking into the dark. I got up lightly and opened the door. I am not sure why. Maybe because it cost him something to share his love of the boy. Maybe because kindness was called for between people of good faith.

"It's snowing, David. It's snowing outside," I said, as I shifted to look out at white under the starlight. "Come in, "I said to him. "Look. It's beautiful. It will make us both feel better."

He was such a huge presence in that tiny bedroom. I sat on the bed as he gazed out the window in the dark. He lifted his head, tilting his nose up maybe to sniff the remedy. He reminded me of that buck in my dream.

"It's all getting covered now, Annie," he said. Then, a look of determination crossed his face. "I need to show you something."

He turned and I thought he might move toward me, but instead he headed out the door with a firm, "Meet me downstairs."

The night was long and it needed to be filled.

David came through the kitchen door all bundled up in his tweed coat and a silly pull on hat with fur around it. Like a Russian commissar.

"We're going for a walk, David?" I said, trying to sound steady. I looked up at his face, grizzled now at the end of the day. He was concentrating on the task at hand, getting out the door, accomplishing his next indicated action.

"Thank you for telling me your story. About your Delly." David stopped and looked at me, slightly embarrassed. Like I had revealed a truth from the Confessional. Once again, the spark of connection sputtered, almost making it over the synapse but falling just shy.

"It's alright. I won't touch you. Unless you fall. I'll pick you up. I won't leave you in the snow. And neither of us is sleeping. Put on your coat." he said resolutely.

I grabbed Eddie's large parka from the kitchen hook. He had gloves and a hat in the pocket and they would suffice.

David opened the door to the kitchen. The night was clear above the gobs of cotton flakes that were showering from the sky. Wherever I looked, edges were softened by fragile white contours. My car had mounds on the roof, the boulders along the gravel road were becoming marshmallow. The porch light on Toby's cabin, splintered into a solstice light, beckoned us forward.

"Come on. I want to show you something."

David set off across the field. We left tracks in the snow. There was a small little road that followed the woods on the far side of the farm and David trudged, puffing steam. He didn't try to speak. He glanced at me only once or twice, keeping track of my progress, I thought, by the sound of my footfalls against the quickly disappearing gravel.

David turned off onto a small trail. He turned on the flashlight on his phone. It was very dark, the darkness forcing movement along the small wire of light. I did not enjoy the closing of the trees behind me, or the way the canopy of sky disappeared a few steps in.

David pushed aside a fallen branch. He shone his light into a patch of trees and there, he stopped, letting the light flick along sticks and pine needles. And then, the beam of his small flashlight hit the glint of a glassy eye. He kept it there, focusing my attention on the head of a large deer that had fallen in the trees.

"I found this yesterday. Before I met you at the restaurant." I looked at the fallen animal, his rack of antlers caught in pine boughs. "I found this," David said. "There were birds circling, and I could feel the small animals sniffing the scent of its death. I stood here a long time. I sat here. Look, see?" He shone his light on a log that had been cleared of branches. "I sat here a long time." The log sat at the base of a very tall tree. I looked up but wasn't sure if it was a maple.

"He's beautiful," is all I could say. It was the same buck in my dream. He was caught and down. "My God, he's so beautiful." My head started spinning. The glassy eyes of the fallen animal found me as I stood there. They knew me. They had seen me before, shied from me in the dream. Remembered stumbling, remembered retreat.

"David, my God. I dreamed about this animal. I dreamed about him. How hard it was for him. How he got tangled in the woods." David did not react to my words. He was lost in his own reverie. He bent down to touch the head of the animal.

"Oh, don't do that! Why would you do that?" I asked.

He left his hand on the muzzle of the animal, his thumb moving gently up and down to invigorate the fur.

"He may feel the kindness."

I stepped back. "Yes. Of course.

"Is this how it happens? With dumb surprise?" David looked up at me.

"I don't know, David." And I didn't really, though the fallen animal so close to the bulk of David's body almost melded with him.

"Look," David said, as he pushed aside some brush. "Look, here?" He kicked at some brush and the accumulating snow. "There's a trap. He stumbled into a trap. It snapped his leg."

The deer's front leg was snapped almost in two. David or someone, must have covered up the wound with branches earlier in the day.

"It's a fucking shame." David finally looked up at me. "God's trick."

He shook his head. I noticed his forehead was sweaty from the effort of slogging into the forest all bundled up. He turned his flash light beam back to the trail. I followed him out of the woods and onto the road. By now the moon was high and I could see through the snow, still falling. It was covering our tracks, the buck in place, probably above sound—if someone was to howl.

David walked in step with me. Deliberately. Neither of us spoke.

I couldn't go back inside. I was larger than space, than the man I stood with, than the buck lying dead. I was closer to the canopy of stars and the white snow falling, falling from above. I stopped and stood gazing up at the sky, letting the snow melt on my cheeks.

I remembered going to the mountains in California. The snow was warm there. I remembered how we played in it without winter clothes. How Jordan made his first snow angel.

"Annie!" I heard him call my name. "Annie! Are you alright?"

"Yes, of course." I was jolted back to the moment we shared.

He grabbed at my arm, and I pushed him. He startled me. He stumbled. There was no ease in his fall, no referencing of the night sky, no release of worldly woes. He was alarmed and then he fell, lying on the ground like a sparking telephone pole. His arms shorting wires, his legs bent and misshapen. His face framed in white light.

David flipped to all fours and pushed himself back up to standing with enormous effort. He turned to me, and let his head come toward my face. There was a small cut above his eyebrow. A little one, like the blooming of an idea. I thought he was going to kiss me but he bypassed my face and headed to my neck, balancing his weight on my shoulder. Holding my body for stability. He was breathing heavily.

"David. David, are you okay? I didn't mean to push you. I was just startled."

He pulled himself back and away from me and held my shoulders, held me at arm's length. "I'm going to kiss you, Annie. I am going to kiss you now."

It felt like a check off item on a to do list. And then he leaned in, his weight rebalanced, and he gently kissed me on the cheek. As I stood still, receiving him, offering no resistance, he moved to my mouth and put his lips against it. I could taste the snow. I could smell the sweat that poured down his face. I could feel his effort to find more than touch in this act, but it ended with that. A movement of skin to skin and nothing else.

That night I dreamt of the large wounded stag in the middle of the farm field. As it raised its head to the moon light, the moon beams struck it's nuzzle and the large stag fell like a cascading set of blocks into the field. First one leg bent and then the others, his muzzle hit the land and his large rack of horns was last to fall, crashing into the earth, shattering, sending dust to cover its demise. David falling into a drift of dusty snow.

Chapter 44

Transition in the Snow

When I rose a few hours later, I saw, from my window, the snow continue to fall. The sun crept up and revealed the sky, still wringing its hands, cleaning its closets. It did not seem to be finished. I dressed and came downstairs to take my coffee out to the porch and watch as it buried and cleansed the world, drifted and leaned into corners that probably appreciated the attention. I wondered if David would come down and we could watch it together.

David did not come down to breakfast. Or for the morning session. I tried to ignore it, allowing David the dignity of privacy if he chose it. His company helped last night. It flung me out of myself and into something larger. The image of the deer on the forest floor loomed large.

It was Mallory who came shooting into the dining room at the coffee break.

"Annie. Come. Annie."

She brought me upstairs. I entered the open bedroom across from mine and there was David, lying in all his majesty, with his eyes closed, his hands folded over his chest. His face a slight shade of grey green.

"Mallory, he's gone. My God." I looked at my friend, standing beside me.

"I knocked and knocked. Toby's cleaning people needed access. I told them to use their key," she said, grim but practical. "I'll call 911. There must be local police with ambulances up here. With the storm it may take some time."

I nodded and she left me with a squeeze and a pause to ask, "You okay?"

I nodded. "Yes."

"Good, I'll tell the others you'll be down in a bit."

When Mallory left, I quietly walked around David's room. He had nicely folded his clothing from the day before. Always meticulous, his toiletries were laid out as if his valet had been there to prepare the room for visitors. I approached the bed cautiously. The room was cotton. I was the only electrical frequency buzzing. I thought it better to leave him. But I was drawn to his bedside. I couldn't stand looking down at him. I brought the chair, the cane chair from the hallway, into the room. I positioned it by his bed so I could feel the clear white light of the storm. I could not sit but could not leave. I went to the window and lifted it a crack to brush away the small ledge of snow that was lining the sill. It was cold on my fingers. I brought those fingers to my lips.

"David. Are you there? Can you hear me?" I whispered. Woefully inadequate these words, worse than the bludgeoned imbalance of recent death. I closed my eyes picturing the stag in the field, opened them to see the overgrown jaw now slack, the large eyes shut easily and noting the perfect relaxation that he finally enjoyed.

I looked out the window and wondered if I should cry. If I would cry. And only realized when I felt the moisture of tears slipping off my chin, that the decision had been made.

Chapter 45

Mallory Makes an Announcement

"It seems David is lying upstairs, dead, everyone. How about that?" Mallory said, straight faced and even a bit more glibly than she had planned.

I heard her as I came down the stairs. I had carefully closed David's door. The room had grown close. Even the cool breeze seemed unable to penetrate the transitioning energies.

They were sitting in the study room. All of them I thought, except David, of course.

Ken looked up at Mallory as if she was crazy. Then, turned to me. "Annie? Is Mallory telling the truth?"

"I'm afraid she is," I said.

"Why would I not tell the truth, Kenny. For God's sake, my humor is not that macabre."

"You don't know what you are saying!" Ken was having trouble. He looked back over his shoulder, feeling the presence of his dead wife, who had lain in such a bed, and who now watched from the spirit world to see how her husband would handle this passing. She had appreciated Ken's devotion at her end of time on the planet, but even in her devolution she did not trust him. He wanted to do this right.

"He's lying upstairs? Is there a hospice person? No? Has someone called someone?"

"I called 911," Mallory said. "The connection was scratchy and they routed me to Burlington. The snow has made all local rescues delayed."

Eddie stood immediately. "I think we can get to the Village. They'll have a fire crew. Someone. I'll try to get to the Village." And he headed to the kitchen to consult with Toby.

Knauta spread her eyes over the assembled, looking for cracks, seeing where she might be needed. "Anita?" she called to the other room. No answer. Out the window Anita trudged through drifts of snow. She was sitting on a round ball that she had rolled, her face up to the wind. Knauta sat quietly, holding space for Ken, for Mallory, for very quiet Amanda. Waiting for their next moves.

"Jesus," Ken said. "Jesus. Jesus." He shook his head, dropping his armor. "Jesus, I'm so rattled. I didn't even know the guy." He looked up at Mallory. "Mal, someone has to sit with him. He shouldn't be left."

Her armor was in place. "Well, I can tell you he's nowhere near this planet. The man was green as a salamander. Yes, Annie?" The group turned to look at me and give Mallory a chance to calibrate her own response, which was erratic and unclear. She was confused by Ken's reaction and a little scared. "I'm going to check on the cleaning person. She was pretty freaked out. Did you see where she went?" she said.

"I saw her trooping out to Toby's cabin." Knauta responded.

Mallory turned to leave and started out to the kitchen.

We could hear her giving orders to Eddie and Toby as they gathered themselves to head to the Village.

"Take a lunch. Some food. You have a backpack, boys?" Mallory insisted.

We heard Eddie's thin reedy voice. It pierced the air like catgut being stretched. Like catgut with no elegance.

"We're fine, Mallory," he said, impatiently.

"Yes, I suppose you are. How fun to be planning a snow picnic when that odd lump of a man is moldering in that bed above us all." Mallory was becoming brittle. I heard it, Knauta heard it.

"Mallory!" Knauta called. "Come back and sit with us, or go see that girl. Leave the boys alone."

There was silence in response. We could see her threading through the small path that Toby had shoveled from his cabin to the main house. We could see the other path that had been carved from his house to the road. We could see the boys, snowshoes strapped to their boots, backpacks with supplies, heading to alert someone in the village.

I was trying hard to find balance and looked from Knauta to Kenny, to Knauta again.

"Sit down, dear," she said.

I looked to the ceiling above me and could finally feel the magnitude of the shift.

Of the loss of balance. David was a big presence. I could feel him tumbling through the roof at me. I looked up again and then stood in the middle of the room, terrified.

Kenny got up and took my hand. He knew about this. He was finding ground now that he had a job.

"Here," he said kindly. "Your eyes are like saucers. Breathe a little, yes?" He took my hand and led me to the seat on the couch next to him. I couldn't stop staring up at the ceiling.

"When I was in India," I said. "They said to understand was to stand under, which was to look up." Kenny held my hand. He made sure I stayed on the couch. I didn't levitate up to the ceiling and through the ceiling and into the bed with the dead man who I had not meant to hurt.

"We took a walk last night. I dreamed of him falling. He tried to kiss me."

"That's a good thing." Knauta said.

I looked at her. "It was skin to skin, Knauta. Little else. So sad."

"Controlled," Knauta said. "Able to navigate his path."

"He told me that the boy, the son of the woman he lived with for a year, that boy committed suicide. He understood sadness. That sadness. He wanted me to know that."

"And you know that. Yes? You get to hold that, his story, for him now."

From the other side of the room, in the armchair by the window, Amanda, who had been sitting quietly this whole time, finally stirred.

"I'll find some candles."

Knauta and I watched her move into action. We both knew her story. We knew she had been here before. She felt this when she reported to jail. When she dropped her purse and keys on the front seat of her mother's car and walked into the State Prison with her brother, Richie. The one who eventually figured how to get her out of there. And then, giving up her clothes. And then having to walk in front of the officer all the time so she could be watched. And feeling the stripping of sympathy as the other inmates watched her at her first dinner. And, the first shower call, at the first yoga class, at the first night in her solitary cell. She knew emptiness. It was like a death.

"Do you have candles?" she turned to Ken. "Do you know where Toby keeps them?"

"In the cabinet. Yes. I think so. Candles, there."

He pointed to the cupboard in the big room and she crossed and carefully selected four of the glasses with wax inside that had been waiting on the lower shelves. The ones from the Botanica that someone had brought with them, thinking the images of Mother Mary, and the Saints were just pretty decoration. That blue was a good color. And so was yellow. And the other white ones were to make everyone else happy.

She took matches, she took platters, she took a bowl of water, she took a kitchen towel and she walked up the stairs. I got up and followed her.

Chapter 46

Amanda Takes Charge

"I'm going to open the door now, Annie. Yes? You ready?"

"Of course," I nodded, mystified at her presence, comforted by her control.

We went in and David was still there. His head had fallen to the side at an odd angle. I went to sit in the chair by the bed and Amanda went to the other side of the bed and righted David's head. She took the comb he had laid out on his dresser and ran it through his grey hair. Pulling it back, getting him ready for his next appointment. Then, she straightened the sheets and made sure the coverlet was smooth, holding David with some kind of respect.

I thought of Snow White in her coffin, of Mao Tse-tung under glass, of my own husband when they let me back into the emergency room cubicle after they pronounced him gone. None of these images helped or fit. I was simply watching as my brain was attempting context and comfort.

While Amanda worked I told her, "We went for a walk last night. It was late and snowy. He came too close and I pushed him aside. He fell in the snow. He was awkward and trying to find his balance. He held onto my shoulders for balance."

Amanda said, "I think we should bless the room."

"There's no phone or Wi-Fi. The snow is very deep out there. The kids are going for help. In snowshoes. Like a Jack London novel."

"Some traditions like to wash the body, but I'm not going there." Amanda looked up at me and I could not make sense of what she was saying. The idea of seeing David naked and inert was unfathomable to her. I realized I had never fantasized about what he might look like naked. Though he was trim. And he probably would have looked fine for a man of his age.

"I'm going to bless the room, Annie." She interrupted my reverie and I was glad of it.

"Yes. Good."

"And then maybe we can leave David here and he'll be alright 'til we get help."

"Look," I showed her a cut on David's temple. "Do you think I caused that? Do you think they will think that I caused that. His heart to break? To stop? Do you?"

Amanda had a flash she could not verbalize. It was something about the absurdity of changing nature, of how the tectonic plates of a moment seem so clear in one moment and then the timeline shifts and we are somewhere else completely.

"Annie. You didn't hurt him."

"Right. Who says I have that power?"

"Come on, Annie. I will stay with him for a while. You go downstairs. Mallory and Kenny are at loose ends. They'll want company. So will you." She saw the loneliness in my eyes. I was carrying it for him now, it seemed.

"We won't leave him." she said. "We'll take turns."

"I'm to sit in the conservatory with Colonel Mustard and Miss Scarlett with the wrench? And wait for the inspector?"

"Annie. You're not making sense. Go downstairs."

I looked at Amanda and saw a blur. I put my hand back on the windowsill and grabbed a handful of snow and put it on my forehead. I offered my hand to Amanda who waved me off.

"Go away now."

I took my chair and sat outside the room while Amanda worked. She opened the windows a bit more but found it hard to turn her back on David. She turned on a bedside lamp even though it was eleven in the morning. She turned and saw that large rocky man turning into green cheese before her.

"Annie. Should I pull the sheet over his head?" Then, answered her own question with a shake of her head. Instead she lit the two candles. The white ones and set them on the desk at the foot of the bed. She arranged the plates beneath them so they would not burn the desk. Then she turned and spoke to him like I had done.

"David? Should I leave a candle at your head? Like in the Gothic mysteries?" He didn't answer. She was trying to be business-like and she felt her own experience of solitude begin to cone her and protect the moment. As she stood there looking at him, I could see her gather her separation and safety. *That was the feeling she was counting on*, I thought. That safety in solitude that she had cultivated and made obedient to her in her years alone.

"I will leave the candle outside on the table. And Annie is sitting outside. You aren't alone." She turned to go, but stopped to say.

"I am sorry I didn't know you. I imagine you frightened yourself as much as everyone else." She turned back. "I want you to know that had you decided to stay on the earth, I would have found a way to tell you that prison is not all bad. I don't think you ever got that one."

Amanda turned and left the room. She closed the door. She lit a candle and put it on the hall table next to me. Then went down the stairs.

Inside, David did not move. Outside, I sat quietly, next to the flickering candles.

Chapter 47

Vigil

I sat at his door for a long time. Amanda came back up with a large, snowy bough of a pine tree she had found. It's freshness filled the hallway, clearing it and offering an alternative to death "I'll put this at the foot of the bed. Like an offering, " she smiled. "Why not? We're making it up as we go along."

She opened the door of David's room and went in. I acknowledged her with a faint smile. I had returned to myself sitting there. Maybe David released me. I closed my eyes more than once and sat in meditation. Thanking him for friendship. Allowing the cocoon of silence to protect us both. Grateful for a muscle that seemed to kick on when I allowed myself to be still and in the present moment. I am not saying that Jordan's face did not swim into my mind eye, or even Ty. I am not saying that I was at peace but I was able to get hold of myself again. Ingest the strength of Amanda's gesture, and the way in which she was operating, fully conscious, from the strength she had clearly won in confronting herself.

"I'll take a turn now, Annie. You go downstairs. Mallory is making some kind of lunch. And there's cocoa, I think."

"Any sign of the kids? Will they bring the police? Will they find someone to help?" I asked Kenny who was doing a crossword puzzle while he waited.

"Not yet. They'll be back soon."

"Where's Knauta?"

"She went back to her room. Anita is in from the snow. They're resting I think."

Mallory came to the doorway with a tray of sandwiches, a pot of cocoa, a bottle of scotch. "Here's food, Annie. I put up a vegetable soup for later."

Out the window we could see two figures wrapped in brown blankets approach the back door.

"It's the monks," Mallory said. "They are back from the Center. They called to say they shoveled out the walks and were heading back. I told them about David."

The young men entered the kitchen, and bowed silently to Mallory who greeted them.

"There's food for you," she said to them.

They nodded and took a sandwich and sat at the kitchen table apart from us, making tea and warming themselves. They remained silent. On a mission. I marveled at their composure and how they kept themselves to themselves as they showed up, fully present. After food, they rose and took their plates to the sink where they washed them. And then disappeared.

Mallory watched them go, and then came back in to us with a plate of cookies she had just made.

I took a cup and filled it with the warm cocoa, and added a shot of scotch that was also on the kitchen tray. I took a cookie and settled in the large armchair that usually was filled with Knauta. Mallory could not sit. She added a shot of scotch to her own cup, which she carried as she moved around. She fussed with the tray. Dusted the table. Went to the bookshelf and took down a few volumes.

"Here, Annie. Here's Mary Oliver for you." She said as she handed me a slim volume.

"How about St. James Bible for you, Ken? You can read psalms aloud." She slapped him with that. "Ah, and the Tibetan Book of the Dead, that should be enlightening!" she said as she tossed the volume over to the couch.

"Mal. Come sit. Enough." Kenny said.

She looked up sharply. "I don't like to sit around waiting for someone to pick up dead bodies, Ken. You might remember that."

He reached out his hand to her and she came to the couch and sat down. Bible in hand.

"I hate this," she said. "I hate it."

Ken turned to me. "Mallory's mom died on her watch. Right, Mal? You sat with her the whole night 'til someone could come."

Mallory was not pleased he had chosen to include me in their circle.

"That was forever ago. She was a miserable drunk. She didn't deserve a witness."

He put his arm around her even though she sat straight and refused to sink into his embrace. "Goddammit," she said quietly.

We stayed quiet then. The room was full. It was slowing down. Mallory took a deep breath and sat back against the pillows. Against Ken. She took another slug of scotch. I opened the book of poems and looked up when I heard the voices of two men and a young woman chanting from upstairs. The monks were bearing witness. Amanda sang from her own perch.

It was settling. We were finding our way. Somewhere the boys hiked homeward or awaited the snowplow to bring out the ambulance. We sipped cocoa and scotch, let voices rise, taking comfort from those still on this side of the divide.

I could feel David's spirit approach us, curious at the open field we held for his departure. I could feel him grateful. I could feel him settle next to me. I sat up a bit straighter but I did not repel him. I did not force him to be alone just then.

Chapter 48

Waiting

I remember the snow as larger than the house. I remember the ice cave the boys built the day after they returned from the village. It would take the ambulance another day to make it through the roads. A tree had fallen about a mile from the house blocking the way. After a good meal, the two young men were restless with the holding energy that surrounded us. They went outside and built a snow cave. Maybe they thought they could put David's body in the snow to preserve it. Everyone stayed to themselves and their own cocoons during the two days we waited for someone to remove his body. Amanda replaced the candles upstairs when needed. And the two monks stayed near David's room, meditating and bearing witness.

We each took walks, but rarely together, as if the sound of our communal voice would disturb the sanctity of this transition place. Ken and Mallory disappeared into his RV and I don't remember seeing them much. Knauta and Anita watched television in their suite. Eddie, Amanda and Toby spent most of their time in Toby's cottage playing Scrabble, I think.

I was left in the house. To rest, think. Keep David's ghost company.

The landline rang a couple of times. The fire house called to say the lines were back up and that the roads to us would be cleared soon. They expected an emergency crew to reach us by nightfall. The second night after his death. And Shamana called. I answered and she recognized my voice.

"Annie? It's Shamana. Shana. Shana Goldstein," she said clearly. "How are you?"

I had forgotten that she was supposed to come up to be with us.

"Shana? Hello." Her voice was strong and she was no longer coy. There was a hint of the directness of her mother. "Did you want to speak to Eddie?"

"Actually no. I told him I was not coming. But I wanted to thank you for the offer of a possible job."

"That's fine, Shamana. Shana. It would have been good to see you again."

She paused a bit. "Maybe. I'm going to Mississippi." She announced this, rather than stating it and I knew I was being given notice of a new direction.

"Yes?"

"A man was killed in Mississippi. A Black man. He was the cousin of my high school friend in Chicago. He had a stroke and was just sitting in his car and the police pulled him out and roughed him up and he just died. And there's a march. And I am going. I am going to go down there and be with his family. They asked me to come and bear witness and I am going to go. And I am going to stay there. And help."

"That's good, Shamana."

Shana sighed. "They're killing us. The government, the white supremacists. I mean, if I am a Jew or if I am Black. They're killing us and me pretending to be someone else isn't going to stop that. It's more important than making gourmet gazpacho, you know?"

"Yes, Shana. I understand. I will tell Eddie. He will wish you well."

"I don't know about that. But I can't stand it, not knowing who I am, who any of us are."

Her tone was almost anguished. "This country is fucked. I have to do something!"

I smiled. "I have had that feeling myself, Shana. Good for you."

"Yes, okay."

"Please give my regards to your mother," I said.

Shana laughed. "Oh yeah, you guys bonded over your fucked up kids, I heard."

"I don't know about that."

"Is it pretty in Vermont?" she sounded almost wistful.

"We've had a blizzard, and there has been a change of plans. Nothing is as it seems . . ."

"Skim milk masquerades as cream," she responded. "Tell Eddie I'm sorry."

And she hung up.

I looked out the window at the afternoon light off the snow. Heard the low growl of another chanting cycle upstairs. Lit another candle to set in the window. And saw the reflection of a red light coming up the newly plowed drive.

Chapter 49

Back to Life

The group left Vermont soon after David was taken away. The ambulance crew gave me David's wallet before they left to take to the local

hospital, writing down contact with next of kin. I found a small photograph of a Black woman and a young boy. This must have been Georgia. And Delly, when he was a young one. There was an address written on the back of the card. I placed it back in the billfold.

Was that my responsibility?

"Well," Knauta said as I asked her that question a month later in her living room. "I don't think so, but it's your decision, of course."

I tucked the card away.

I had enough to keep me busy, I kept saying. I had been in touch with the embassy to see if they had word of Jordan. Nothing. The windy hallway of his absence loomed.

Months passed, Anita and Knauta left for Austria. Mallory, Amanda and I made dinner for them before they went.

"Catch me up on all the news," said Knauta, after a couple of glasses of wine. "I want to know everything before I head off to my new life and forget you all!"

"I'm moving in with Eddie," Amanda chirped, a little red faced. She was on her second glass of wine as well.

"Wow! When did that happen?" I said. "Why didn't you tell me?!

"We've been meaning to but, you know. Eddie is working on new job applications, I'm busy at the library. And now I'm shipping all of Anita and Knauta's things for them!"

"Yes, yes, well, congratulations! My goodness. That's great news!" I said, taken aback.

"We'll have you over when we get our new place!" she said, throwing me a bone.

"It will be fully furnished," Knauta said. "Just take all the furniture. No need to sell it!"

"We don't have a place yet!" Amanda cried. She looked flushed and happy with all her plans. "It's all happening so quickly! We may move to the country. Get a house in Western Mass! I'm looking at new jobs out there. Eddie wants to be closer to Amherst and Emily Dickinson land."

Knauta piped up, "There was an amazing little bird! I've always loved her poetry"

"Eddie is up for a job with the House. And could teach some adjunct classes near by. It would be such a dreamy change for us both! And, of course, we have a house full of furniture, thanks to you guys!" Amanda smiled at Knauta and Anita. She was animated by the new beginning but there was something more in her energy. This was a big deal for her. Normalcy after a very tough time. I could give her that.

I was surprised to feel as stunned by this news as I was. Eddie had always kept in touch but since the workshop in Vermont and the start of the serious relationship with Amanda, he had pulled back. They both had.

Mallory was watching me closely. As we cleared dishes and stacked them in Knauta's sink, she squeezed me. "Sorry, you're feeling a bit isolated, my friend. I can see that."

"Oh, no. It's fine." I said, not at all fine. Mallory waited.

"It's just . . . since Vermont, things have shifted. Eddie and Amanda have been busy. I see that now. And you are up there in Vermont. Busy with the new meditation center."

"And living at Toby's. Well, living with Ken and Toby. Ken will stay and help with the lodge. It made sense to be with them. Him." She stopped and wondered how to describe what she was feeling. "I appreciate being with people who know me. From before. A long time. I don't have to explain myself. Or fling myself so desperately at the world with wild abandon. I feel lucky. There's a place for me to be. And a person who is willing to let me be there."

"You know how great I think that is, Mallory." I shook my head.

"Yes. It was getting pretty exhausting being me on my own. I am happy to have the beauty of the countryside, and friendship, and a sleeping partner. I have people with whom to share breakfast and who will actually eat a plate of cookies if I leave them on the counter. I never thought I would have that luxury."

Her words moved me. I didn't realize how much I wanted the same thing. The simplicity of being somewhere you belonged, mutual bonds, mutual concern and care. I had been trying for that but one by one, the distractions of my students, their lives, their stories, the details of earning a living had pulled me away from the central ache in my life.

The party was breaking up in the other room. "Bye, Annie!" I heard Amanda call from the living room. And then, Knauta and Anita sending her off. And then Knauta, "Turn on the eleven o'clock news. Let's see how much closer we are to Armageddon." The click of the remote, the murmur of the television, the slight noise of Anita gathering more plates, throwing away wine bottles.

"That fucking bastard," we heard Knauta scream at the television. "Anita, can you believe it? When will someone in the Republican Party grow some balls and stop this bastard?"

"Shh, Knauta. We are leaving the country!" We heard Anita answer.

"Not a moment too soon! Come here. Sit with me. Listen to this!" And Anita ceased her busy work while CNN droned in the background.

I turned to Mallory. "The night before David died, he sat outside my door telling me how he had no way to hold the sadness of the suicide of his son. I just lay there and listened to him."

"And then you went for a walk with him. I remember."

"It was because I understood him. How he couldn't hold such random events. How his love for that boy did absolutely no good when it came to the boy's fate."

Mallory started to put the dishes into soapy water. "Have you heard anything more?"

"The embassy has no word. They are searching prison records now to see if he has been incarcerated. But the system is very tight. And I'm not so sure they are concerned about tracking someone who might have been involved in murder."

Mallory shook the plates after she rinsed them and set them on the sideboard. She took a deep breath and then said simply and directly,

"Sorry, Annie, but in the end it's not yours anymore. He has made his own choices and gone down his own road. It's just that you want something from him that's the problem. You want him to love you or include you somehow. The kid sounds so lost in his own labyrinth he has not an inch for you."

I looked up at her. "Is that true? Nothing left for me?"

"Nope," she said, soapy and busy.

"Mallory, forgive me but you've never had a child."

"No, but I've been a child. And I'll tell you, my mother and her problems did nothing but fuck me up. Okay, I am happy to have compassion but at a distance, a very far distance. You have to change your story, Annie. This story, the one where you're a perfect mother, misunderstood by an errant son who turns around and loves you in the end. That story is not happening."

I was quiet after that. Maybe she was right. Maybe there would be no end, no easy way to tie up the loose ends of loving. I picked up a dish and carefully wiped the dish towel against it. Knauta was leaning in the doorway, Anita behind her.

"That's a little tough, Mallory. Even if you're right." Knauta said. She extended her arms to a big embrace. "Put down the dishes, girls! Please go home! Anita and I are sleepy and getting ready to get out of Dodge." We all came together with arms extended. The circle was as closed as it could be at that time. Everything is approximate.

Chapter 50

Cape Again with News

It was quiet after that. Mallory dropped me a line from Vermont. It was getting into their high season so they were busy with the Lodge and the retreats she was organizing at the Center. Eddie and Amanda moved out to Amherst and were setting up their life there. They were excited to come out to the Cape for the last weekend and I looked forward to that. No word about Jordan. Through spring and early summer I remained in Boston, teaching classes, a summer school seminar at a local community college. And, then it was time to head to the Cape again.

I arrived with my car full of groceries and good intentions. I vowed to read good books, eat good food and leave the world behind. The days were warm and I started them as late as I could manage, rarely rising before the fog left the beach. The nights surprised me. The nights were easier. But, the morning news still showed up on my door.

The radio reported on the killing spree of two young men in British Columbia. It seems there was a robbery that got out of hand. The boys fled and were found dead, by their own guns, a week later. The father of one of them had predicted that. "Oh, he'll go out in a blaze of glory," the news reports offered. And so it was true. The boys killed themselves and left a recorded confession of their crimes at their death scene.

I thought of that mother, not surprisingly, unquoted. What does a mother say about such things? Such losses. I remembered seeing that TED Talk with the mother of the Columbine shooter, and how she lived with her guilt and trauma and anxiety every day of her life. How she reframed her son's act as a murder-suicide so she could properly include herself in the paradigm of grief as well as guilt. Her enormous regret was excruciating.

The end of the first week I received the email from the embassy. I was asked to call a Laurence Backman. He was a young man, from his voice.

"Ms. Simon. Glad we are able to connect. I have news for you."

And he proceeded to explain how Jordan was in custody and had been since soon after we heard from him in January of last year. He was not being charged with murder, as far as Laurence knew, but rather that he had been arrested and detained because of his connection with the murder attack in Tokyo.

"Yes. I understand he owned the car. But was he there that day?" I asked, failing to believe that my voice was masking my terror.

"As far as we know, they are investigating him as an accessory but we have sent a lawyer to the prison to follow up and we hope to have more news soon. I must warn you, the Japanese penal system can be very rigid. They won't allow visitors so I don't suggest that you fly there. They can hold him as long as a year, even with no charges. There is little we can do."

I searched for that TED Talk again and watched the tortured mother of Dylan Klebold try to make peace with her responsibility and her right to a guiltless conscience. She could not find it. It was painful to see the strain she hefted in getting her words off the index cards she held and into the camera. That was all she could do. Acknowledge she was still alive and standing, and making an effort to live. That was it.

At least she had it worse than I did. Jordan had not committed murder, though he was being held in relation to one. An accessory, flirting with giving permission for the murderer, to take out his fury on another human.

My thinking was circular, fiery and continuous. It rattled me behind bars, twisted me around barbed wire. I started spinning from the moment I hung up with young Lawrence Backman—he turned out okay, didn't he? Did his parents comfort him when he cried?—through everything I did. Even walking the grocery store aisle, feeling the refrigerated air on my arms, all I saw were bars across windows. The metal of the shopping chart bumping against others when shoved back in place, reminded me of the clanging of metal doors. My scuffling feet felt shackled.

Jordan's situation was another part of what we were all trying to figure out, what the world writ large, was trying to find out. He was searching for some way to make a dent in his world and couldn't find it.

Eddie and Amanda finally arrived. He looked tired, she looked rosy. Small talk and finding the right pillows for the bed consumed us for a while. I kept wondering if they could see me altered, carrying this news about Jordan, bowing under its weight. But they had their own baggage. They were not looking closely.

I could hear Eddie shoving the metal bed to the other side of the room so they could look out the side cabin window. I guess his memories of sex with Shamana, under a different moon, needed adjusting. I served dinner, moving carefully. Avoiding loud noises, ignoring doors closing, chairs scraping. We floated on faux laughter and self-conscious glances from one to the other. Each sore with our burdens. When Amanda refused to finish her first glass of wine, and Eddie grabbed his third beer, I knew they had finally landed enough to have a conversation.

"Amherst is good?" I said. "A big change I imagine."

Eddie blinked and looked up. "Yes. I am teaching. That's great. I am working at the Dickinson house. That's great."

Amanda continued, "I am up for a job at the Amherst library. That's great. And I'm pregnant." She grinned at me with all her teeth. I wasn't sure if she was showing happiness or the grimace of a tiger protecting her young.

Eddie took a pause and then a forced grin and said, "And that's great, too!"

My head whipped around to find Eddie's eyes. The pupils had constricted and looked tiny and tight. Amanda said nothing, pulling her T-shirt down, self conscious already with the way she was filling it out.

"A baby? Really? Now? My goodness. Are you ready?"

Amanda now got me in her sights. "There is no way I am having an abortion. There is no way I am giving away this baby. This is mine. I have earned this child. And she will be mine if Eddie doesn't want her."

I looked over at Eddie. "I never said I didn't want this baby," he said. "I just said it's complicated now. It's early. We don't even know if . . ."

"I'm almost in my second trimester. I am carrying to term. This child is heading from heaven right to my lap!" The wine had given her a wacky ease that combined with her hormone load, was serving her up as a hearty stew of maternal desire. I felt like her breasts might start dripping at any moment.

"Wow," I said. "A new baby. That's something."

"We're not getting married, Annie. If that's what you're thinking," she said, simmering.

"No," Eddie quickly agreed. "No, we'll live together for now and until the baby comes and if it doesn't work out, we'll co-parent somehow and we'll make it work."

"Right. I am not getting an abortion. Everything is fine." Amanda said it again, like a mantra, and then she clamped her lips shut, willing them to contain her desire.

There was silence then and I tried to smile and push away from the table and grab a plate for the sink. *Conjuring a child?* I thought. *Did they really mean to conjure a child?*

"I'll do the dishes, Annie. You talk to your nephew. I think we're tired of talking to each other." Amanda was resolute.

Eddie laughed. "Oh, that's not true." Amanda laughed but she still got up to clear the table and head to the sink.

I poured another glass of wine, settling my own simmering pot and waited for Eddie to speak. We could feel the airplane diving. "What have you been doing out here all by yourself? Have you had a good time?" he asked, gamely.

"Sure," I said. My eyes steady.

I tried to pull up from the dive, imagining Eddie overwhelmed with a new baby, a new relationship, a new career. All that weight made it tough.

"Happy?" I asked him, with a forced smile.

"We're taking it one day at a time," he said. And Amanda wheeled back around from the sink.

"I told you, Eddie. You don't have to be part of this. I told you that!" She was armed and ready for combat. The wine had tipped her resolve into fury. "I deserve this chance! I'm not abandoning another child as long as I live!"

"I didn't know we were talking about a landscape of littered children, Amanda." Eddie responded. I hadn't seen him in this mode. The intellectual, cynical warrior.

"Hang on," I said. "You guys might want to settle this without me sitting in the room?" I offered.

"You can stay, Annie. You have a child. You know how important Jordan is to you." Amanda threw over her shoulder at me.

I took a beat. "He has enough trouble of his own making without me putting all my hopes and dreams onto his back. You want this baby to solve all your problems?" I said.

Amanda was quick to take up the fight. "Just because your kid decided to go off crazy and violent doesn't mean all kids will. All kids do!"

"Don't, Amanda," Eddie said, ready to protect me.

I stepped back, took a breath. "I'm just saying it's not always so easy. I'm sure your mother hadn't planned on having to mother you through your time in prison. How does a mother do that? How do you know she didn't try?" I said.

"My mother is a wimp. She says she loves me but backs off when I'm caught up in something I had no control over. Her own feelings are more important than helping me out. So be it. I'm a grown up and I'll do my own clean up."

"You don't know the first thing about it, Amanda. Really! You just don't know!"

Amanda was stunned by my rebuke but before she could answer, Eddie spoke up.

"On the back of our baby? Your own clean up? That's so not fair!" Eddie spoke up, like this just occurred to him. Like he finally put a finger on why the conception of this child was out of joint.

Amanda turned, stunned. "You think I got pregnant to make a point? To make my kid pay for the shit that I went through?"

"Our kid!" he thundered. She stopped. He went on. "I don't know what I think, Amanda!" He shook his head and spoke quietly, firmly. "This baby is an accident!" Amanda was struck by that, but Eddie went on. I'd never seen him so cracked open. "This baby carries the mistakes of you and me. Is it fair to ask this baby to come in with that legacy? And then heal you to boot? Jesus Christ, that's a whole hell of a lot."

The room was silent then. Very silent. Thick and steamy and a conjure pot of the so many souls that had come before all of us. The ones that had come in as people and the ones who had stayed hidden and now floated next to us as sparks of memory tucked into the back of the dusty bookshelves that lined the room.

"The night Jordan was conceived, Ty and I had had a huge fight," I said. "Mostly we fought because when we met, it was like falling into a fire pit. When you try to drink fire, you are consumed. That was what our love affair was like. It was like fire. And we couldn't get enough. But, nobody can live at that temperature.

When we married, we tamed ourselves into eating breakfast and going to work and doing the laundry, but we would sometimes flare at the strangest time. We would fight like hell, pissed at being domesticated by our marriage. Pissed that we could never satisfy each other. Or ourselves. That we had surrendered to just living our lives like everybody else.

But, that night, we made love with a fury and a contempt for all the compromises we had made. And, that was the night Jordan was conceived. Jordan was conceived, as a panacea for our shortcomings." I looked up at them. "He was made from the stew of who we could never be. How can a kid ever feel they are enough with that kind of legacy?"

They didn't respond. I didn't expect them to.

"Jordan's been in prison since January. They don't know when he will get out. I heard from the Embassy a week ago." I didn't look at them, but they heard me. "Sometimes I feel like Joan of Arc's mother. Or maybe her father, because her mother could not watch the flames licking at her child's body. But like her father, then, watching the flames, licking and sizzling his child's flesh and having nothing but the smell of the sacrifice to hold in memory." It was quiet then. I shook my head slowly and started to get up and said to the room, to myself to the beloved children. "A child conceived as compromise or booty will carry that conception mark for the rest of their earthly and heavenly lives. Don't be so cavalier with saddling these soul sparks as they travel to the world. It's so very much for them to carry."

I walked back to my room off the back deck of the house and left them. I sat on the wooden bench under the stars.

First, there was a chill and I thought of David and why I had wanted his reserve in my life, his control, as a north star. How it soothed me to feel someone so armored. How I had used him, not wanting his passion too close, but recognizing him as someone who lived in the pit of the Coliseum, a gladiator perpetually preparing for slaughter on the playing field of his life.

What hubris we embody in our attempts to live. Finding people to use as our fortress, creating children to act as our warriors.

"Oh my God, Ty." I felt him next to me. The heat on my arm, the dribble of his warmth now growing to an embrace.

Barefoot, I walked down to the sand and stood a distance from a beach fire crackling into embers, watched by a young man I had never seen before.

"Sit," he called. "It's okay."

And I did. He got up and put his hands out to the embers.

"I used to burn my hands when I was a kid. My parents really worried. But one day my dad gave me matches and my mom gave me a bucket of sand and left me to figure it out. And I did." He grinned at me.

I closed my eyes and then opened them again to see a shooting star, and the moon with a smile. Three drops of water hit my face.

"Tears from the man in the moon," a voice said, as I pushed the water away from my eyes and onto the back of my hands. "They always fall to bless the truth."

When I looked again, the boy was gone.

Chapter 51

January 2020

E. B. Simon was a month old. Amanda insisted on Evelyn, with a long E. And the initial B for "baby," Eddie said. Eddie said he always wanted a child with an initial for a name, so he could keep track of him, like in a file folder. Bebe was his mother's name, and I bet he didn't mind that connection either. My brother, Charlie, had a big empty house in San Rafael since his second wife divorced him and Eddie took up his dad's offer of free housing for a year

Amanda and Eddie had come to an uneasy but loving peace. Amanda wildly grabbing onto the chance of this new baby. Eddie unable to see himself as someone who could abandon something, someone, he created. And so they began. Uneasy, but willing.

I was called in as the surrogate gramma. Amanda's mother still was not in contact, even more horrified by a child out of wedlock. Eddie's mom had died when he was a baby. I was anointed.

And then the email came from Jordan.

Mom. I am out of custody and no charges. Needless to say, it's time to leave Japan. I am heading to Australia with a group from the community. I will be passing through Los Angeles and have to do some

visa stuff. I spoke to Eddie who told me about the kid and that you might be going out in January. We could meet in the L.A. airport. Let me know.

I made my way out of the plane and down into the terminal. L.A. was always so bright, no place to hide. Even at the airport. I rolled my computer bag along the tile floors there in Terminal 5 and stood, uncertain, in the line at the women's bathroom. I wondered if Jordan would recognize me, if I should put on makeup, play this like a forties movie and be lovely and Loretta Young in my embrace of my wayward child. That idea evaporated with the shove from the lady behind me to take the next stall or forfeit to her demanding bladder.

Wheeling my bag back out the door and into the terminal I scanned the food court and spotted Hibachi-San. By the window was a tall boy who had recently become a man. He was twitchy. A little scrawny, eyes a little wild. But, then, I bet this meeting was as tough for him as for me.

He gazed steadily out the big windows onto the tarmac. His hands were large and competent. One set down his small teacup and joined the other one on his lap. Composed. Composing.

I remembered the teacups at Descanso Gardens. I remembered how he liked to sip from them and cradle the whole cup in his hand, feeling its warmth, as he had grown larger. I remembered holding his hand after he set down a cup, and it was warm and open.

"Hello, Jordan. Hello, Son." He turned and tried to focus.

"Hi, Mom." He blinked a few times as if the composite angles and skin flanks that composed my form were not in his computer data bank. He had to reach to find my image in his brain. Then he smiled a crooked smile. "There you are," my image finally clicking.

"Yes." I said.

He swung his black hair back away from his face, I think, but my eyes seemed to be leaking.

"Oh God," I said, scrambling to find the chair and get myself seated." Sorry."

"No. No. It's okay."

I finally got enough courage to look into his face. It was open but rough, some of the crust had been worn off of him.

"So," he said, simply. Turning and facing me head on. He took a deep breath and started his speech. "I guess I missed Dad. I mean I missed Dad a lot. And so I went away and . . . and, then I figured out that he was always going to be gone and you weren't." This was clearly rehearsed. I wondered if some girl had helped him figure out what he was feeling and how he would talk to me. "So I sent you an email. Instead of Eddie. It's good to see you."

He waited to see how that landed.

"Yes, Jordan. Yes, I miss him, too. Dad."

"Yeah." I'm not sure he had scripted the meeting for himself past this point.

"It's good to see you. Jordan. Really." I unconsciously moved my hand to the place on my chest that ached. I think I must have smiled and just gazed at him. He looked out at the tarmac again, but it was okay. He was allowing me to scan his body, to reacquaint myself with the proximal feel of him.

On the plane I had reviewed the last five years of theorizing about Jordan's departure. Then, I had begun learning "acceptance." Nothing worked at this moment.

"Can you tell me where you are coming from?" I tried. "What's ahead for you?" I was being asked to meet my son in motion, rather than in the luxury of a consensual stillness. I was not being invited inside his life, I was being allowed a viewing.

I shook my head and the words poured out before he responded. "I just don't know what I may have done to make you go away for so long?" And then I put my hand to my mouth. I did not want to ruin this, have him skitter back to shelter at my probing.

"What makes you think it was you who did anything? Dad gave me money and I wanted to travel. That's all." His eyes went to challenge and then to a dead bead, a stare I recognized from those recalcitrant farmers I had met in Michigan.

"I was in jail." Again, it felt rehearsed. "In prison, Mom. I spent a year in prison in Japan. It was only because I knew the guy not because I did anything wrong."

"Yes. I know."

"It was awful. I couldn't breathe there. For a whole year. I didn't."

"They wouldn't let me visit you."

I shifted in my chair. I couldn't imagine what a Japanese prison might be like.

"It wasn't like a Zen monastery," he said. "It wasn't romantic. The Japanese are very . . . rigid." He searched for the word and his body constricted. His face so bleak, and ashamed. He was exhausted by the restraint it must have taken for him to survive. Away from everything that ever gave him comfort. I couldn't catch my breath, watching him.

"Oh, Jordan," I said. "Oh, my son." I reached cross the table but his hands remained in his lap.

"I am fine. It was okay. I improved my Japanese."

That was it. That was what I was going to get from him. It was all he had really. My son who had never been able to look at the details and find delight in nuance or hope in aberration. Instead he had built walls against whatever he was feeling, moved away from what made him unique and strong and no matter what I had done or not done as a mother, he had chosen this difficult path to keep himself from himself. I withdrew my hands and sat up straight again.

"Eddie has a baby. He's a father. He sends love."

"Yeah. I spoke to him."

"He became a writer. And now with the baby, and a new partner everything is up in the air. They called me to come and help. A surrogate gramma."

Jordan softened. "That's nice for you, right?"

"Sure. Yes. I'll stay a couple of weeks and help take care of the baby." I looked up at him and everything started swimming. "I'll get to hold a baby again." I smiled, seeking ballast but, slosh! I was bushwhacked. The memory of the weight of a child in my arms. The way we sat on the swing under the eaves late at night. Swinging in the moonlight to stop him crying. Cooing to each other to soothe each other's fears. How he clung to my body.

"Mom," he said, rescuing me from the memory. "Mama." I looked up. He had not called me that since he was a little one. "I'm sorry, I'm just . . . sorry. I . . . love you. I missed Dad. I missed . . . I don't know." He slid his hand across the table and I grabbed it.

He squeezed my hand so tightly, trying to wring the truth about himself from me, his source. It was impossible. Neither of us knew the answer. His grip eased and I saw that a tear, maybe two was welled at the rim of his eye. They slipped now, fell across his face, slid down, parting his thick eyelash, shining his beautiful eyes as if they were luminous marbles, allowing light into their interior for the first time in many years.

"Oh God, I love you, Jordan. You have had a rough go. A very rough go." Then, it was quiet and he let a few more tears fall from those eyes. I squeezed his hand again and looked deeply. Reaching him. Yes, reaching him. "Thank you, darling boy. Thank you for letting me hold your hand again."

He grinned, sniffing, like he did when I knew him. Blowing his nose now, wiping at his face.

"You know, you are very beautiful, my boy." I smiled, taking a breath, feeling more space for words. Jordan almost smirked, an involuntary response even he recognized and wiped it away. "You look like you did when you were little and we used to go to the beach every summer together. Swimming so far out into the bay."

"Yeah. You would always swim out and find me."

"Yes," I said. "Yes. That's what I'd do."

We sat quiet for a moment. Then, he said "Those summers were fun. I remember that. They were fun." Like he put that memory back in the memory bank. Like this thought could accrue interest. It could grow for him and make him richer.

"Good," I said. "I 'm glad they were fun. That's good."

"Yeah," Jordan laughed. "Something to build on, my mom would say!" Jordan turned and smiled. "Yeah, that's what you would say."

"Yes, Jordan. That's what I would say."

We both sighed, pushing away the very difficult preparation that we both had done. We grabbed both hands now and held on and were quiet.

And then, the moment of grace passed. I sat, hoping the door would not close again, but my son looked up, moved his hands back to his lap. Wiped them on a napkin.

The door clanged shut. I wondered if this is what Jordan felt when the bars closed on him for the night. He could see me thinking that. He couldn't stand the idea of his mother, this woman he could not understand and yet who knew him too well, inside his head.

I pulled back. But it did no good. Jordan knew that I knew him. And this complete knowledge of him still felt like the best reason to reject me.

"You going to San Francisco?" he asked.

"Yes. My flight is at five." I lied. I had not booked my onward ticket. It was too heartbreaking to think of being so close and then being far again.

"I have to get to another terminal," he said.

"Where are you going again?"

Jordan stood and started to gather his backpack and jacket. "I'm going to work with some friends. To Australia. Start a new enterprise." He smiled. "We met at the monastery and I am going to meet these guys, and a girl too." He smiled. "And start a farm, maybe."

It was everything for me to stay still and not call out. Not ground him. Tether him.

"Well," I said. "Australia!" Calculating the miles between us.

"Yes. We were going to go to China, we know people there, too. But there is a bad flu there. A plague or something. From bats. They wouldn't let us visit."

"Oh," I said. "Australia." I smiled, too brightly. "Koalas. And kangaroos."

"Right," Jordan said, awkward again.

Jordan stood and I did too. He was tall, my son. Still standing straight. I felt like a willow blown by his presence. He came close and held me. Tightly. His arms wound round me like a tree.

"Thanks for coming, Mama. I'm sorry. I'm really sorry."

And just like that, he turned and loped out of the restaurant. I stood and watched him. He turned and waved. Then, he came back to where I was standing. "I love you," he said.

I looked up at my tall grown boy. "I love you, too" I said.

"Good." Jordan turned and left me, nodding his head. As if it was enough.

I ordered a bottle of warm sake and felt it snake through my body, like a covenant.

Chapter 52

The Baby Born

I spent a week and then another and then another with E. B. and his parents. My brother, Charlie, was cordial. We hadn't been together for many years.

"Thanks for looking out for Eddie, all this time." he said.

"Yes. The pleasure was all mine. I've come to count on him."

"Will Jordan come back?" He asked me simply.

"Eventually." I heard my voice equivocate. "I don't know," I said simply.

Charlie just smiled. He had had his share of such endings. And they had caused him to pull away from his son. And I had stepped in and so the circle was completed.

We spent our days rocking the baby, cooking for the kids. Eddie was job hunting, Amanda was exhausted, sleeping when the baby slept. We traded off nights and there were four of us, zombies walking in service to new life.

The house was full of angled furniture and hard edges. Charlie had lived alone for so many years, the guest bedrooms were disgruntled at having to shake their dust and welcome breathing humans again. The garden, full of palms and bougainvillea, featured a maze of California succulents, twisty giants surrounding the house. It was like Sleeping Beauty's castle keep but in fog and sunshine.

We couldn't keep the world out totally. The impeachment of the president was heartbreaking—or his non-impeachment—and we agreed to turn off the news.

I was exhausted from the odd hours of caring for the baby and a routine that never established itself. It had been all motion since coming west, since parting from Jordan, since reacquainting myself with the chunky rhythm of nurturing new life. Everything frayed edges, the bits too short to reweave.

I took a night off and drove out to Fairfax and Spirit Rock, the meditation center.

There was a dharma talk with handsome people, poseurs and aficionados both. Some quietly applauded themselves for the way their legs bent so easily into lotus position. Smug at their attempt at oneness they seemed to miss the walls of ego that kept them from leaping forward. But I was tired and hadn't the energy for any more outrage.

The windows in the chapel were full of wheatgrass shifting in the breeze. They made me dizzy as they swayed. The speaker, a young woman, wound in blue fabric with a hollow voice, was a soporific. I crept my way out the door into the lobby catching myself before nodding out.

My brother had given me several hundred dollars when I arrived to say thank you for the help I had offered his son. And for my plane ticket and expenses.

I took the money out of my purse and put it on the table in front of a young man, skinny and dwarfed by black glasses and a stocking cap. He wore monk's robes and he made me smile.

"I'd like to make a donation." I had to do something to honor these years, move forward somehow into new life.

"Wonderful. Are you honoring anyone in particular?"

Oh, I thought. *Sure.* I looked at him and began to spout the names. "I'd like to make a donation in my son's name, Jordan, and my friend who died, David. And Mallory." The names started flooding me as I stood there looking at this eager young man.

"Great, you can write them all down on the list on the wall. Okay?"

Yes, I want to add more people, too. I want to add my husband, Ty. And my friend, Sylvia and the new baby, E. B., and his parents. And can I add my brother, too? Charlie. Can I honor them all?"

I realized that I was rattling off these people's names with urgency. Like if I named them, honored them, I could somehow come to understand them, keep them wrapped around me for protection and light. Affirm them and move ahead to whatever was next.

The young monk smiled. "The more the merrier. I'll even give you different colored pens."

I looked around embarrassed. "Sorry. I get carried away."

He laughed. "No. They carry you. They carry your heart."

I smiled at him and the phrase that cemented his work. I set to inscribing the names on the wall.

As I wrote I thanked them all for the ways they had embraced me, the ways in which they showed me how I needed to gather myself again. The needing, the defending, bearing false witness, thinking my arms alone were the ones that would solve their dilemmas. All these ways in which I needed to wind the whirlwind back into myself, and higher, somehow. Away from the landscape, erupting with carbuncles, shattering, shifted beyond recognition.

It was that way for all of us. Everyone in our country. We were spinning like mad Sufis but without the focus of the dance. Our edges were frayed and had given way. The threads limp, unfamiliar in their dissolution. The threads defying the weavers. We tried. We are trying. We are tried.

And then came the plague.

Acknowledgments

Much like Annie Simon, I was deeply disturbed at the shift in the political climate in 2016.

And, I, too, volunteered for the Hillary campaign and saw first-hand what the rest of the country is seeing only now as I write in 2022.

I want to acknowledge the many people who allowed me to see with open eyes, feel with open heart and make the attempt to find the words that characterized the shift in our country between Trump's election and the pandemic.

So, Joshua Alvarez, thank you for hiring me onto the campaign. Angela Locke, who brought the early version of this work to the UK and allowed me to hone my American perspective with a British community. To Jacqueline Schultz, who shared my horror and the discomfort of finding a way to breathe as we saw the writing on the wall about our crumbling democracy. To my daughter, Sofia Shultz, who is my teacher in so many ways. To Jule Selbo, strong, true, constant and a standard bearer for possibility. To Barbara Bottner, always with clear eyes, strong eager words and a heart that sustains me when mine fails.

My Beta Readers known and unknown.

And first, last and always the New York and Los Angeles Writers Bloc. My home, compass, mirror and the soul salon that lets me be an artist.

[blocpress] is a small press that supports the work of the writers of the New York and Los Angeles Writers Bloc.

Originally founded in the 1970s by playwright and critic Jeffrey Sweet, the New York Writers Bloc, is a supportive safe haven writers group growing from a small group focused on work for theatre practitioners only—with actors and writers offering support and development—to work supporting fiction, non-fiction, memoir, television, film and theatre. Original members included Jerry Stiller, Anne Meara, Percy Granger, Donald Margulies (Pulitzer) and Merson, among many others.

In 1984, Susan Merson, Jane Anderson and Tony Shultz established the Los Angeles group which became home to several award-winning writers including Jane Anderson (Emmy), Noni White and Bob Tzudkier (Tony for *Newsies*), National Book Award Finalist, Janet Fitch, Kim Purcell (YA NPR Award), Jennifer Castle (Disney Books) and Barbara Bottner (Award-winning children's book author and YA honoree for *I am Still Here*).

The Bloc is still active on both coasts, moderated by Susan Merson in New York and Barbara Bottner in Los Angeles.

www.ingramcontent.com/pod-product-compliance
Lightning Source LLC
Chambersburg PA
CBHW051136130726
47988CB00005B/1856